COLLISION

THE ALLIANCE SERIES: BOOK THREE

EMMA L. ADAMS

1

ADA

"There's a ghost in Jeth's computer!" Alber's shout came through the open window of the attic room, just below where I lay on the roof. Groaning, I rubbed my eyes. I hadn't meant to fall asleep up there, but it was peaceful, even with the distant roar of London traffic and the smell of exhaust fumes. And for once, my sleep was free from screaming nightmares. I slid out of the improvised pillow-nest I'd made, picked up the pillows and the paper-back I'd been reading, and climbed back into my room through the window. My seventeen-year-old brother Alber stood in the doorway, blinking at me with contact-less violet eyes.

"You were asleep on the roof?"

"I dozed off," I said, shutting the window behind me and dropping the blankets on the bed.

Alber shook his head. "You're mental. It's freezing out there."

I shrugged, though I was barefoot and wearing pyjamas, which didn't help. "I had blankets. What's going on?"

"Jeth's computer's freaking out. We reckon it's a ghost."

"Of course. How'd you figure that one out?" I put slippers on and followed my brother down the rickety ladder from the attic to the landing. Loud swearing came from behind Jeth's slightly-open door. He cursed at full-volume, in Karthonic, the language of his homeworld.

"No other explanation. If Jethro the genius can't figure out what it is, it has to be a ghost, right?"

"Wait, he really *doesn't* know what it is?" I pushed Jeth's door further open and went in. "It's the end of the world as we know it."

"Very funny," said Jeth, tapping the screen. The floor around his leather-backed computer chair was a tangle of wires hooked up between computers, monitors, and dubious-looking pieces of shiny offworld technology. My older brother was a certifiable genius who worked in the Alliance's tech department. Since we'd moved into this new house, he'd claimed the biggest room to set up all his computers. And I'd asked for the attic. If I couldn't have my old room, with the stars I'd painted on the ceiling, a window that opened onto the roof was more than enough to make up for it, even though I couldn't see the stars here in the middle of the city.

I leaned in to see the screen, which had frozen on a blank page covered in what looked like white squiggly lines. "What did you do to it, anyway? Did you put parts of offworld tech in there, by any chance?"

Jeth was forever messing with different worlds' technologies to see what would work on Earth, and he'd created devices even the Inter-World Alliance didn't possess. Not that it was entirely legal.

"It was working fine until a few minutes ago," said Jeth, rapping his knuckles on the monitor. "Whatever it is, it's totally locked down the computer. I can't fix it." He slapped the desk with the side of his palm. "Dead. *Dammit!*"

"Wow," said Alber, lounging against the doorway. "Chill

out." At a distance, he and Jeth could have been related. They were both tall, tanned, and fair-haired. Nobody would have guessed they came from different universes.

"I was working on something important," Jeth muttered. "And yeah, I did put a couple of… enhancements in there. But it's worked fine for the past year!"

"RIP, computer," said Alber solemnly. "Shall we say a few words in its memory?"

"Shut it," said Jeth, regarding the screen with a forlorn expression, as though he'd lost a beloved pet.

"What in the world is going on?" Nell came upstairs and peered round the doorway.

"Jeth killed his computer," said Alber. "We're in mourning."

Nell sighed, running a hand through the strands of hair straggling loose from her bun. "It's almost quarter past eleven. Ada, didn't you say you were meeting someone at half past?"

"Ah, crap," I said, taking a step back and tripping over a wire. I steadied myself against the side of the desk. "Lost track of time." I backed out of Jeth's room and all but flew up the steps to the attic. Fifteen minutes to make myself look presentable before I went to New York.

I ran the quickest shower ever, changed my outfit seven times, panicked that I'd lost my communicator, then remembered I'd left it on the roof, jumped a mile in the air at the sound of a motorcycle outside, and ran downstairs so fast I almost knocked Alber flying.

"Whoa," he said. "What's chasing you?"

"Very funny." I grabbed my coat. Though I opted to go without my guard uniform, I grabbed my magicproof leather-style jacket to keep off the chill winter air.

The sleek and shiny cycle hummed in front of our house. Removing the helmet, Kay looked up, his dark hair ruffled from the wind and his usually pale face flushed in the cold air. He wore the typical uniform of an Alliance guard—black gear, his jacket embossed with the silver cuffs of an Ambassador.

"Hey," he said.

Alber came to the door and gaped at the motorcycle. "Holy hell, that's *awesome.* Can I have a go?"

"No chance, Al," I said, before Kay could answer. "He failed his driving test," I told Kay. "Thinks speed limits don't apply to him."

"Yeah, but you can't even drive," said Alber. "So."

Kay set down his helmet. "We good to go? The bike stays here," he added. "No racing this time. Sorry, guys."

"Dammit," said Alber. Twice, Kay had managed to get hold of temporary permits to allow Alber to join us in one of Valeria's capital's famous hover-zones, where you could rent magic-powered hover bikes. They were automatic models, which came as a relief to me. I'd never learned to drive because we had so little money it didn't make sense to spend it on something mostly unnecessary in London. But I'd still managed to cause a pile-up when the bike stalled and flipped upside-down in the middle of the track, much to Kay's and Alber's amusement. The two of them had ended up racing each other around the track.

At least it had redeemed Kay in Nell's eyes somewhat. To her, Kay meant both the Alliance, which we'd tried to avoid our whole lives, and the council who'd doomed our home-world. Considering Kay's father, the currently-absent Lawrence Walker, had issued the statement against interfering in Enzar's war in the first place, I wasn't sure she would ever actually *like* him. Then again, Nell trusted no one outside our family. As a former servant to the sadistic rulers of Enzar, who'd have used me as a human weapon if she hadn't smuggled me out, she wasn't given to showing overt affection.

Nell appeared behind me and hugged me suddenly, startling me. "Take care of yourself, Ada."

"Uh. I will." This new Nell was kind of freaking me out. She'd always kept barriers up even with her own adopted children, but after she and Alber had been kidnapped by the Conner family, she'd been far more open with us than before. It took some getting used to.

Kay gave me a questioning look when Nell returned to the house. "You okay?"

"Huh? Yeah, it's just weird." I lowered my voice. "It's like living with an alien. Until a few weeks ago, Nell hadn't hugged me since I was about four. Unless you count teaching us headlocks, but I'm pretty sure that doesn't count."

"Useful life skill, though," said Kay.

"Ha," said Alber, turning to wave at Nell before she closed the door. "To be fair, it *is* weird. Maybe she's had a personality transplant. Pretty sure that exists on some universe, right?"

"Maybe the one with haunted computers," I said.

"You know what Jeth's like, he probably put too much incompatible offworld technology in there. He's like a mad scientist," said Alber. "Anyway. I've always wanted to go to the States. Bet you Alliance Ambassadors get to travel all over."

"On assignment, mostly," said Kay. "All Alliance bases are open to Ambassadors. And everyone in the Alliance can apply for an offworld permit."

Even I could, though my application had been delayed due to my not having legal identification until I'd joined the Alliance. Some worlds barred outsiders from entry, some required a crap-ton of paperwork, and others were listed as "hostile" to offworlders. I'd only been to Valeria and Aglaia so far, but as soon as I made Ambassador, the Multiverse would be open to explore. Like I'd always wanted.

The three of us made an odd group as we passed by crowds of tourists and shoppers, mobs of bikes and over-enthusiastic taxi drivers wheeling around corners. I couldn't quite get used to living right in the middle of London rather than on the outskirts, but at least it meant I didn't have to travel far to work now. Central appeared as a dark shape against the sky, a black skyscraper taller than any of the surrounding buildings and reflecting the sun from its gleaming surface. Alien and yet familiar.

The street we headed for, however, appeared deserted, the houses abandoned to disrepair. Most bore the damage a rampaging wyvern had caused when it got out of the Passages concealed behind a sliding metal door on the back of an old factory. Wide, high-ceilinged corridors lit with blue light linked the entire Multiverse and covered hundreds of miles.

"No monsters this way," Kay said, as we entered the corridor. "We're sticking to first level."

"Good," said Alber. After being abducted by the Conner family, my brother wasn't as keen on risks as before. He *said* he was fine, and we'd rescued him before he'd been seriously hurt, but I knew from my own experience the worst scars weren't on the outside.

For most of our lives, we'd used a hidden lower level Passage that cut right through the territory belonging to the monster-infested world of Cethrax, so it had been strange adjusting to using the Passages as an Alliance employee. The cold, blue-lit corridors on this level were safe, relatively speaking, because this part of the first level belonged to the allied worlds, the members of the Alliance. Second level belonged to the worlds which, for whatever reason, hadn't joined the Alliance or had even been barred from membership. And the lower levels were given over to the many door-ways leading into the swamps of Cethrax. As an Alliance guard, it was my job to hunt escaped monsters down, when I was on duty. Lucky I had this weekend off.

We skirted around the main Passage to Earth, not wanting to get caught up in the cross-world traffic, instead heading for a side-corridor which led the same way. The Passages were a shortcut across the worlds, for Alliance employees at least, and a two-hour walk to New York was far more reasonable than flying.

At an intersection, we met Simon, a friend of Kay's who'd also graduated from the Academy. He worked at the New York Alliance and had helped with setting up the links from the shelter to Enzar. His blond hair caught the blue Passage light as he waved at me.

"Hey," he said. "I should warn you, the New York guards are jumpy as hell thanks to the whole invisible goblin debacle."

"Yeah, same at Central," said Kay. "The number of acci-dental injuries is through the roof, because people keep attacking each other, thinking it's a goblin. And there are rumours of a serial prankster who keeps sneaking up on people in the dark tunnels. Ridiculous, of course."

I glanced sideways at him. "And that definitely isn't true?"

I wasn't sure if he'd told Simon, but Alber didn't know Kay could turn himself invisible now. I understood why he wouldn't want the whole Multiverse to know he could do something that was supposed to be impossible, but it was still pretty freaking awesome. And yeah, he'd tried that trick on me before. I wasn't amused.

"Might have happened once."

"Ha," said Simon. "At least that dickhead Aric isn't around anymore. Has no one seen him since?"

Kay shrugged. "He's either stranded on Aglaia, or he made

it back into the Passages. If he did, he might be anywhere, on any world. His family's all in jail now anyway."

"Good," said Alber vehemently. Aric's cousins and sister had tortured him. Wynn Conner was dead, killed by the centaurs, and Kay had apparently spared Aric's life in the forest—which I didn't quite understand, given that they'd hated each other ever since they'd been at the Academy. Kay had almost accidentally killed Aric two years ago using magic, while Aric and his sister had retaliated by setting a wyvern loose in the Passages, which had left Kay permanently scarred.

"Hmm. I wonder about that," said Simon. "Where do fugitives go?"

Kay shrugged. "I don't know, he probably ran off to another world and got himself a false identity. I'm not too worried, to be honest. Idiot has no sense, he'll get himself arrested within days."

"You don't think he'll attack the Alliance?" Simon asked sceptically.

"Alone? No. Without his family's name to protect him, he's nothing. He'll probably claim he's innocent."

"Dickhead," said Simon. "Never mind him, anyway."

As we rounded a corner, a group of black-uniformed guards appeared from the shadows, armed with stunners.

"Only me," said Simon. "Jesus, point that stunner somewhere else, Dave. I told you I was bringing people."

The muscled guy he'd spoken to eyed Alber. "He's not Alliance."

"Oh, lighten up," said Simon. "We're visiting the shelter, not Central. He's Ada's brother."

Dave stared at me, and so did the rest of the guards. Nothing new there. The number of versions of the story of how I'd come to work at Central in London was probably bigger than the number of worlds in the Multiverse, and typically, the more dramatic parts had spread the furthest. I supposed it did sound odd that an illegal magic-wielder from a highly classified world who'd been arrested for dangerous magic use and trespassing ended up as an Alliance employee only weeks after breaking out of jail. Though I'd told as much of the truth as possible to people at Central, I was fairly sure a lot of people either saw me as a danger or a lunatic.

"All right," said Dave, and the guards moved to let us past.

This doorway opened into an alley. The sun peeked over the skyline, reminding me we'd technically travelled five hours back in time. Simon led the way, but once we reached the alleyway's end, Kay wandered off alone. He'd pulled out his communicator again, but still somehow managed not to walk into anyone on the crowded pavement.

"The shelter's doing okay?" I asked Simon.

"Yeah. They were struggling a bit until a couple of months ago, actually," said Simon. "I didn't know much about the place until Kay called me up, asking about setting up the link to Enzar. Not long after, they got an anonymous donation. A *massive* one. It lifted them right out of debt."

"Really?" said Alber. "From who?"

I poked him in the arm. "Al, don't you know what 'anonymous' means?"

"Shut it, you."

"It came from someone in the Alliance," said Simon, jerking his head in Kay's direction.

"You think?" I said.

"Yeah... I reckon he did it. Same happened back in London, now they're opening a whole new shelter network."

"I forgot about that," I said. "I've heard it mentioned at Central, but I guess I didn't think how they'd fund it..."

Simon nodded. "It's something he'd do, for sure."

A pang went through me. When I'd first met Kay, I'd

assumed he was a callous Alliance guard out only for his own interests. It wasn't the first time my tendency to speak without considering first had swung around to hit me in the face, but it didn't help that my family had also jumped to the worst conclusion. Specifically, Nell and Jeth. I'd had words with them about not blaming him for the times I'd nearly got killed, but we'd been at an impasse for a while, as I'd adjusted to working at Central while Kay went offworld with the other Ambassadors.

"Huh," said Alber. "I'd want everyone to know, if it were me."

I rolled my eyes. "Figures."

A sudden electric jolt shot up my spine, like I'd trodden on a plug. My head snapped up. I knew that feeling… but it didn't happen on Earth. It *never* happened on Earth.

Magic.

Kay turned back, and from the expression on his face, he'd noticed, too.

"What's up?" asked Simon.

I stared around, at the shops lining the street, the yellow cabs standing out amongst the traffic, the crowds passing by. Nothing out of the ordinary for New York.

"Alber, did you feel that?" I asked.

"Feel what?"

Maybe I'd imagined the sensation, but I'd have expected my younger brother, who was mageblood—the magic-wielding Enzarians on the other side of the conflict to the once-ruling Royals—to be able to sense magic, too.

We caught up to Kay at the street corner next to a convenience store. "That was a shift," he said. "I'm sure of it."

"Anyone want to clue me in?" asked Simon.

"I thought I felt… magic," I said. "A shift?"

"Like something boosted the magic level. I can't feel it

anymore." Kay put his communicator in his jacket pocket, frowning.

"Eh, probably nothing," said Simon. "There's a bunch of offworlders living in the area, I'll bet one of them brought something from another world in."

"Hmm. There are magic-wielders at the shelter?" said Kay.

"Yeah," said Simon. "I don't know the specifics. People come and go."

"Huh. Might be worth checking out."

We reached the shelter, an apartment building at the street's end. It looked no different from the other buildings on either side, but through the windows, most of the people I saw were offworlders —some easy to recognise by appearance, such as clawed hands and feet, wings, or odd-coloured eyes, some less so. The door flew open and a blond girl, around ten years old, ran out, shrieking.

"Get back here, Isa!" A blue-skinned woman ran from the building. Simon blocked the girl's way before she ran into the road.

"Whoa," he said. "Easy there. I'm not gonna hurt you."

The girl rotated on the spot, wild-eyed. "Rick electrocuted me!"

Oh, crap. It sounded like magic, all right. First level was a mild static shock, and usually impossible even for a magic-wielder here on Earth. Unless you were like me, and from a high-magic world. But even I couldn't use magic here most of the time.

"No I *didn't!*" yelled a teenage boy from the upstairs window.

The girl stared at us. "Have you come to take us away again?"

"No," Simon said quickly. "We were just checking things out. What happened?"

"I'm not sure," said the woman who'd chased after the girl. "You're from the Alliance, right? I've seen you here before."

"Yeah," said Simon. "These guys are from Central. They helped out with linking us to the cut-off worlds. If this is a bad time, we can leave…"

Another sudden jolt of energy rushed through the air. I looked at Kay again, alarmed. At that moment, the boy from upstairs ran out the house, too, and didn't stop.

The woman followed. "*What* is going on?"

"No idea," said another boy, of around twelve, who'd appeared from the house. "Rick's hands started *sparking*. It was wicked cool."

"Magic," said Kay. "He's a magic-wielder, right?" He directed this question at the blue-skinned woman. "From one of the outlying worlds?"

"And who are you?" she asked, instead of answering. "I didn't think Earth people were interested in magic."

"What just happened isn't normal for Earth," said Kay. "Even magic-wielders shouldn't be able to… that was a second level shot, wasn't it?"

"He was glowing," said the boy. "Kind of freaky."

"Damn," Kay muttered, with a glance back at me. "It definitely isn't normal for Earth."

"We can take care of this," said the woman, with a protective glance behind at the children who'd gathered in the hallway and behind the windows to see what was happening. I guessed she was in charge. "We don't want the Alliance shutting us down, you hear?"

"That's not going to happen," said Kay. "Can you let the Alliance know if anything else comes up? Magic can be dangerous."

"We can handle this." She started herding the curious children back into the house.

Kay turned to Simon with a shrug. "Should we clear off, then? I don't think we can be much help here."

"Sure." Simon turned his back on the shelter. "Let me know if anything else happens, okay?" he said to the woman.

"Weird," I said, as we walked down the street, back in the direction of the Passage entrance. "Are you sure it was second level?"

"Pretty sure," said Kay. "If it was first level, we wouldn't have felt it."

And third level was destructive and invariably fatal. A shiver ran down my spine.

"Hmm," said Simon. "I always wondered how the whole magic deal worked. Can you sense if someone else uses magic, then?"

"On Earth, yeah," said Kay. "But that's because it's low-magic so it stands out a mile."

And because he, like me, had some kind of magic in his blood, thanks to an experiment the Alliance—his own father, in fact—had engineered.

"Hang on." Kay turned back. "Right... you guys go on ahead. I have an idea."

"Here we go." Simon rolled his eyes. "Does it involve hijacking vehicles or crazy stunts?"

"Nah, I'm gonna go and check back there." Kay indicated the shelter, where a bigger crowd gathered outside. "They won't see me."

Not if he's invisible. Any of us could use the Chameleon devices for temporary camouflage, but Kay could make the effect last as long as he wanted to.

Simon shrugged. "If you like. We'll wait."

Alber stared through the windows of a video game store. "I'm gonna look in here," he said.

"You know you don't have the right currency, don't you?" I said. But he'd already gone inside.

"One of the perks to being an Ambassador is the offworld credit card," said Simon. "It has like ten thousand currencies logged into it, you can withdraw in whichever you need. I can't wait to get one."

"Ah, I guess I never thought of that," I said. *Awesome.* I made a mental note to check on the rules about cross-world regulations to see what I could legally bring back to Earth. Before I'd joined the Alliance, I'd spent a lot of time at the black market for offworlders at Covent Garden, where Jeth bought most of his offworld technology parts.

"I reckon you'll make Ambassador soon. You've been offworld more than once already, right?"

"Yeah, but my boss doesn't like me. Then again, I suppose she doesn't like anyone, so…"

"Ah, Kay told me about the dragon," said Simon. "Come on, you're a celebrity."

I pulled a face. "Can you not do that?"

"You're just like him," said Simon, shaking his head. "He hated attention at the Academy, but there was no real way to avoid it, considering he was the youngest in our year—only sixteen when he signed up. I realise it's none of my business, but you know, I'm kind of surprised what happened with you two. I thought—eh, never mind."

I stifled a sigh, checking over my shoulder to see if Kay was nearby. No sign of him. I didn't think he was the type to invisibly eavesdrop, though. "Yeah. He said I have to take care of myself first."

Simon let out a breath. "I don't know what crap you're dealing with, but it's true."

"Yeah. I got that. He said the last thing I needed was to be around someone like him."

"He did?" Simon blinked. "Damn."

"Take it that's not normal for him? I got the impression he had kind of a chequered history…"

He pulled a face. "Not really. Kay might act like a shame-less flirt sometimes, but if he really likes a girl, he takes bloody forever doing anything about it."

"Hmm." I huddled inside my coat, shifting from one foot to the other. Then I spotted Kay walking back towards us. So he wasn't invisible, then. But I supposed we were in public, so he couldn't exactly appear out of thin air in the middle of the street.

"What was that about?" I asked, as he caught up to us.

"Later," he said in a low voice. "Where's your brother?"

"Looking at video games he can't buy. What happened?"

"Trouble," he said. "Or, magic. Simon, you should tell your boss about this. Not report those kids or anything, but there's something off with the magic level. I'm going to ask if there's anything similar going on in London. Central will know."

"If you say so." Simon shrugged, and pulled out his communicator. "You're heading back there now? Aren't Ambassadors allowed weekends off?"

"Someone has to do it." He started to walk back towards the alley.

"Wait." Alber appeared from the shop. "When are we going to get our tour?"

"I'll give you one," said Simon. "I thought he'd disappear on us. You're in denial!" he shouted after Kay.

Kay turned back. "Technically, we're in New York."

"All right, smartarse, have it your way."

"Huh?" said Alber blankly. "What did you mean by that?"

"Absolutely nothing at all." Simon glanced sideways at me.

"Cheers," I muttered.

"He *is*," Simon said quietly, as we continued down the street. "I know it. Don't you rule out hope yet, Ada."

Hmm. I didn't know whether to believe him. It had been weeks since I'd inadvertently thrown myself at Kay while

15

under the influence of Aglaian wine, and since then, he hadn't so much as looked at me in a way that suggested he wanted anything more than friendship.

I shrugged, doing my best to sound offhand. "If magic's making trouble again, I can guarantee we'll both end up involved in it sooner or later."

I couldn't see the future, but I didn't need to, not wherever magic was concerned. Kay was dead right when he said trouble and magic went hand in hand.

2

KAY

"Let me get this straight," I said to Ms Weston across a mile-high stack of paperwork I swore had materialised overnight. "Someone thought it'd be a good idea to sell a *unicorn* on Earth?"

"They thought it was a horse," said Ms Weston, moving a stack of papers to one side. "So did the buyer, it seems."

Well, damn. Just when I thought the job of an Ambassador couldn't get any more bizarre.

"And now it's loose and gone rabid, you want *me* to go after it?"

"I admit I didn't expect such a magic-related issue to come up on Earth, but yes, if you would."

Just another day at the office. I shook my head. Only Ms Weston could keep a straight face while discussing escaped unicorns.

"We need a magic-wielder on the case. Two, ideally. In fact, take Ada with you. It'll be good experience."

I blinked. "You're thinking she'll make Ambassador soon, then?"

"She certainly qualifies." Ms Weston still didn't emerge from stack of papers.

She'll be happy about that. She'd wanted to see the other worlds her whole life. We had that much in common.

"Should I ask her? Now? Or is there anything else you want me to do here?"

"No... I think we can manage without the two of you. Markos will keep everything organised."

I nodded. "Sure, I'll tell Ada."

I found her in the open booth of Office Fifteen, surrounded by yet more paperwork. Markos turned around from the filing cabinet he stood beside.

"If it isn't the ghost," he said, shuffling more papers.

I rolled my eyes. The centaur was one of few people who knew I could become invisible. No one was around to over-hear, so the rest of admin must be on patrol or in the other offices. It was quiet in Office Fifteen these days, since I'd been promoted. My Ambassador duties meant I only came to Central to report to Ms Weston after assignments.

Probably for the best, given that being in close proximity to Ada made it damned difficult to focus on paperwork.

Ada looked up at me now, chewing on the end of a pen. "Please tell me you know Valeria's year-dating system. It's making me cross-eyed."

"You're in luck," I said. "Ms Weston says we have to go and investigate an escaped unicorn."

Ada blinked. "Did you say what I think you just said?"

"A unicorn? Yeah, some idiot bought it thinking it was a horse. Don't ask me why. Those things are dangerous when provoked anyway, so it's up to us to deal with it."

"Wow," said Ada, setting the pen down on top of the files. "That wasn't in the job description."

"Tell me about it. But she reckons you might be ready for a promotion soon, so..."

Ada jumped to her feet in a second, a grin spreading across her face. "Seriously?"

"Those were more or less her exact words."

"Oh my god," she said. "We're leaving now? I need to get my guard gear, but I'll only be five minutes." She ran from the office.

"Someone really wants to go offworld," Markos commented. "I can't say I see the appeal. It would be nice if there were people as enthusiastic about helping me with this." He indicated the cabinet of endless papers. I didn't envy him one bit, but then, he was the one who'd volunteered to keep Central's admin system in order.

"You're missing out."

"Yes, she reminds me of someone else." He gave me a significant look. "Someone who drove us crazy for a month with constant pacing. Is the Multiverse everything you hoped for?"

"Hell, yes. With or without the unicorns."

"You might change your mind about that," said Markos. "I heard about one that got loose in the Passage and skewered seven people *at the same time.*"

"Thanks," I said.

"Good luck, humans," said the centaur.

Ada reappeared, clad in black faux-leather gear, her jacket half-zipped in a not-unflattering way. I dragged my eyes away, but not before I saw her flush.

"All right," she said. "Let's go catch us a unicorn."

"See, that sounds downright bizarre even here," I said. "In the company of a centaur."

"And a dragon," Markos added.

I glanced in the direction of Ms Weston's office. "Is she aware of that nickname?"

"If she were, my head would be mounted to the wall," said Markos.

And on that note, we left the office.

~

"Whereabouts is this place?" Ada asked, as we walked out of Central through the automatic doors.

"South of London," I said. "Middle of nowhere. An estate owned by this family, apparently. Question: would you rather take public transport and walk three miles, or ride on this?" I indicated my motorcycle.

Ada's jaw dropped. "Wow. Safety helmet?"

I passed the spare helmet over to her, and she eased it over her bright-red hair.

"I've seen you on a hover bike," she said. "I'm amazed you and Alber got out in one piece."

"Hey, now. I've never crashed a vehicle on Earth. Not even with a wyvern as a passenger," I said, referring to the time a wyvern had come out of the Passages near Central and tore my car to pieces.

"Yeah, that was some pretty neat driving," she said, fastening the helmet. "Okay. I'm set."

Yeah, and I'm gonna go crazy within the hour, I thought, as her arms wrapped around my waist and I revved the engine. Apparently, the universe got a kick out of putting us in compromising situations. If it had been any other girl, there'd have been no problem. But we were colleagues, to say nothing of the fact that since she'd met me, she'd nearly died several times, her brother and guardian had been tortured, and she'd seen a side of me that scared her half to death. After that, I didn't know why she would even want to associate with me. I'd never dream of hurting her, but there was no denying I'd done a pretty thorough job of fucking up her life. Sure, she *said* she didn't blame me and she wanted to be friends, but that couldn't undo what I'd done.

Once we left London, the speed limits relaxed enough that I pushed the bike's limits further than I had before.

"Hell. Yes," I said, as we reached a deserted stretch of country road.

Ada yelled in my ear, "I thought you said you were a safe driver?"

"Perfectly safe," I said, grinning back at her. "I'm within the limits."

She yelped as we shot down a steep road, steering around tight corners through woodland, and down another sharp drop.

"Jesus Christ," she gasped, hands gripping the front of my jacket. "You're insane!"

"So they tell me." But I slowed down as the speed limit dropped. I pulled up at the roadside to check the directions again. Not far now.

Ada relaxed her grip on me. "Okay, maybe that was kind of fun."

"See? Nothing to worry about. We're almost there, anyway."

The manor was even more extravagant than I'd expected. A dozen windows stared insolently. I didn't particularly care for the memories the arched glass windows and terraces conjured up, though it looked nothing like the Walker estate had before it had burned to the ground.

"Wow," said Ada. "How many rooms are in there?"

"Approximately too many," I said, checking the details on my communicator again. This was the place. Three cars were parked in the drive, and it bordered on a field containing several horses.

"Can't see any unicorns," said Ada, echoing my thoughts as I rang the doorbell. "But—wow. Who lives here?"

"Mr and Mrs Anderson. Three kids, five horses. And one unicorn, apparently."

Ada laughed. "Who mistakes a unicorn for a horse?"

"I think we're about to find out."

Two people came out of the house—a balding guy in a smart suit and a woman whose eye-wateringly green attire screamed "designer". Figures.

"You're with the Alliance?" She looked us up and down in a way that made her opinion clear in half a second, and Ada shifted beside me.

"That's right," I said. "Something about a unicorn?"

"Some trouble with one of our *horses,*" said Mrs Anderson, giving me a disparaging look.

"The Alliance only deals with offworld-related problems," I said, "so, I'm taking a wild guess that this horse of yours came from an offworld dealer."

"That is absolutely none of your business," said Mr Anderson, glaring at me.

"Someone contacted the Alliance," I said in my calmest tone. "That makes it our business. Where is it?"

Still glaring, Mr Anderson pointed across the field, to the woodland on the other side of the river. "It ran. Could be miles away, for all we know."

Brilliant. "Okay. We'll sort it." Turning my back and heading that way, I pulled out my stunner, which had three shots, more than enough to disable a magic-using creature. Or anyone, really. The stunner acted as a less-harmful version of a Taser, using second level magic instead of electricity. Ada hesitantly reached for hers.

"Does this not count as animal cruelty?" she asked, turning the rectangular device over in her hands.

"If it's as much trouble as Ms Weston said, then no," I said.

A scream echoed across the river. A wooden bridge crossed it and on the other side, two small children ran in and out of the trees, pursued by…

Well, shit. It really was a pure-white, storybook-style

unicorn. Then I saw its face, and all storybook resemblance faded. Mad, red eyes, drool dripping from pointed teeth, and a gold spiralling horn the length of an Alliance dagger.

"I'm pretty sure it's rabid," I said. "Just brilliant." Stunner in hand, I crossed the bridge.

"You have got to be kidding me," Ada muttered.

At another scream, I sprinted after the unicorn. Sparks shot out from the stunner even though I hadn't pressed the button. *Damn.* I hoped those kids were out of the way. At least the trees slowed the unicorn down, enough for me to catch up and see the two kids, boy and girl, had managed to climb a tree. The unicorn circled below, hissing and tossing its head.

This is ridiculous. I approached it as quietly as possible, stunner at the ready.

"Who are you?" shouted the boy. He must have been around eight years old or so.

The unicorn turned to face us, mad eyes rolling in its head.

"Thanks for that," I muttered, backing up. Ada reached my side, her own stunner aimed forward.

"Don't hurt my horse!" the girl screamed.

"That," I said, "is not a horse." And if those kids didn't shut up, we'd all be impaled. I didn't like the odds.

The unicorn charged, and I threw myself aside, aiming the stunner at its flank. I hit it with a spark of level two magic that made my own skin tingle, but the unicorn whinnied in pain, its entire body shuddering.

"Stop it!" The girl jumped to the ground, running at us. "Let him go! He *is* a horse."

"You do realise 'he' was going to stab you?" I said, approaching the unicorn warily and going for the leather harness over its head—seriously, who the hell had put a harness on? I tugged on the leather reins, and Ada hesitantly grabbed one, too.

"This is officially the weirdest thing I've ever done," she said. "And I've never been near a horse in my life. Or unicorn, come to that."

"Yeah, well, me neither," I said. "Unless you count centaurs. Which I wouldn't, in front of Markos."

"Let him *go!*" The girl tugged at my arm.

"I really wouldn't," I said. The unicorn shifted again, its hoof kicking in a remarkably centaur-like way, and I prepared to give it another zap.

"Your parents shouldn't have let you run around in here," said Ada. "Did they have no idea it isn't a horse?"

"He *is* a horse," snapped the girl.

The 'horse' snorted and bucked to the side, and I gave a sharp tug on the reins. Letting go with one hand, I moved the stunner, before it swung its horn around and knocked someone out.

"Stop!" The girl grabbed at the stunner, and jumped back with a yelp as sparks flew from the end. I hadn't pressed the button, but the magic level surged up again.

The unicorn roared, more like a lion than a horse, and charged, hoofs pounding against the forest floor. It was all I could do to hang onto the reins, trying to get my stunner close to its skin. Ada and I were forced to half-run alongside it, without colliding with trees.

"I am never getting a horse!" gasped Ada. "I think I prefer centaurs!"

"That's debatable," I said, as magic shot from my stunner, missing the unicorn but creating a starburst of red sparks. The second time, I managed to hit the unicorn, which collapsed to its knees at the forest's edge.

"Yeah, I take it back," said Ada. "*This* is the weirdest thing I've ever done."

By some miracle—and not at all helped by the two children getting under our feet and the occasional random spark of magic—we hauled the unicorn over the bridge and locked it up in the stables. Mr and Mrs Anderson looked on, unimpressed. They hadn't even moved from the doorstep once we'd got the unicorn under control, watching us as though we'd invaded their house.

"Someone will be along to take it away shortly," I said, going over to them.

"You can't take him away!" wailed the girl from behind her father in the hallway.

"Tough," I said.

"Don't you speak to my daughter that way," snarled Mr Anderson.

"It would help," I said, irritated, "if you kept track of your obnoxious offspring."

Ada made a noise of choked-off laughter. I thought the old dude might explode with rage. Instead, he slammed the door in our faces.

"You're welcome," I said, and turned to leave. I pulled my communicator to send a message asking for some mode of transporting the bloody unicorn out of here, and back to whichever world it came from. It'd be useful if the Alliance *did* have a pest control department.

"God, Kay," said Ada. "I can't believe you said that." She pressed a hand over her mouth, shaking with laughter.

"What? That kid was a brat, and her parents were worse."

"True. But come on, how could they not know it was a unicorn?"

"I have no idea," I said. "Idiots who don't know anything about offworld, I'd guess. Maybe there's a scammer going around hoaxing people. I'll call up Ms Weston, anyway."

One conversation later had me even more nettled than before. "It's not the only one," I said, as we went back to my motorcycle. "Things like that are happening all over the country. Apparently the unicorn went crazy because of the magic level. I thought I felt something before."

"What, there's unicorns all over the country?" said Ada, sceptically. "I'd never even seen one until now."

"Nah, not just unicorns. Anything magic-related seems to be acting up." And that meant bad news for the Alliance. What could cause a shift in Earth's magic levels? "There have been a few flying cars, apparently. People who added offworld tech to make their engines run faster, I guess."

"Seriously?" Ada laughed. "I bet I know where they got that idea."

"Huh?"

Ada fixed me with a glare. "If you tell me you haven't read the *Harry Potter* books, we're no longer friends."

I rolled my eyes. "Yeah, of course I have."

"Good."

My communicator buzzed. Message from Simon: "Dude, there's a GRIFFIN on the Statue of Liberty!"

"Seriously?" I said. "Just how many people own offworld species? It's barely legal as it is."

"No clue," said Ada. "What happened?"

"Griffin on the Statue of Liberty," I said. "Yes, a griffin. I'd blame Alvienne for that one." On that particular world, griffins were as common as house cats, only more feathery and less well-trained.

"Wow," said Ada. "Is the magic level off all over the world?"

"Sounds like it." I shook my head. "Jesus. I don't think this has ever happened before." I didn't know for certain, of course, but definitely not in the Alliance's recorded history. And definitely not on Earth.

"Wow. Maybe that's what messed up Jeth's computer. He put offworld tech in there."

"Could be," I said. "Which world?"

"No clue. He used to buy spare parts of tech from the market..." She cut herself off, guilt flashing across her expression.

"You mean, illegally," I said. "Come on, Ada, I'm not going to arrest any of you now."

"I know. Old habits die hard, I guess." She gave me a smile, which made me forget my plan for a moment. *Focus.*

"Right. I'd say we head back to Central once the Alliance picks up that unicorn. I want to know if it's just Earth, for a start. This kind of disturbance doesn't come out of nowhere. Either something magic-related's going on somewhere here on Earth, or a bigger upheaval offworld had a ripple effect."

That was the most likely option. A big disturbance on one world could affect the Balance across the Multiverse. A very good reason to keep magic on a tight leash. When the Campbells had tried to use Ada as a weapon, Earth's magic levels had spiralled, and I'd only found out much later it had been global, not just in London, and it had spread into other worlds, too. Magic-wielders here on Earth could do things they wouldn't normally be able to—even use third level. Sounded like something similar was happening now, but not on the same scale.

We'd sure as hell know about it if it was.

Ms Weston called me when we were halfway back, forcing me to pull over and answer my communicator. Apparently, half Central were being sent out to investigate these incidents. The Council was up in arms. And she wanted all magic-wielders to come to her office, *now*. Didn't take a genius to figure out we'd be dealing with most of the trouble ourselves.

As it turned out, seven magic-wielders were present at Central. Out of two hundred, this seemed an absurdly small number, especially as two were technically from offworld and two worked in other departments. None of the Council members were magic-wielders. *Interesting.* Though it made sense in the interests of staying unbiased. Earth's Alliance had a history of magic-averse leadership, probably because it had remained secret for so long. Until my grandfather made a public speech about the Multiverse's existence in 1988. Right now, it looked like we'd reach that level of worldwide panic by the end of the week.

Ada and I were joined by Carl, head of the Alliance guards, and two Ambassadors, Raj and Iriel. I'd worked with both of them on investigating an illegal trade operation between Klathica and Earth last week. Iriel was originally from Klathica, but her blue skin and webbed hands made me pretty certain she had Zanthan blood somewhere. She'd transferred from Klathica to Earth a few years ago.

"Right," said Ms Weston, regarding the group with her steely gaze. "As I'm sure you're aware of by now, Earth's magic level is inexplicably fluctuating, resulting in anything originating from offworld with links to magic reacting to it —technology, mostly, but also offworld and cross-world specie. We're headline news, actually." She held up her communicator screen to demonstrate, switched to a sensationalist online newspaper topped with photos from all over the world. Some showed people who appeared to have lightning coming out of their hands. A griffin lay in the middle of a busy road. Two people appeared to be flying around a city in a minivan. Wait, that was Piccadilly Circus here in London. Despite myself, I turned to look out the window. Nothing odd appeared over the river. We must have missed it when Ada and I were chasing the unicorn.

"Well, damn," I muttered. "Someone's gonna have points on their licence."

Raj laughed. "Yeah, tell me about it. The guards didn't

catch them till the engine gave out near Westminster. Nearly crashed into Big Ben."

"Whoa," said Ada, and then everyone took a step back as Ms Weston slammed the communicator onto the desk with such force, a sheaf of papers fell. She caught them one-handed with a surprising reflex.

"That is *enough*," she said. "This is no joke. The Alliance is at the centre of attention across Earth, and we seem like imbeciles who don't know how to handle our own technology. News like this could result in mass panic."

So could her temper. Raj stood as close to the door as possible without walking into it, while even Carl looked cowed. Ms Weston had that effect on the unprepared.

"Naturally," said Ms Weston, her voice a touch calmer, "where offworld is concerned, it's our problem. But there are so few magic-wielders amongst us, few qualified to deal with any threats, and we have not yet established whether the same problem is affecting other worlds. And, of course, we don't know *why* this is happening, on Earth or otherwise. Either a magic-wielder or magic-based operation has caused a severe disturbance on Earth—unlikely, as the Alliance would have heard about it by now—or the reason lies offworld, and with whichever world is responsible."

Silence fell over the room. If she was right, and we didn't find out which world was responsible, things could get *really* tricky in worlds which relied on magic remaining at a stable level. Valeria would be okay, because using magic outside of technology was mostly illegal. But worlds where it was legal to fire a magic-shot at someone… We'd need to figure this one out quickly.

"So," said Ms Weston, "I'm going to need you Ambassadors to go and speak to the guards for as many worlds as possible. Go to the main Passage. Carl, I'm asking you to go into the Passages, too. Take Ada with you, and call a patrol, but warn them about the magic levels first. I have asked the two other magic-wielders in the Offworld Defence Division to inform the other Alliances on Earth and keep the newsfeeds up to date. Any questions?"

Everyone shifted uncertainly, but nobody spoke. Ms Weston was in full-on manic mode, and no one dared argue with her.

"One quick one," said Raj. "Is someone watching the magic levels? Is there a pattern? Because if there is, it might help to predict when it'll happen next."

"Yes," said Ms Weston. "The trackers work to an extent, but we'll certainly put the tech team on the case."

"Are all the incidents being reported, then?" I asked. "I think the Alliance ought to make an official statement, and quickly, before the rumours get out of hand."

"And before our reputation takes another hit," Raj added. "Is that the council's plan?"

"Naturally, it is," said Ms Weston. "The last thing we need is more bad publicity, both on Earth and offworld. The newspapers have had quite a day with stories of griffins and flying cars."

"And unicorns," added Ada.

Ms Weston gave her a stern look. "Yes, and unicorns. Kay, Raj, Iriel, go to the main Passage. Carl and Ada, gather your patrol in the entrance hall. Pick reliable people who are used to dealing with magic and won't panic if things go bad. And take stunners—more than one each."

Ada nodded, her face set. For all we knew, the disturbance might have come from the Passages themselves. They certainly contained a crap-ton of dispersed magical energy. But it didn't come from nowhere. Something *must* have happened on another world. For all the ridiculous headlines, no way could the actual cause of the event be on Earth itself and not get picked up by the Alliance. But why an offworld event had had such an effect on Earth was a mystery.

The group parted in the entrance hall, Carl and Ada heading to the guard office. I fought down the urge to remind Ada to be careful. She knew already, of course. But like me, she was linked to magic, and it had almost killed her before. She'd been scared half to death she'd accidentally hurt someone—a fear I knew too well, because up until recently, I'd thought magic turned you into a lightning rod, striking down anyone who got too close. But that was only true in unstable magic zones like the Passages. In worlds where magic was commonplace, it could be controlled. In a way, that made it even more dangerous, because if something went wrong, it *really* went wrong. Like Ada's homeworld, Enzar, where the nonmages had exploited magic-wielders, or magebloods, until they'd rebelled and tore the world to pieces in magical warfare. That world was too far out of reach to have a major effect on the Balance. *I think.*

What if one of those distant worlds *had* caused the ripple effect? It was far from impossible, even though if the doorways were kept closed, none of the raging magic could reach the Passages. Ada had said the Enzarian refugees reached the Passages via a transition point far from the actual war zone.

Still...

Raj, Iriel and I made for the doors. No flying cars greeted us outside, but the distant sounds of singing and shouting drifted from the direction of London Bridge. *Tourists.* I spotted a crowd gathering outside the front gates, but guards stopped them getting into the car park. As for the back gates, guards stood at both ends of the back street to stop over-curious people wandering over here. Central had had enough media attention already. West Office, in the heart of London, was more well-hidden, but Central was like a beacon. Add in the war that had almost erupted on our doorstep and it didn't surprise me that the souvenir-toting stalls from the centre of London had migrated over here like they expected a West End show.

Inside, the Passages were louder than usual. The noise grew as we followed the route to the main corridor, where chaos greeted us. Usually, the twin rows of doors to the various worlds were open, though guarded, and the space between filled with people travelling between the worlds. Now, however, the normal crowd became a panicked crush. People—humans and non-humans—jostled and shouted and trampled each other in an effort to cross from one door to another.

"Hey!" I called to the nearest guard, who I recognised as one of the group who usually stood outside Valeria's door. "What's going on?"

"You Earth people should get out," said the Valerian guard. "Magic's going crazy in here."

"It's happening on Earth, too," I said. "Level's way higher than it should be, and fluctuating. We've been dealing with issues all day. How's it on Valeria?"

"Heightened. No accidents yet, but there's a lot of contention in the offworlder communities."

At that moment, a bolt of red lightning shot over our heads, making every nerve in my body respond as though I'd handled an electric switch.

People with an internal magic source will be in real trouble.

"I can imagine," I said, peering over the crowd. No way to tell where the bolt came from, but the panic level climbed. The crowd jostled one another and a green-skinned guy had started a fight with dude who had a coat of real feathers growing from his arms. Punches flew left and right and several people staggered back, away from the magic bolts sizzling from the green guy's skin.

"Stop that!" I shouted. "If you use magic in here, you'll knock off the Balance even more."

"What's it to you?"

Ignoring caution, I edged my way between them. Behind me, Raj sighed with exasperation. The green-skinned guy glared at me, magic flaring from his hands. Klathican. They'd recently patented magic-based implants for super-speed and whatever other enhancements people wanted, and the black market had got hold of ones with questionable effects almost immediately. Idiots. I'd worked with Raj and Iriel to get them shut down, but some of the people who'd bought the temporary boosts illegally must have gone offworld.

I had to deal with this fast.

The feathered guy glared at me, too. "Move it. This is none of your business, Alliance guard."

"Ambassador, actually," I said, "which makes it my business."

The noise around had quieted as people saw the action and realised they were about to get some free entertainment. Great.

"You watch it."

The feathered guy threw a punch, which I blocked with my forearm, stunner already in hand. I fired a shot at the green-skinned guy as he crept up behind me. He collapsed, swearing, and two metal-armed Klathican Alliance guards dived on top of him. Blocking a second hit from the feathered guy, I zapped him with the stunner, too.

By now, more Alliance guards had gathered, and the second guy crawled away as he saw he was far outnumbered. Klathican Alliance guards locked both guys up in cuffs. I didn't take my eyes off them until I was sure they were secured. Technically, with an internal magic source, both had the power to blast the corridor to bits. Lucky most people didn't know that.

"He shouldn't have been able to do that," said the Alliance guard holding the green-skinned guy, to his partner, in Klathican. "Those implants don't work offworld, even the dodgy ones."

"Clearly, they do," I said, also in Klathican. "I'd put a ban on people with them coming out here until this mess is sorted."

"That's the plan. You're Earth, right?"

"London, yeah. We've offworld devices acting up worldwide. I don't suppose anyone knows where the disturbance came from?"

"No. Our Alliance team's looking into it."

"Same with ours." I glanced around for the others and saw Iriel speaking to several people with blue-tinted skin and webbed hands—must be pure-blooded Zanthan. At least the crowd had dispersed somewhat, as the Alliance representatives from various worlds got things under control. And all the doors were closed. *Good.*

Raj joined me as I went over to Iriel. "Do you have a death wish? That guy could have had anything implanted in him. Bloke in here a minute ago knocked three people out cold with a super-strength booster."

"I had the stunners," I reminded him. "They work twice as well on magic-wielders with implants like they had."

"Still." He shook his head. "I don't like this. Never been something on this scale before, unless you count the ruckus at Central."

Yeah, and at the time, it had taken days for the other worlds to get the details on what exactly caused the disturbance. But it had mainly been contained on Earth.

A jolt went through me, making me look up sharply. *That was almost second level.* Several people jumped, and someone screamed. A group of tourists from Alvienne fell to the ground, writhing in pain.

Shit. If not for the magicproof uniform, I'd have been hit by the same thing. As it was, my hands tingled so much I could barely keep them steady on my stunner.

"What was that?"

An Alliance guard ran into view at the corridor's end. Carl. "There's a rogue magic-creature upstairs!" he shouted.

Ada had been with him. I moved quickly, ignoring Raj's protest. "What happened?"

"Kay, we need backup." Carl punched the communicator touch screen. "I'm putting a call through. We've seven of our people up there already. I'll give you three authorisation. We need as many magic-wielders as possible."

"Got it," I said, drawing my stunner.

"Right." Carl tapped his communicator. "Use your stunners—they're the only weapon that'll work. Second stair on the left!" he shouted after me as I ran, Iriel and Raj on my heels.

The second floor meant nothing good. It meant volatile worlds like Enzar.

A wave of magic slammed into us, throwing everyone off their feet. The stunner dropped from my hand as the magic surged through it, the skin of my palm searing like it was on fire. I came upright to see a bolt of lightning fly overhead, bouncing off the walls.

"Stay down!" I shouted.

Behind me, Raj swore. "That's third level!"

Third level. Someone was aiming to kill.

3

ADA

The moment we entered the Passages, I knew we were in trouble. Magic surged around me, making the hairs on my arms stand on end. It had climbed at least one level since I'd last been in here, and I hoped I wouldn't have to use the stunner. The Alliance's magic-based weapons overreacted when I used them at the best of times. Even though I knew I *could* control magic, it seemed too much like tempting fate to use it in the Passages under normal circumstances, let alone now. Our patrol moved closer together as we veered away from the path to the main Passage—the sounds of a commotion echoed from that direction, but Carl shook his head.

"We need to make sure nothing's happening around the second level."

My heart dropped. The second level was reached via hidden staircases, but only elite guards were allowed to patrol up there. I'd not worked at Central long at all, but I guessed the circumstances called for it, seeing as there were so few magic-wielders. I'd known magic was a rarity, but when I'd seen the small group of us gathered in one room, it really hit me. *There must be magic-wielders at other Alliance branches*. Surely.

And Carl didn't know—no one at Central knew, except Kay and perhaps Ms Weston—that I could feel magic levels when they rose in intensity, and if I fired the stunner, I might well lose control of it.

The tunnel-like staircase ended, and the second floor's blue-lit corridor appeared deserted. The Passages blocked all natural sunlight anyway, but this level felt like all warmth had been leached from the air. I'd been here too many times to count, to meet with Delta and help refugees sneak through to the hidden Passage on the first level behind another concealed stair. But I'd never sensed magic this strong around here before.

A noise ahead. I tensed, and Carl held a hand out, indicating we slow down and keep quiet. Our padded shoes made no sound on the polished floor, and as we crept around a corner, a blurred reflection passed by in the wall, too quick to make out what it was.

I pulled out my dagger, heart beating faster. The stunner vibrated in my pocket. *Crap.* I didn't dare use it, not with the magic level this unpredictable.

The shape passed by again. At first, I expected the shadow of a chalder vox or another Cethraxian creature. But they didn't normally venture near the upper level.

Smoke gathered in front of us, bringing the group to a halt. Shadowy reddish smoke formed the outline of a lion-sized beast. *Pure magic,* I thought, with a shiver. Then: *oh, shit.* Regular weapons didn't work on these creatures. Like the gigantic kimaros from Aglaia. But to beat that, I'd needed stable magic. And there wasn't any here.

Heart in my throat, I pulled the stunner. Sparks immediately shot from the end, and I winced.

Carl struck at the creature with his stunner. An electric

jolt split the smoke and the creature yelped. A creeping feeling curled around my spine, and I turned in time to dodge a second pair of insubstantial fangs as they snapped inches from my head.

I aimed the stunner at the beast and fired, a jet of red-purple lightning sparking off the walls. The creature screamed, but a louder noise overlaid it: a tremendous roar from ahead.

"Watch out!" Carl yelled.

I spun around in time to see an even bigger monstrosity rise from the smoke—red and long-limbed and snarling.

Where did it come from? Stupid how that was my first thought, but panic made me freeze up for a moment. It lashed out in a sea of sparks, and several guards fell, lightning encasing them. Carl swore, backing up, and other two monsters appeared alongside it—*where the hell did* they *come from?*

"My stunner's out!" Carl yelled. "I'm calling for backup—if you run out of shots, just *run!*"

I had five shots left. Ignoring my pounding heart and shaking limbs, I ran at the nearest creature, which advanced on the fallen guards, and shot it with the stunner. A blast of magic far stronger than the stunner should have hit the creature in the face, sending ripples of magic pulsing outwards—only by pure luck did it miss the guards on the ground. *Damn.* If it hadn't been for the adamantine in my blood, the backlash would have probably knocked me out. I wasn't in control.

"Guys, stay back!" I yelled at two other guards who'd come to stand alongside me. "It's not stable."

I'm *not stable.*

But I had no choice. I struck with the stunner, sending a searing bolt of lightning at the nearest beast. Except the lightning didn't come from the stunner. It came from my hand.

A nearby guard swore. "I'm out of shots."

"Take mine," I said quickly. "I can fight without it." Magic seemed to want me to.

"Thanks," he said, blinking like he was surprised I'd give away my weapon, and caught the stunner.

A snarling bundle of red smoke descended on us. How many of these things were there? For every one I knocked down, two more appeared, sparking and trailing smoke. I struck another with a bolt of magic, aiming at the floor to make sure I didn't hit any of the other guards. The beast dissolved in smoke... and then divided in two. Like some ghastly hydra. Both halves growled at me, sparks flying out from their clawed, smoky red hands.

Shit. I backed away, thinking hard.

A rumbling sounded, and the ground trembled under my feet. *What the hell?* I'd thought the reinforced floor was impervious to any kind of hit. *The magic. It's got to be the magic.* Lucky my shoes were magicproof, too.

"I'm getting outta this corridor!" someone shouted, and the sound of running footsteps clattered on metal.

A growl sounded, but before I could strike the two smoky creatures down, both dissolved into a formless red haze. Through the fog, guards ran everywhere, shouting, while I struck out with magic, to no effect. The magic-creatures had turned themselves into smoke, and it was like trying to beat up a cloud. At least we all looked equally ridiculous, I thought as I spun on the spot in what probably looked like an undignified ballet manoeuvre. Another guard face-planted, while a second tripped over him and brought the two of them crashing into a heap.

And the floor shook again, the smoke coalescing in the

centre to form one formidable beast, filling the space from floor to ceiling. A shower of purple-red danced off the walls. I jumped back, but not before a spark grazed my forehead. The pain was more sharp than electric. Wincing, I braced myself against the wall, out of range of the magic. I still couldn't see the creature. It was made of pure magic, and didn't have a solid form. But I could feel the energy burning, and it was all concentrated in one place. The monster had pulled all the magic in the area into itself. *It has to burn out. It can't keep going like that.*

But the monster didn't show any signs of slowing down. Stunner shots mingled with the sparks, and inhuman screams told us at least one hit the target. My hands shook too much to risk aiming another magic shot, even as I felt the creature's magic surging through the air. A bolt of pain shot through my forehead. I reached to touch the skin, and found it blistering hot. *I thought magic couldn't hit me!*

I thought I could absorb it—magic and antimagic both, because of the adamantine in my blood. Whatever that creature was made of didn't follow the normal rules.

I spun around in the dark, not daring to fire in case I hit a person instead of an enemy. I had no weapon now.

A hand reached from the darkness and closed around my neck. I screamed as my skin burned, and kicked at the shadows. I fired a shot of magic, hoping the wall was where I remembered so it wouldn't rebound and hit anyone. A howl echoed in my ears and the grip around my neck went away, though the burning sensation remained. The brief flare of light illuminated the corridor, and a person running towards us.

Kay.

The light went out again. Kay swore, and sparks flew again, forcing me to back away, arms shielding my face.

"There's backup on the way!" Kay shouted over the chaos. I couldn't see him anywhere, and several people shouted as sparks from the creature rebounded off the walls again.

"We've got it!" someone yelled. "Quick—everyone with a stunner get over here!"

Kay shouted, "Everyone get down!" The corridor lit up in a flash of lightning, outlining three guards in the act of wrestling a bear-sized creature to the ground. In the gleaming light, their hands and faces were marked with vivid red burn-like marks. I edged towards them, but I couldn't hit the creature at close range with so many people nearby. The magic emanating from the creature buzzed in the air—it writhed underneath the guards, and I knew, with certainty, that it was about to burn out.

Several stunners fired at once, and the creature exploded. Fragments of metal scattered on the ground, and the blazing light faded as the blue sheen slowly returned to the walls and ceiling.

Whatever the creature was, it was dead.

"What the hell was that?"

"Did any of you get hit? Fucking *burns*."

I bit back a cry as pain tore through my neck again. A burning sensation hit my forehead, too, and I pressed my hand to it, biting down on my lip.

"Ada?" Kay was at my side. "Shit. *Shit*."

I winced as his hand brushed against my neck. "I got hit," I said. "I thought..."

I thought magic couldn't affect me. But I was wrong. Dead wrong.

Luckily, no one was seriously hurt, but several others had those burn-like marks on their hands and faces—the uniform blocked any more damage. Every minute or so, a sharp sensation jolted my forehead and neck and made my skin tingle all over with pain. Magic?

Kay steered me towards the stairs.

"You don't need to do that," I said, pulling away and climbing by myself, Kay directly behind me. "I'm fine." As my feet touched the ground, another sharp pain sent me staggering into the wall.

"Ada... damn." He touched my forehead lightly. "That's magic burn." His fingers brushed my neck, then his fist clenched. "What did it do to you?"

He seemed more agitated about it than I was. It wasn't like it was serious—*ouch!* I instantly took that back.

"I hit it, don't worry."

"Wish I'd taken it out myself," he said through clenched teeth, eyes flashing back to the marks on my neck.

"You didn't get hit, did you?" I asked him.

He shook his head. "I got here too late." He took my hand. His was freezing cold, but then, so was mine. "Hang on. We're getting out of here."

"What *is* this?" I said, touching my neck. It didn't hurt to touch, oddly, but the skin felt tender, white-hot. "It was just a spark."

"Magic burn," he said. "That creature was pure magic. Did you see where it came from?"

I shook my head. Another sharp pain made me clench my fingers around his. "Why does it keep—*ouch!*"

"Because it's magic burn," he said. "I hope it's not long lasting. It'll keep shocking you until it wears off."

"You've got to be joking." I stared at him. The blue Passage light gleamed in his eyes.

"It's like when you get hit by backlash," he said. "I've no idea what power that creature was drawing from, but it shouldn't have been able to hit you."

"Well, it did." *Ouch.* "And this is going to keep happening? *How* long?"

"I don't know."

"That's really helpful," I snapped.

"You're lucky it wasn't worse. At least you can still walk."

"At least *what?*" And there I was, expecting one degree of sympathy for a second… wait a minute. "It happened to you?"

"Twice."

"When… the backlash hit your hands." It had slipped my mind that when he'd used third level magic to kill Janice, the backlash had burned the skin off his hands. I hadn't realised magic had an aftershock, too, because I'd been in a coma at the time. "Sorry."

"Don't worry about it."

Ouch. "How long did it last for you?" Suddenly, I wasn't sure I wanted to know.

A pause. "Two weeks."

Damn. "Seriously? Like, day and night?"

He nodded. "On and off."

You didn't say anything. But I shouldn't have been surprised.

Pain seared across my neck again. "Can't I put an ice-pack on it or something?"

"You can try, it might help."

"It didn't work for you." And now I felt guilty for snapping at him on top of everything else.

Kay's hand steadied my shoulder as pain made my knees go weak. "No, but it might not affect you as badly."

My head throbbed. "Uh-huh." I let him rest his hand on my shoulder. I was tired, and I'd have appreciated it more if not for the pain.

"I'm an amplifier. That probably made it worse. You're…"

"Supposed to be magicproof," I said. "Adamantine. It's my real name, actually."

"It is?" He looked at me, as if surprised I'd told him. But I wanted him to know.

"Yeah. Nell's fault. Lucky it's not on my Alliance ID. That'd get everyone talking."

"They'll already be talking," he said. "About this. I've no idea what that thing was."

"Me neither. It was like the kimaros on Aglaia, but more... sparky." But if it could break through adamantine protection, the Alliance were in major trouble.

"Sparky," he said. "Ms Weston will be thrilled if you put that in your report."

I groaned. "I'm not reporting now. She can't expect me to fill out files like this." My hands shook, and I was grateful for Kay's steady hand on my shoulder for balance as we made our way through the corridors.

We wound up back at Central, and Kay walked me down to the infirmary before going to report to Ms Weston. From what I gathered from the others, the main corridor in the Passages had been in chaos, because this magic-related issue rebounded across the Multiverse.

The Alliance's medical division had their work cut out. One nurse, Saki, gave me a Death Glare that puzzled me until I remembered I'd attacked her when I'd been held prisoner. Oops. I'd forgotten to apologise. But now wasn't the time. Complaints and yells of pain filled the infirmary, where instead of lying on the beds, the guards were dashing around moaning loudly about the magic burn.

I was sick of it already. Every time I relaxed, another spark of pain reminded me. The nurse told me the marks would fade quickly and wouldn't scar, but the pain would carry on until it ran its course. Apparently, it was very rare that the medical staff dealt with magic burn, which was why they didn't know *how* to deal with it. Only sympathy for Kay having to put up with it for two *weeks* kept me from joining in with the complainers. Once the nurse had checked me for other injuries, I was free to walk back upstairs to the entrance hall.

"Ada!" Jeth ran over to me, communicator in hand. "They wouldn't let anyone downstairs. What happened?"

"It's not serious, I'm fine. The marks'll be gone in a few days."

He scanned my forehead and neck, fist clenching around his communicator. "Shit. Does it hurt?"

"Not much—ow." I stepped back as he touched my forehead with a forefinger. "There's no cure for magic burn, it'll go away on its own. I'm *fine*, Jeth."

"What's going on in there?" asked Jeth, indicating the stairs down to the infirmary. Guess he'd heard the noise.

"A bunch of people complaining. No one's seriously hurt, but there was this freaky magic-creature. I'm not sure even the Alliance knows what it is."

"Damn, Ada," said Jeth, worry creasing his forehead. "It's not safe in the Passages now, is it?"

I shook my head. "I don't know. They say this magic level chaos is happening all over the Multiverse." *Ouch.*

"Ada?" Kay crossed the hall towards us from the guard office.

"I'm fine," I said wearily. "They checked me over, let me go."

"I thought so. Iriel and Raj had to break up another fight. It's madness in the main Passage. I think they're going to lock it down." He held his communicator in one hand, and tapped on the touch screen.

"She's still hurt," Jeth snapped. "They're letting her go in this state?"

"There's no cure," I said quickly. "I told you." Unlike Alber, my older brother hadn't warmed up to Kay and me being friends. Kay himself glared back, while I rolled my eyes at the pair of them.

"I'm not on my deathbed," I informed Jeth. "It's magic burn, not the plague. What's the plan for tomorrow?" I asked Kay. "Half the guards got taken out, by the look of things."

Kay tapped his communicator screen again. "Ms Weston says you don't have to come in tomorrow. I told her about the magic-creature. You can if you want, of course, but you're exempted from patrols."

Given that I flinched with pain every other minute, that was probably a good move. It still annoyed me.

"Great," I said, suppressing another wince. "Ms Weston said my handwriting is illegible anyway, let alone when I'm being electrocuted."

"Is there really nothing you people can do?" Jeth asked.

Kay shook his head, putting his communicator back in his pocket. "It'll go away on its own." He addressed me, not Jeth. "Distract yourself. You have my number, anyway."

I stared. I *did*, but he'd never brought it up before.

"You should go. I'll see you soon."

He'd gone before I could so much as blink. *Okay...* Apparently my social skills had nose-dived since I'd started working here. Then again, it wasn't like we'd exchanged numbers at a bar. My communicator stored all Alliance members' codes automatically.

Jeth looked at me. "You have his number?"

"I have everyone's numbers," I said, a little too quickly. "Our communicators are linked up to all the staff, remember?"

He shook his head. "Sure. You be careful, Ada."

"Bit late for that." I tapped the marks on my neck. "It won't scar, don't worry," I added hastily, and started to walk towards the exit before he started worrying over me again.

The front doors slid open. "I hope they do lock the Passage down," said Jeth. "It's not safe, is it?"

Ouch. "Talk to me about something else," I said, shivering as we walked outside into the pouring rain. "Distract me. What're the tech team doing?"

"Now? Trying to track the magical disturbances," he said. "It's a bit annoying that we got interrupted, we were about to test out our new offworld communication apps. They're based on the Chameleons."

Ouch. "How d'you mean?"

"Earpiece translators for offworld languages. We've a whole bunch of them, but we haven't got clearance to use them yet because of all the craziness happening. They're fine, though, most of our technology is. It's just certain types of magi-tech that are playing up."

"Weird," I said, huddling in my jacket and wishing my coat had a hood. "I can't believe no one knows what's causing it."

"Hope they get it sorted soon," said Jeth.

"Me, too."

Nell descended on us as soon as we got in the house. "What happened to you?" she demanded, instantly fixating on the marks on my neck and forehead.

"A magic-creature," I said. "I don't know what it was, but there's something weird going on with the magic, everywhere. I guess you've probably seen it on the news?"

"Your brother almost set the house on fire," said Nell.

"It wasn't my fault!" Alber came out the kitchen into the hallway.

"What did you do?" I asked, eyebrows raised.

He shifted guiltily. "Tried to light the stove using magic."

I rolled my eyes. "Idiot."

"It used to work!" he protested. "I didn't know magic had gone crazy."

"The whole Multiverse knows now," I said, rubbing the back of my neck as another sharp pain hit me. I shrugged out of my jacket. At least that hadn't suffered any damage.

"What happened?" asked Alber, following me into the kitchen. I quickly explained while I ran cold water on a cloth and pressed it to my neck, hoping it might help.

"Magic burn," said Jeth, switching on the light. "I can't believe there's no cure."

"It doesn't normally happen on Earth," I said, moving the cloth to my forehead, which twinged again.

"Yeah, but the Alliance deal with offworld all the time." Jeth pulled his communicator from his pocket. "I'll look it up in the files."

"There won't be anything there," I said. "Whatever that thing was, it sure wasn't normal, even for the Alliance. And it might be worse for me because I have an internal magic source."

"Damn," said Alber. "That's because you're Royal, right?"

I winced. "Sort of. It's not just me…" But he didn't know Kay had experienced something similar. Nell had guessed, but I was pretty sure I was the only person who knew that now Skyla and the other victims were dead. *Ouch.* "Okay, this feels like being poked in the neck with a red-hot electric wire every minute. So I'm sorry in advance if I yell at anyone."

"They ought to stop you from going into those Passages," said Nell from the doorway, eyes narrowed. "Those magic-creatures are more dangerous than the usual monsters."

"Someone has to deal with them." But I shivered, thinking of the way it had looked so much like that creature on Aglaia. A deadly killer. We were lucky no one had died.

It was hard to feel lucky at one in the morning when the

bloody magic burn *still* hadn't gone away. I set up camp on the roof again, complete with a book and sleeping bag. The cold had never particularly bothered me. Maybe because I'd been going into the freezing-cold Passages for so many years. I set my communicator down next to me, but hesitated on using it. Did Kay want me complaining at him all night? I skimmed the newsfeed instead, which updated every minute or so from the various Alliance branches worldwide. An offworld update feed showed the news from nearby worlds, and like Earth's, it was going haywire with reports of the magic level fluctuating in a way it shouldn't be.

And zapping me. Ouch.

Sighing, I scrolled through to Kay's number and sent a message. *"Are you awake?"*

A couple of minutes later: *"Yeah. Want me to call you?"*

So he'd meant it? Not that he'd suggested otherwise, but I didn't think we were at the calling-one-another-in-the-middle-of-the-night stage of friendship. Then again, I wasn't exactly an expert on the subject.

"Okay."

The communicator buzzed in my hand, at the same time as the magic burn decided to blaze across my neck again, making me drop it. *Crap.* I caught the shiny piece of expensive tech before it fell over the edge of the roof. "Hey."

"What was that?"

"I nearly dropped my communicator off the roof."

"The roof?"

"I like sitting up here." And now I sounded like an idiot.

"Just don't fall off."

"Fall off? I'll have you know, I have an awesome sense of balance."

"I know you do. I've seen you climb trees."

I smiled. "Oh, yeah. You're pretty good, too. Even invisible. Did you learn invisible stealth at the Academy?"

"Nah, I dropped out of ninja finishing school."

"Very funny. Ow." I rubbed my neck again. Even the cool air didn't help, though the shocks occurred less often than before.

"It's still happening?"

I couldn't deny Kay's concerned tone took some of the sting off.

"Yay me. How did you stand this for two weeks? Wait, you said it happened twice?"

There was such a long silence, I thought he'd hung up. "It wasn't the first time."

Ouch. "What... what happened?"

"When I hit the wyvern with magic, I didn't have any protective shield, so I got the full backlash."

"Damn." As I'd heard the story second hand, I didn't know he'd been hit by magic as well as almost getting torn to pieces.

"I know, right?" His tone was light. Almost too much so.

"Ow," I said, lamely. "Sorry." Holy hell. Guess I'd been lucky the creature had only touched my neck.

"Don't worry about it."

I rubbed my forehead. "I was thinking..."

"Yeah?"

"I'm supposed to have adamantine inside my blood," I said. "So the sparks shouldn't have been able to hit me. But maybe it doesn't apply to surface wounds. Those sparks just grazed me."

"Good point. If you were magicproof on the outside, then you wouldn't be able to use magic at all."

"That's what I've been wondering... but adamantine isn't really magicproof, is it? It's partly magic itself. So I'm not a shield, not really. More of a conduit."

"Good point," he said. "I think it does act as a shield on the outside, because it stops higher levels from harming you."

"Just not lower levels," I said. "Makes sense, since I've always been able to sense magic, in the Passages. What about your amplifier? Does it work on anything else, apart from the Chameleon?" *And me.* Because I could absorb magic, I could also absorb the effects of any other source just by touching it. That included Kay's own abilities, because he was a human amplifier—almost a source himself.

He paused. "Maybe. A lot of the Alliance's equipment is partly made of adamantine, but I can't affect that."

"It worked when you amplified *my* power," I pointed out. "But that might be because it's an internal source... that explains it."

"Explains what?"

"Why it didn't kill me to channel that much magic." I fidgeted, swapping my communicator to the other ear. "You know when we sent that kimaros back into the Passages on Aglaia? That was easily as much power as I used when the Campbells..."

"Not exactly," he said. "You were pushing on the magic already there, externally, not absorbing it. Same with the lustre source. It only amplifies what's there."

Like the Chameleon. "Good point." I frowned. "Okay. I'll keep that in mind. I really need to find out more about this stuff. I know how it works for magebloods, because it's all external. But it seems like magic gets more complicated by the day. Wish it was more help when we fought that creature."

"It's saved your life before."

"I know, but I always wanted to fly."

He laughed quietly. "Yeah, can't do that. Sorry to disappoint you. You'll have to stick to your hover boots."

"I suppose it'd be *too* awesome," I said. "You can't have all the superpowers, that's unfair."

"Nobody said the Multiverse played fair." He said this

lightly, but I could detect an undercurrent to his voice. The Multiverse hadn't played fair at all, considering neither of us should have had magic in the first place. "You should probably try to sleep."

"Why are *you* awake? Do you not sleep at all?"

"When the Multiverse plays fair."

"Guess that's not really happening right now." I sighed, tilting my head to the night sky. Lights from the high-rise buildings obscured the stars.

"I could send you a link to some Valerian music if you like."

Huh? I couldn't tell if was being serious or not. "Depends if it's relaxing."

"It sounds like a train falling off a cliff."

"Then, no."

"I was joking."

"Hmm. I couldn't tell." Yep. I definitely needed to work on picking up social cues. It'd be easier if we were speaking face to face. "You know what, lecture me on the most boring subject you can think of."

"You want me to talk you to death?"

I laughed. "Nah." I'd asked that question when he'd been my interrogator. "I used to fall asleep at school, is all. Guess that accounts for my crappy grades."

"You passed the Alliance's entry exams with high scores. Ms Weston told me. Where'd you learn to speak Klathican, anyway?"

He'd been asking about me? "Nell taught me. Said it's the easiest language to learn in the Multiverse."

"Yeah, the Klathicans tried to install it as a cross-world trade language a few decades ago. Didn't take. Now there are a hundred variations."

"And you speak... how many languages?"

A pause. "What level? Seven fluently, six semi-fluently, and I know odd phrases in a dozen more, maybe."

"Holy hell," I said. "Seriously, how do you have your shit together? You're barely older than I am."

"Did I tell you how old I was?"

"Simon said you joined the Academy at sixteen." *He also said you were in denial. Just say the freaking words, Ada.* "Ah. Wait a minute—I haven't been shocked in a while." *Way to chicken out.*

"Maybe it's wearing off. It only grazed you, right?"

"I hope so," I said, though a twinge of guilt reminded me I'd had it easy. There was more I wanted to say, much more. Even in the forest on Aglaia, if we hadn't been interrupted, I didn't know what would have happened. He'd probably have stopped me... well, given how he'd responded, maybe not. But then, I imagined most guys wouldn't turn down a direct come-on, and pursuing that line would make me look pathetic and desperate. "I'll see you soon?"

"Yeah, if I'm not sent after another unicorn."

I wiped raindrops off my face, picking up my book before it got splashed. "Wonder if they caught that griffin?"

"Wish they'd sent Simon after it," said Kay. "I'd never have let him forget it."

"Was any of this stuff in *your* job description, by the way?"

"Nah, but it's the Alliance. If magic's involved, it's our problem."

Another drop of water splashed onto my face. "Guess so. I'll see you tomorrow, anyway."

Yawning, I returned to my room via the window. In the mirror, the marks on my neck and forehead had faded already. *What did that?* Maybe it was because the adamantine in my blood had finally kicked in. Or this magical instability had finally stopped.

Wishful thinking.

4

KAY

Once again, Ms Weston called an early-morning meeting of all Central's magic-wielders the following day, and we were to be ready to go offworld. Naturally, the message came through at five in the morning, thereby killing any chance I had of getting to sleep.

Then I got a message from Ada. *"I got Ms Weston's message. I'm coming to Central. Can I meet you outside?"*

"You sure?"

"Yeah, of course. The magic burn's gone and I'm not sitting in admin. She said to be ready to go offworld. I'm gonna need a caffeine hit."

"I can take care of that. Espresso okay?"

"Please."

The question was, if we were going offworld, did that mean the Alliance had tracked the magical disturbance to whichever world caused all this chaos?

I waited for Ada outside Central, two coffees in hand. She arrived, clad in guard gear with her bright-red hair ruffled by the cold wind. Jesus, the universe was really trying to torture me today.

"Hey," she said, coming over to me. "You're a lifesaver."

I handed her the espresso. "You got lucky."

"Yeah. I did." The marks on her forehead and neck had faded already, though the thought of them made me feel like hitting something. That blasted magic-creature was lucky, too, that I hadn't been the one to finish it off.

I drank half the scalding-hot coffee. "We should go see what the dragon wants."

"Yeah." She yawned. "What was worth pestering me at this godforsaken hour? It must be urgent, 'cause yesterday, she said I didn't have to come in."

"Yeah." Especially since she'd called in all the magic-wielders. That either meant we were being sent out to somewhere on Earth, or offworld. "I suppose it's because there aren't all that many magic-wielders at Central."

"So we're the magic-wielder crack team." She grinned at me.

"It's in the job description. Right under 'unicorn-catcher' and 'wrangler of runaway goblins.'"

Ada laughed, and I was kind of tempted to stick around and try and get that smile out of her again. But I didn't want to test the dragon's wrath at this hour in the morning.

In Ms Weston's office, we found Raj, Iriel and Carl waiting. All, aside from Ms Weston, wore guard gear.

"We have been discussing the incident in the Passages yesterday," said Ms Weston, without preamble. "The magic-creature came straight from a source world. Carl used a tracker to analyse it and the tech team have been working to get more details. We've found that it didn't come from the second floor of the Passages, it came from below, on the boundary with the first level. And we've found that the source of disturbance across the Balance also came from this direction."

"One world in particular," Carl added.

"We've pinpointed it," said Ms Weston, picking up her communicator from her desk and tapping the screen. "It's a world registered with the Alliance but which has refused to apply for membership. The peoples of Vey-Xanetha migrated there from another world entirely after a cataclysm a thousand years ago, using the help of the Alliance as it existed at the time. There is an Alliance base there, but it's more of a research base. We don't currently have any Earth operatives there, but it's functional, if a little isolated. And that's where the disturbance is coming from." She turned the communicator around so we could all see the bullet-point list of notes under the name VEY-XANETHA.

"From the base, or from that world in general?" I asked, frowning at the list. As I'd expected, the world was listed as high-magic. But I'd never heard of it before.

"The whole world recently experienced some kind of magical upheaval. Even the people at the base don't know the specifics. Vey-Xanetha is high-magic in a very unusual way. They believe their three nature deities shaped their world and interact with them using magic. There is proof of this in the nature of the world itself."

I blinked. "Seriously?"

Ms Weston arched an eyebrow. "So it would seem."

Well, damn. Definitely not a world I was familiar with. Not that I knew every world in the Multiverse, but a detail like that would definitely have stuck in my mind. The Zanthans worshiped an actual, living sea serpent, and most worlds had at least one culture where certain humans were regarded as living gods. Magic-wielders, usually. But magic deities as a living thing—as creators, even?

"These deities. Who are they, and what exactly do they do?" I asked.

"I don't know all the details. The Vey-Xanethans have done a remarkable job keeping to themselves, all things considered. According to records, they were an advanced people when they were forced to leave the world they originally inhabited a thousand years ago, and were effectively forced to adapt to a hostile world nothing like what they were used to. At any rate, these deities are the core of their existence."

"So is this upheaval linked to these... deities?"

"Perhaps. That's why I want you all to travel there today. The council have called a meeting with representatives from the other allied worlds, but none feel the situation is urgent enough to merit sending in a team. Earth, however, has been affected worse than the others, and the council have permitted me to assign you to Vey-Xanetha as Earth's representatives. I've asked the other two magic-wielders to stay here and keep an eye on the situation on Earth, and Carl, I want you to watch the Passages. Kay, Ada, Raj, Iriel, you're to head to Vey-Xanetha and talk to people at the base. Some of you have useful skills which might help you determine what the problem is. There's clearly been a magical disturbance, and the quicker we find out what it is, the quicker we can find a way to deal with it. If it affects the Balance, it becomes the Alliance's problem."

Yeah. Except a world that had already opted out of joining obviously had some issue with us. Even Aglaia had allied with the Alliance, and the leading centaurs couldn't stand the sight of us.

"You're to observe the situation, for now. With the current instability, anything you do there may—no, will, have consequences. Is that understood?"

She looked at Ada, but she'd directed the question at me, too. Everyone nodded.

"We've anticipated some communication difficulties due to the lack of links with other worlds—the people at the base have learned the native language, but of course, none of you will know. So we'll be field-testing these." She handed each of us a metal clip-on earpiece.

"They're translators?" I guessed.

"Oh, they're what my brother was working on," said Ada, examining the device. "Don't they automatically translate any language?"

"In theory. Don't lose them. We have only a few in Central."

I clipped on the device. "Someone say something in another language."

"Like this?" said Iriel, uncertainly.

I pulled off the earpiece. "What was that?"

"Zanthan," she said. "You understood?"

"Yeah. Guess these are updated versions of the communicator app? Or the sort the council uses for cross-world meetings?"

"They eliminate the need for computers," said Ms Weston. "And on low-technology worlds, they will be much less likely to stir up content." She turned to Ada. "Your brother certainly has a flair."

"I'll tell him," said Ada, clipping on her own earpiece.

Raj did likewise. "This is pretty neat," he said. "So it works with all languages?"

"All the ones registered," she said. "You'll have to speak slowly, mind. There are bound to be misunderstandings, but this is the best we have."

"Awesome," said Raj.

"Right," said Ms Weston. "It's Door 11, in an obscure Passage area, not one we usually use. There's only one doorway to that world. I have to emphasise: you aren't to leave the compound unless I send you further instructions. The dangers are unrecorded, but it's registered as unstable."

And on that note, we were dismissed. But I almost saw

worry in her expression as we left. She hadn't said to expect trouble, but with magic, it went with the territory.

"Unstable?" Ada asked, as we headed downstairs with the rest of the group. "How does the classification work, anyway?"

"Unstable means it's barely hanging onto a connection with the Alliance," I said. "The level above that is 'dangerous.'"

"Like Enzar," she said.

"Yeah."

A wave of noise hit us before we reached the entrance hall. Crowds swarmed in, and a large number of people headed in the direction of the Complaints Division. Most didn't look like they worked here, given the high number of offworlders amongst them. Central must have opened to public complaints now. Someone was going to have their work cut out. At least we were going to do something useful, rather than answering queries or rounding up escaped unicorns. We skirted around the crowd to the doors.

"I've never heard of Vey-Xanetha," said Ada. "But Door 11... I think I've seen it before." From the flash of guilt in her expression, I guessed she'd been near that door when using the Passages illegally before she'd joined the Alliance.

"I think I've heard the name," said Iriel, "but I didn't know anything about them until today."

"Me neither," said Raj. "But I can't pretend I know every non-Alliance world."

"Nor me," I admitted. They must have worked hard to keep themselves secret from the Alliance. "Living deities?"

"Forces of nature, according to the file," said Iriel. "I've heard of that kind of thing happening when magic and nature mix. Seems like a recipe for disaster if I ever saw one."

"Magic usually is," I said.

∼

Vey-Xanetha had definitely done a good job hiding their door in the most labyrinthine part of the Passages, and if not for my knowing every inch of the place, we'd have been lost for longer. The door itself was at the back of a dead-ending corridor near one of the staircases to the second floor.

"About bloody time!" said Ada, as I pushed the door open. Before she followed, her gaze darted to a corner, where a faint shimmer showed a hidden stair to the lower levels. One of the routes to the hidden Passage she used to take, probably. Now the Alliance knew the Passage's location, we didn't use it anymore, but they hadn't closed it, for some reason. I supposed it might work in their favour to have an extra doorway into London.

"Yeah," I said, deciding not to bring that up in front of the others. "Okay. Someone's meeting us on the other side." The door opened onto the side of a mountain, on a steep path barely a metre wide. I stepped out carefully, testing the ground first. The path wrapped around the cliff with no railing between us and a steep drop. Below lay a forest, masked by low-hanging white clouds. The sky above gleamed purplish-red, which was usually a sign of the level of magic in the atmosphere. This mountain was part of the range dividing the one continent on Vey-Xanetha. It was one large landmass, apparently, the one place all the inhabitants had migrated to after leaving their old world. We did have a map logged into our communicators, but it was most likely out of date. Still, they'd have up-to-date information at the base.

I sensed the magic here, like on Aglaia—subtle, right now, which didn't fit in right with the description Ms Weston had given us of this being a high-magic, unstable world. Maybe the levels fluctuated. I'd be on guard, anyway. I didn't trust magic as far as I could throw it—and I sure as hell wouldn't be doing *that* here. Magic shots weren't illegal, actually, even third level, but that meant encountering magic-wielders here might put us in a world of trouble.

The base itself sat higher up the mountain; they'd built it next to the one Passage entrance. The others groaned when they saw we'd have to climb a steep stone staircase cut into the mountain itself.

"What," said Raj, "is the point in using Passages for convenience if we have to climb a bloody mountain?"

"Could be worse," I said, indicating the forest. "We might have ended up down there in the jungle."

The temperature here was much higher than Earth, more tropical than anything, and in guard uniform, we were all sweating within a minute. The climb didn't take too long, though Raj kept muttering how he hadn't signed up for this when he'd become Ambassador.

"None of us did," said Iriel. "Welcome to life as a magic-wielder."

"Luck of the bloody draw," muttered Raj.

Yeah. That's one way of putting it. Personally, if I could stop Earth getting overrun by rabid unicorns and griffins, I'd take on the goddamn mountain.

As we came to a steep incline leading up to a large stone structure, the mountain shifted under our feet, so abruptly Raj tripped over and Iriel staggered against a wall. I barely kept my balance, and Ada backed up a few steps. Magic flared, making my hands tingle with static. There was the instability.

"What was that?" asked Raj, getting to his feet.

"Felt like an earthquake," said Ada, with an uneasy glance at me. Of course, the other two wouldn't be able to feel it—only people with an internal source could.

"No clue," I said. "I reckon we ought to get up there."

I took the lead and we climbed quickly, keeping close to the wall alongside the path in case another earthquake—or whatever it was—took us by surprise. Reaching the top, I turned back to make sure the others were keeping up. The forest looked even more extensive from here. According to the map, it covered half the continent, and wasn't properly mapped out. I hoped we didn't end up having to go there, because offworld GPS didn't work in worlds without a satellite licensed by the Alliance. This world didn't look like it'd be launching rockets into space anytime soon.

I couldn't see further than the jungle. Above, I swore the sky had gone a deeper red in the last few minutes.

A shadow moved in the corner of my eye, and I instinctively shifted my hand towards my dagger. I'd rather avoid using the stunner, but Ms Weston had described this world as "hostile", and that was reason enough to be on full alert.

I turned towards the shadow, but there was nothing there. Maybe I was being jumpy, but I never doubted my own instincts.

"Be careful," I said to Ada, who reached the top next. "I think I saw something move over there."

Raj and Iriel caught up. "Time out," said Raj. "*And* we have to walk all the way back later."

"Quit whining," said Iriel. "How many Alliance members from Earth have seen this place?"

"No one in the past twenty-five years," I said.

"We should get a photo," said Ada, grinning at me. "Come on, it's pretty awesome."

I rolled my eyes. "The council won't like it."

"What, does Vey-Xanetha have a ban on photography?"

"Minimal interference," I said. "It's part of the Ambassadors' mandate."

"And we're in a dangerous job," said Raj. "It's not a holiday."

"I know that," said Ada. "Is that the base?"

The building's tower-like shape cut into the burnished

bronze-coloured cliff face, probably the same height as my apartment block. There was real glass in the windows, but it must have been brought in from offworld, because there didn't seem to be any other kind of habitation on the mountain and the jungle looked impenetrable. The metal-plated bronze-coloured door opened, and someone stepped out.

"Civilisation!" Raj proclaimed.

The claw-footed man who greeted us was presumably part-avian, from one of the west-lying worlds. He seemed nervous, shifting from one clawed foot to another and anxiously glancing up at the sky, and hurried us into the building. He walked with a pronounced limp and bandages were visible above his scaly ankle. A recent injury.

"I'm Avar," he said. "I work in research here."

A bronze-skinned man with violet eyes joined him, a native of Vey-Xanetha named Mathran. The pair of them were assisted by various people from other Alliances, but at the moment, only the two of them were present at the base. We clipped on the spare earpieces we'd brought, so everyone would be able to understand one another without complications. Before, we'd have had to rely on communicator-translators onscreen. I couldn't help being impressed by Ada's brother's ideas—pity he was such a dick.

The room designated for the meeting overlooked the cliff's edge. The plain furniture was made of some stone, the same coppery colour as the mountain. A working ceiling light flickered above. So this world had electricity.

"How does that work?" Raj asked Avar, spotting it, too.

"We use solar energy here," he explained. "We decided that in the interests of noninterference, we'd make this base self-sustaining."

Mathran said, "We are glad of that decision now. The world outside is hostile."

Avar shifted, revealing the bandage on his leg was faintly

stained with blood. In fact, Mathran himself bore several scratches on his face. Had something attacked them? Maybe that was why the others had left the base.

"What even lives down there?" asked Ada, peering out the window.

"There wasn't anything about the wildlife in the files," said Raj. Thinking about it, we hadn't seen a living creature yet aside from the people at the base.

"It's a little complicated," said Avar.

"The first thing you need to understand about my world is the gods," said Mathran. "They shape our lives here, more than anything else. My people migrated to this world a thousand years ago, and found it hostile. The gods protected us. Aktha, Veyak, and Xanet. I am a summoner—magic-wielder, you call it—and I am linked to Aktha. Each of us is attuned to one of the gods."

Three kinds of magic-wielder? This was a new one.

"Everyone on this world?" I asked. "Your people live in the jungle, right?"

"Some do," he said. "My birth city is much further north than here, on the plains, at the present time."

"At the present time?" Odd thing to say. The memory of the earthquake came to mind, for some reason.

"Yes. Our continent shifts and reforms itself at the whims of our deities."

Huh? I blinked, glancing at the others out of the corner of my eye—Raj and Iriel exchanged surprised glances, while Ada's eyes widened.

"Really?" asked Iriel. Of the others, she looked the least shocked.

Avar nodded. "We have seen it happen," he said. "The mountains are a constant, perhaps because this part of the world is tethered to the Passages, but the rest of the continent changes, drastically, every twenty days."

"Damn," said Raj.

That pretty much summed it up. There might be a million worlds in the Multiverse, but most followed the same natural laws, even the ones with high levels of magic. Magic was a law in itself. Of course, there were countless uninhabited worlds or ones inaccessible to anyone in the Alliance due to hostile conditions—but ever-shifting continents were a new one on me.

"So, what's going on with the magic level?" I asked. "Our supervisor told us a disturbance was traced to this world."

"Yes..." said Mathran, trailing off as if hesitant. "We would never have reported this to the Alliance if there wasn't something fundamentally wrong—the fact is, the last continent shift is late. Five days late. It's never happened before."

"And the magic levels?" I asked. "The Balance is being affected throughout the Multiverse."

"The Balance?" said Mathran, brow furrowed in confusion.

Does he not know what the Balance is? Impossible. Avar appeared confused, too.

"*The* Balance," said Raj. "Of magic? The way magic on each world is always at the same level? This world is third level, right?"

Mathran's expression remained confused. Maybe there wasn't a Vey-Xanethan translation.

"Third level," I said, "is what we call worlds where it's possible to channel a high amount of magic." But there hadn't been much information in the files on what exactly was possible on this world.

He blinked. "I do not know this 'third level'. Magic is a word we use to describe the actions of the gods—*hathet.*" The word must not translate into English. Were 'magic' and 'miracles' interchangeable? And did that mean *people* couldn't use it?

"What seems to be wrong?" I asked.

"The deities," he said, "are not responding to us as they used to."

Responding? "Did they used to speak to you?"

He shook his head. "The deities do not speak our language, no, but *hathet* links us. It is different for each of them. Akatha lends us strength to rebuild our towns when the continent shifts. He is the god of earth, and also fire and metal. We rely on him to keep our machinery running—in the cities, everything has ground to a standstill, or so we inferred from communications before most of our technology shut down. But I haven't been able to get there, because of the jungle. It's impassable to outsiders because of the hostile creatures within."

Damn. Even I couldn't figure out how magic was involved in this, though it was pretty clear it was, if the whole Balance across the Multiverse had been affected.

"We'll see what we can do here," I said. "There are three deities, you say?"

Mathran nodded. He seemed to have decided I was the group's leader, though neither he nor Avar had reacted at all to the name *Walker*.

"The summoners devoted to Xanet, the deity of nature, tend to work as healers, if they are gifted enough. Xanet can even stave off death, in certain cases. Those who serve Veyak are predominantly farmers and weather-summoners. Everyone acknowledges the presence of the trio, but if you are chosen as a higher summoner, it's your duty to serve the deity who chose you above the others."

"But you're allowed to live up here?" Raj asked. "With Alliance members?"

"The deities permit us to do as we like, provided we do not directly violate them. Although," added Mathran, "it is true that I don't have a great number of friends amongst my own people. I have set myself apart by allying with the Alliance. My people are progressive, but life here is difficult enough without adding in outside interference. We have been uprooted from our world before, and it will not happen again."

I knew from the absolute conviction in his tone that it would do no good to argue.

"Okay," I said. "So, what *can* we do? Obviously, the Alliance has no intention of interfering more than we need to, but if there's anything we can do to find out what exactly went wrong…"

I concentrated on my sense of the magic level and felt no difference. It didn't feel like a high-magic world, either. But this—whatever it was—only happened five days ago. I wasn't sure how that measured up to Earth's concept of 'days'.

"Firstly, the summoners of Aktha were late crossing over the mountain. I was once part of that group and they recognise me as a friend. They're nomadic, and travel around the mountains according to the continent's patterns, and every three cycles, they pass by this base. But this year, they haven't. We have not been able to leave and find out if they simply decided to stop after the disturbance, or if something else stopped them."

"You can't leave?" asked Ada.

He inclined his head. "Unfortunately, the wildlife has turned against us, and there is no other means of transport from here. Ordinarily, the continents would have shifted to allow it. I can go out into the Passages, of course, but I will not leave my own world to suffer."

Of course not. But the Alliance had the technology to temporarily create doorways from the Passages to different parts of any world. Ada had used one of those when she'd come to Aglaia, and the Conner family must have used a version of the same to move between Valeria and Aglaia. In fact, maybe the Alliance could even temporarily create a doorway on Earth...

"We may be able to find a way around that," I said. "I don't know for definite." Because the doorways might well work at random. Except the Conners had been pretty precise in building theirs to lead right into centaur territory on Aglaia. I never did find out how they learned to do that. They weren't *that* deep in the Alliance. Still, I supposed certain knowledge was open to magic-wielders. Like us. But Vey-Xanetha was a different world, with different rules. And no source listed in the files. They must use magic only in pure form, through these deities... but where did that leave the reverse reaction?

To ask him to demonstrate magic might violate some rule or other. I debated voicing the question anyway, but he moved towards the door, after glancing out the window.

"For now, our only option is to remain here. You shouldn't stay much longer. Our day-cycles are shorter than what you will be used to, and the hostile creatures come out at night. We are safe in this building as it was constructed at Aktha's blessing."

"You mean, your god directed you to build it?" asked Raj.

"The building was shaped by Aktha himself," said Math-ran. "The world and everything on it shapes itself according to the deities' will."

So that's why it looks like it was cut into the mountain. Unless someone was following directions. The summoners, he'd called them. Who were they—priests? Priests and magic-wielders, I'd guess. This was far from the only world where magic and religion were tied together, but I'd never heard of actual gods having a physical presence.

"It's true," added Avar, sensing the general scepticism in the room. "I have seen it with my own eyes, as have the others here at the base."

"This… Aktha keeps machinery running, too?" I asked.

"In a way," said Mathran. "I suppose it's comparable to what you Earth people call electricity—the machinery runs indefinitely as Aktha does. It's quite remarkable."

"But it's stopped?"

Mathran nodded, and Avar shot him a glance that wasn't lost on me. "We have computers here, but the one that still works uses Klathican technology, not Vey-Xanethan. There are communication devices like this one—" He placed a round, metal object on the table, covered in shining blue plates. I reached and picked it up, turning it over in my hands.

"It's like this?" I asked, pulling out my communicator—I figured they weren't familiar with the word 'telephone', but 'communicator' spoke for itself on most of the allied worlds. "You could use it to talk to people?"

"Yes, and send written messages," said Avar. "The last one we received, from a researcher who used to work here at the base, said, 'The city has stopped'. That was the last we heard."

I examined the device, like it had some answers. "If this runs on the power of Aktha, is that your energy source here, too?"

"That, and energy from the sun," said Avar. "And the rivers. The deities were more than enough—until now."

"If this… Aktha controls the machinery," said Iriel, "what about the other two?"

"Veyak is the deity of the heavens, who brings storms and night and stars. One of the first differences we noticed after the continents stopped was that the birds no longer flew. And Xanet is the deity of life, of healing and renewal. He brings the dawn of day, and can even heal those who are close to death—though I suspect summoners of Xanet are experiencing a similar problem to those who follow the others."

Living deities or not, one word came to mind to describe this world: alien.

"There have been no storms, as there would be if Veyak were active. The lightning normally strikes over that way." He pointed over the trees. "I have not heard a word from the other people of the cloud forest, though ordinarily, their activities are visible from here, if we look down on the trees. No movement has been seen in six days now. And the same can be said of the other people of the forest, the followers of Xanet who live in the city of Sekth. We always get at least one visitor from there, but nobody has come. That was where the message came from."

"How many people on this world interact with the base?" I asked, curious.

"Few do," he said. "Most simply do not have the interest. Our daily concerns are enough without adding in worlds unknown, especially after losing our old world. The Vey-Xanethans do not forget their history. But there is one other base, in the city of Sekth, run by a good friend of mine. They have a machine like ours, but like everything else, it has stopped. All we can do is wait for a sign."

Avar glanced out the window at the sky. "Less than thirty minutes. You should leave before the sun goes down."

"Your councils will be willing to discuss options, I am sure," said Mathran.

Hopefully, the council would have a plan. Though it bugged the hell out of me that I couldn't even begin to think of a solution. A whole continent grinding to a standstill. Magic acting out… This was bigger than us.

The sky had darkened in the time we'd been inside the building, though it hadn't been more than an hour. Time zones always worked in an odd way in the Passages, where you could get from one end of Earth to another and only skip a few hours, or alternatively, lose a whole day in here. It wasn't raining, though as we emerged from the building, another flash of lightning lit up the sky.

We made our way downwards in silence. I couldn't begin to think of a solution to this one. Now I could definitely feel a hint of the magic beneath the surface, though—a shiver under my skin, like the Passages but not quite the same. Not what I'd expect of a high-level world, but by the time we reached ground level, the air around us seemed red-tinted. I caught Ada's gaze, and I could tell from the tension in her stance that she'd felt the magic stirring too. But there was no sign of anything resembling a living god.

A *screech* echoed, and a dark shape dropped from the red clouds overhead. I instantly drew my weapon, dropping into a defensive stance, and the others followed suit. Whatever approached us was winged, and I'd guess around the size of an eagle—no, bigger, and growing by the second.

Mathran moved quicker than I'd ever have expected, pulling an object like a sharpened metal stick, and hurled it at the bird-like creature. It dropped with another screech, flipping over in the air and falling like a stone. Another bird-thing dropped from the cliff above. Three pairs of claws extended, three beaks snapped, three pairs of eyes glared murder at us. *They weren't kidding when they said the wildlife was unfriendly,* I thought, preparing to strike. Luckily I'd been up against weirder monsters from Cethrax.

The three-headed, three-clawed monstrosity plunged towards us. I slashed out with my dagger and caught its claw before it connected. Raj's dagger sliced the edge off one beak, and it withdrew, screeching, blood spattering the ground. Mathran threw another metal stick and this one pierced an eye on the left head. The beast screamed, dropping in the air, wings flapping frantically.

A second rose up to join it and dived for Ada, claws

outstretched. Ada was ready with a strike of her own, sending a spray of blood into the air.

"There will be more of them," Mathran said, grimly. "You should leave now."

He hurled another stick-like spear, getting the bird through the neck. It soared up out of range, one head dangling limply.

"Leave!" said Mathran, throwing another stick and piercing one beating wing. The bird dropped over the cliff's edge, towards the jungle.

Raj didn't need any encouragement. He pelted through the doorway and almost ran full-tilt into the wall, then collapsed against it. Iriel, close behind, shook her head at him, while Ada waited for me. I hung back to make sure Mathran and Avar had the situation in hand, but they'd disappeared.

"Kay, come on." Ada hovered at my side. "They've got it."

"Yeah." I pushed the door closed.

"Damn," said Raj. "I guess that's what they meant by 'hostile'."

"And we haven't even seen the gods yet," I added.

5

ADA

"Hope the old guy's okay," I said, as the door closed on Vey-Xanetha. I rubbed my arms, not quite daring to put my weapon away. "And I thought Cethrax was unfriendly."

"He'll be all right," said Kay, making sure the door was fully closed before turning to me.

Raj leaned breathlessly on the wall. "That was a close call."

"Tell me about it," I said. "I didn't feel anything off with the magic level."

"Yeah, that's what bothers me." Now Kay had his communicator out. "Do any of you have a signal?"

I checked mine. "Out of range. Why can't doors lead from one end of the Passages to another? It'd save time."

"Yeah." Raj rummaged in the pocket of his jacket and got out his own communicator. "You'd think so. But the senior Alliance members are the only people who get to access any behind-the-scenes information about how the Passages works. I'm surprised no seniors were sent to supervise us. Aside from Avar. But he's not from Earth."

"But then, Carl's the only senior staff member at Central

who's also a magic-wielder," said Kay. "Someone has to check the Passages, especially after yesterday."

But the magic level felt normal in here as we began the walk back. Nothing out of place. When it became clear there weren't any monsters around the corner, I checked my communicator again and found its inbuilt clock had stuck on UK time.

"Does the clock not adjust if you go offworld?" I asked the others, to fill the silence.

"If you set it to," said Kay. "But most worlds measure time differently anyway."

"Zanthar does," said Iriel, and I was pleased I'd managed to guess her homeworld right on the first go. Her blue-tinted skin and hair and the hints of webbing between her long fingers suggested she came from one of the semi-aquatic worlds. Her eyes gleamed dark blue, her pupils white instead of black. But her north London accent suggested she'd been living on Earth at least a few years. Raj, the tall skinny British-Indian guy, was definitely Earth through and through.

"Yeah. Does it not get confusing?"

"All the time," said Raj. "And I've been doing this for two years. You accept you're always going to be out of your depth. Nobody can be an expert in every world in the Multi-verse. You'd never know as much as a native even if you lived there."

"Absolutely," said Iriel. "I'd never claim to know as much as an Earth native. But you, Ada... sorry, I'm curious. You've always lived in London?"

"Since I was a year old. I don't remember my homeworld at all." It was probably for the best that I didn't.

"You were adopted?"

"I was, but my foster mother's from Enzar, too." The Ambassadors, I assumed, knew more than most Alliance members about my bizarre circumstances. "She brought me here."

"And learned English?"

I nodded. "Yeah, she learned before she moved here, and there were tutors at the first shelter we lived at."

It didn't escape my attention that Kay watched me out of the corner of his eye as we walked. Curious? He'd never asked me about my life before Central had taken me on.

"These shelters…"

"Yeah, they were illegal," I admitted. I'd figured everyone would know by now. "Technically. They're registered under the Alliance now."

"And there's another one opening," said Raj. "In offworld district, right?" He directed this at Kay, who must know who'd been responsible for setting all this up.

"Yeah," said Kay. "If the Law Division files the paperwork. Might check on it when we get back."

"Once we've reported to the dragon." Raj put his communicator away.

"One of these days, she's going to hear someone calling her that," said Iriel. "She's a terror, isn't she? I'm glad she's not my usual supervisor. I've never spoken to her before today, and she told me I'm forbidden to activate my eye-scanner in the building."

"Activate what?" I said, and then jumped a foot in the air when Iriel turned to face me and her eye spun in its socket, revealing a web of wires behind.

"What in the Multiverse is that?"

Her eye spun around again, revealing an ordinary blue iris again. "Cyber-eye. Every Klathican tech has one, but she acted like I'd brought a live fish into the office and skewered it to the desk."

"I wonder why." I shuddered, and Kay shot me an amused look.

"Weston's not keen on offworld technology," said Iriel. "So why was she was assigned to this mission?"

I hadn't thought about that, actually. She was officially in charge of admin, but seemed to be involved in everything else at Central, too.

"Probably to keep an eye on us." Kay smirked at Iriel's eye as it twisted around again. "Seeing as we cause all the trouble."

"True," said Raj. "Also, let's face it, she's the only supervisor at Central who actually gets things done. The others are scared of the council and knee-deep in paperwork."

"I'm pretty sure she repels paperwork," said Kay. "That, or has a secret army who does it all for her."

"There's a theory in Office Twelve that she's a cyborg." Iriel's eye rotated again.

I snorted. "Nah, she can't be. Her sister works at the training complex and she seems normal enough."

"True," said Raj. "I'm kinda worried about Earth in general, since we left. If we're going to find Central overrun by griffins."

"Or unicorns," I added.

"Yeah," said Kay. "There aren't enough staff in Earth's Alliance in general to deal with all the crap that went down yesterday. Complaints Division people are going to be run off their feet."

"Guess it comes with being low-magic," said Iriel.

"I'm striking that place off my holiday list," said Raj. "Do you reckon she'll send us back there?"

"Probably," said Kay. "If this magical disturbance is still happening."

As it turned out, however, no new disasters had made the news, though the Alliance was dealing with the aftermath of yesterday and catching various offworld creatures which had got loose. The Complaints Division was overrun by people yelling about their offworld tech malfunctioning. And a worldwide videoconference between all the Earth's Alliance councils was in place on the fourth floor, which meant telling the council what we'd heard on Vey-Xanetha would have to wait.

"I expect a report from each of you," said Ms Weston, dismissing us from her office. "This may be an isolated incident, but we can't count on that. I've already spoken to the council about giving us an easier way to access Vey-Xanetha if this happens again. The long route through the Passages isn't a safe method of travel."

Yeah. We were lucky not to have been attacked in the time it took us to cross the Passages. Kay had remarked that it was a pity we couldn't travel using Valeria's hover-tech. The material the Passages were made of stopped most technology, or it interfered with the magic too much to risk using it.

Back to Office Fifteen. Markos was at a standing desk, sorting through heaps of paperwork.

"Enjoy your adventure?" he asked me, as I laid the report files down on the desk. Raj and Iriel took up seats as far away from Markos as possible.

I flipped over the page. "I've had better. The three-headed bird spoiled the view."

"Yeah, and we didn't get to meet any gods," added Kay. "What a letdown." He turned to the new pages and started filling out the forms. "Best get this over with. I doubt anyone ever reads this crap, but I can check on the other information they have in the archives when I file it."

"Speaking of," said Raj, "what's the boss looking for in there? Didn't she rearrange the whole place the other week?"

"Thirty-year-old records," said Markos, "and even I can't find them."

"Hmm." Kay frowned at the papers. "Thirty years old?"

"No idea," said Markos. "I think she's trying out for a

council position and wants to read up on certain key developments."

"She'd be better at the job than half the council," said Kay. "Let's face it, she practically runs the place when they're offworld, which is every other week, these days."

I'd never spoken to Earth's council, but half of them weren't even *on* Earth at the moment. I'd ask Kay about it later. He'd spoken to them more than the rest of us, after all. Visiting Vey-Xanetha had reminded me how little I knew about magic—how little anyone did—and now I remembered I hadn't had a thorough look in the archives yet. Mostly because the archives had been out of bounds while Markos had been rearranging them.

"How long have you been Ambassadors?" I asked Raj and Iriel, out of curiosity.

"Year and a half," said Raj. "And in that time I've been arrested seven times and had to be bailed out by the Alliance twice. It's not an easy job, but there are perks."

"Arrested?" I glanced at Iriel, who shook her head.

"He keeps losing his Alliance ID. If you're on a hostile world, it's the only thing between you and grim death. I offered to superglue it to his forehead."

"Not all of us have it implanted in their *eyeball*," said Raj. "And no, I'm not asking for an upgrade. The staff at the Klathican Embassy hate me, they'd probably give me a chalder vox's eyes instead."

"That's a thing?" I said.

"Some people have more money than sense," said Raj. "Which, by the way, is another perk—offworld currency. Have you been to Valeria yet?"

"Yeah, I've been on the hover bike track."

"Of course you have," said Raj. "I'm surrounded by lunatics."

"Okay, Mr Safety Inspector." Iriel's fake eye rolled around

again, making me dizzy to watch. "What about the griffin incident on your first mission?"

"Did you have to remind me?" Raj groaned. In response to my quizzical look, he said, "My first mission was on Alvienne. Long story short, a griffin got into the Passages and caused havoc. They'd already caught it so the questioning was supposed to be straightforward, but the griffin escaped in the middle of interrogating the suspects."

"And he ran screaming," said Iriel.

"Thanks," said Raj.

I grinned. "Nice. So why did you sign up as an Ambassador? Griffins aren't in the job description?"

"With the Alliance, there's always a risk," said Raj. "And as a magic-wielder, even more so. We get access to places no one else does."

"A magic-wielder," I said. "But you're from Earth?"

"Yeah, I'm one in a million." He shrugged. "Not as much as Iriel, though. I want to know how your parents met. A Klathican and a Zanthan walk into a bar..."

"Very funny," said Iriel. "They met at the Klathican Embassy, I think. I'm half Klathican," she added in explanation, "and they tend to stick to their own world. They wanted dibs on what's left of Zanthar when it's fully buried under the sea... that'll be interesting."

"It's high-magic, right?" I asked. I'd helped some Zanthans move out of the problematic areas before, because the Alliance restricted immigration.

"Yeah, and stable, for a wonder. Would have been a different story if the Zanthan natives hadn't won the first continental war."

I didn't know their history, but I knew how easily a high-magic world could be swept up in conflict.

"So you knew you were a magic-wielder... when?"

For most Earth magic-wielders, they didn't know until

they went offworld. For me, I couldn't remember ever *not* feeling its presence when I went into the Passages.

"Since I was about five," said Iriel. "I moved to Klathica when I was quite young, but I got a lot of grief when I joined the Alliance."

"So you decided to come and pester us on Earth," said Raj. "I knew someone in the Alliance, that's how I got in, but I sure as hell didn't know about the whole magic deal until then."

"How did that happen?" I asked, curious.

"I accidentally electrocuted someone. They were fine," he added hastily. "But I got arrested. Happened on Klathica, so I had a crap-ton of security mechas on my back."

"Security mechas?"

"Their scary-as-hell security guards. They make that eyeball look like a fluffy kitten."

I giggled at Iriel's expression.

A minute later, Kay stood. "I'm going to the archives. I'll see what else they have on Vey-Xanetha. Just in case."

"I'll go, too," I said quickly.

Once in the elevator, he said, "Did you feel the magic level change? At all?"

I shook my head. "No. And not since we got back, either. Not since... last night. But I didn't really notice under the magic burn."

His jaw tensed a little at the mention of magic burn. "It stopped early this morning," he said. "But on Vey-Xanetha—I can't think of anything at all. Any solution to whatever happened there. If even *they* don't know, then I don't see what we can do."

"It's weird. I wish I'd tried to use magic there. I'm sure it would have worked, but... something feels off. Like it shouldn't be disturbed."

"Yeah, I got that vibe," he said. "I think we ought to see a demonstration of what they actually use magic for over there. What their summoners do."

"Talk to the gods?" I said. "Wow. Guess you can't do that with an earpiece. I'm surprised they didn't start acting up with the magic level rose."

"They're portable," he said. "I'd guess your brother tested them first."

I smiled. "Yeah. That'll explain how he almost blew a hole in the wall the other week. Like the Chameleons. Do you still have yours, by any chance?"

He shook his head. "The battery ran out. I had to return it to the tech team. I can only amplify sources if I'm touching them."

"Still," I said. "Must be pretty handy." Maybe I was reading too much into it, but Kay didn't talk about magic to anyone else the way he did to me. Sure, there were only a handful of people who knew he could become invisible, but I kind of liked that I was the only person with whom he voluntarily discussed the subject.

"Yeah. I wish I knew *why* it works like this. Earth has nothing on magic-related abilities, and most other worlds keep the information under wraps. There's literally nothing on amplifiers in the archives here."

"So... when did you decide you wanted to understand?" I'd been wondering that for a while. "When we first met, you didn't use magic. You hated it, actually."

I'm not interested in magic-wielders had been his exact words. Of course, that was before the Campbells and Skyla had forced him to use the ability he'd probably hated for years, or at least since the wyvern incident. While I'd grown wary of magic, he'd started actively looking for information.

"I don't trust it," he said. "But knowledge is an advantage. It's dangerous to have this kind of ability and not know anything about the limits. I'd bet there are people who *do* understand magic out there, on some worlds."

"Like… Enzar's Royals," I said. "Yeah. They wanted to use me as a weapon. And Nell told me I had the choice. I get to decide what to do with it. I used it for years without knowing."

Kay shook his head. "Ada, you never tried to hurt anyone. You're not…"

"A monster? I know." *But* what *am I?* I might know how dangerous magic was now, but I *did* want to know more. Maybe it could help us solve the problem in Vey-Xanetha. Or maybe I just wanted an excuse to hang out with Kay. I decided not to examine that notion too closely.

The lift stopped at the top floor, and we walked out into the archives. Rows of dusty shelves covered the entire floor. At some point soon, I'd probably have the joyless task of rearranging things in here. Admin was usually in charge of updating files.

"Would it be under 'Vey-Xanetha'?" I wondered aloud, scanning a list on the side of a bookcase.

"Yeah, if there's anything at all," said Kay, leading the way down the nearest aisle. "I've been in here a few times. They don't have a *lot* on magic, but it's always worth checking."

"So you've read everything on magic sources?" I asked in an undertone, though the dusty air was quiet.

"Everything here," he said. "But Earth's behind the other allied worlds when it comes to that kind of thing."

And high-magic worlds guarded their secrets well. I'd thought I knew everything about magic back when I'd assumed I was mageblood, but now it felt like re-learning a whole identity. No other Royals had escaped Enzar. I had nobody else to learn an example from. Nell had no magic, and avoided talking about our homeworld if she could help it.

"Yeah," I said. "Wonder what happened to that griffin?"

"Simon messaged me. New York's Alliance caught it. Half the world's Alliances have been here in London today, talking to the council. Simon's stuck here until they clear the path he normally uses to get back to New York. Assuming nothing else happens, we're heading to the Blind Wyvern. You should come and join us."

"Oh," I said, looking at him sideways. "Sure." I'd been there a couple of times with Jeth and the tech team, but Kay never stopped by longer than to say hi, before going back to playing darts with the off-duty guards and Ambassadors. At first I wondered if I was somehow too uncool to fit in with the Alliance's elite crowd—though he and my brother didn't exactly get along—but I'd been in the Alliance long enough now to notice how people reacted to the name *Walker*. When curiosity finally got the best of me, I'd asked a couple of the guards what they knew about Kay's father. "Scarier than Ms Weston," one of them had said. I hadn't quite got the nerve to ask Kay himself, but if I carried that kind of reputation around with me, I'd make more of an effort to be sociable with everyone, too.

Still. He'd actually asked me to spend time with him. That had to count for something, right?

Turned out there was nothing else on Vey-Xanetha in the archives, though we searched thoroughly.

"So much for that," Kay muttered, running a hand through his hair. "I can't think of anything else... wait." He paced down a different aisle, and I followed.

He stopped before an aisle of filed reports. "The last mission to Vey-Xanetha was twenty-five years ago," he said, scanning the shelves. "These are general mission reports from back then. Maybe it's here."

There were too many newspaper clippings and reports to

count in that year alone. But none we found were even vaguely relevant. Nor did they mention magic.

"Hmm. Guess it was a long shot," he said. "Earth was barely involved. Other worlds' Alliance branches might have more information, but we probably wouldn't be allowed into the high-security stuff, and if it involves magic, it'll be under lock and key."

"Which Alliance branches?" I asked. "Not Valeria? Surely they'd let us have a look, if it's an emergency."

"After what happened with the Campbells and the Conners? I can't see them letting anyone into high-security stuff for a while. Even Alliance members. Well, Conner was from Earth, and so was Campbell, a couple of generations back."

"He was?" I blinked. "I didn't know that. And they were linked with the Alliance, too."

"Standard, really," said Kay. "No one outside the Alliance will have got close enough to a potent source of magic to imagine screwing around with it. That's why this mass outbreak is bad news."

"Too true," I said. "Power corrupts. Or magic."

"Either works," said Kay, absently scanning the files again. "This doesn't add up, though."

Ah. I'd seen Kay act like this before. Once he ran into a problem, he immediately wanted to find the answer. He hated inconclusiveness. Then again, I wanted to know what could have caused a shift in the magic levels, too. I checked into the online files on my communicator, but they had only the basic information. I ran a finger along the files on the shelf, stirring a cloud of dust. Most were labelled with the same names.

"Ambassadors filed these?" I asked Kay.

"Yeah. Except the really confidential parts. Those are reserved for the council."

"And the council won't get involved with this mission?" I asked.

"Nah. There are only three of them here at Central, and they're too busy reassuring everyone we've got this magic level situation under control and in videoconferences with the rest of the Alliance branches. Or hiding from the rabid unicorns."

"Odd," I said, remembering one of the absentee council members was Kay's own father. "What do they do, sit in the office arguing all day?"

"Pretty much." Kay shrugged. "They're more figureheads, representatives of their homeworld. Some are permanently based offworld, but it wouldn't be practical to have to change leadership every other week because the council members were all dead."

"Every other week? Is that how often Ambassadors are killed?" I hadn't seen the official job description, but that wouldn't exactly be a winning sign-up form.

"I might have exaggerated a little." He absently looked back at the shelves. "Depends on the mission, whether high-level magic is involved... a lot of things."

"Wow," I said.

"Still wanna sign up?" He gave me a half smile.

"You *were* exaggerating." I pretended to hit him and moved out of range before he could grab my arm. "Gotcha. That wasn't funny."

But maybe there was some truth in there. Ambassadors *did* venture into hostile territory. A lot. Even more than guards did. An unspoken question hovered between us: his father was a council member. Offworld. Where? But I didn't want to push Kay away by bringing up his father. I'd learned there was no quicker way to shut down a conversation.

Still, I made a mental note to check out the mortality rate for Ambassadors before I took the job.

6

ADA

Ms Weston waved me away from her office without even looking at my report. I decided to go to the training complex, where I was pretty sure Kay had gone, rather than hanging around for two hours to wait for my brother.

The training complex was two streets away from Central, surrounded by high fences to stop passersby wandering in. The Alliance-only simulators used technology from offworld, and I wondered if they'd had any difficulties since the magic levels had started fluctuating.

There was no one in the reception area so I went exploring, looking for Amanda. Probably training novices. I didn't really feel like going into a simulator, so I wandered around the upper floor instead. There were surprisingly few people around, though the guards would still be dealing with the aftermath of the chaos in the Passages yesterday. I checked the newsfeed on my communicator again, shaking my head at the ridiculous articles popping up online about unicorns and griffins and god-knew-what-else. Probably half of them were fake memes created with Photoshop. I couldn't help laughing at one that made claims of an offworld conspiracy to sell England to another universe, in which they managed to get the names of every Alliance world wrong. Though the scary thing was, judging by the comments, at least a handful of people actually took it seriously.

I stopped near one of the training halls, peering through the glass above the door. Kay sparred alone, striking invisible enemies with the speed and precision of an expert fighter. *Whoa.* I put my communicator away, staring. I'd seen him take down an enemy with a single strike before, of course. Not unusual for an Alliance guard, especially an Academy graduate. They were lethal by definition.

But Kay fought like if he paused for a second, he'd die. It was almost hypnotic to watch. Every single movement had a purpose. His face was the picture of intense concentration—he hadn't seen me, though I was sure if I entered his peripheral vision, I'd become another enemy. Only one other person I knew fought with that level of focus: Nell, who'd used those skills to escape a war zone.

Kay paused, wiping his forehead, running a hand through his hair, and I quickly shifted out of view and nearly collided with Amanda.

"Sorry." I moved away from the door.

"No worries." She smiled at me, not commenting on the fact I'd been blatantly ogling Kay from the sidelines. Because that wasn't creepy at all.

"I wondered where you were." Amanda was one of the training instructors, and the first person at Central I'd become close to—apart from Kay, of course. I wasn't much of an expert on friendships, given I'd been doubly betrayed by two of the few people I'd called friends. Delta and Skyla. Both were dead now. And Kay and I had been responsible. The aftermath of what happened had left me a wreck, and it had taken me too long to admit it to myself. Amanda had taught me how to use the Alliance's custom-built simulators to deal with the panic attacks I'd suffered after being kidnapped by the Campbell family. It helped to be able to talk about it with someone who didn't think Valeria was called "Vagabondland" like a certain tabloid did.

"I've been around. Checking the simulators. How've you been, Ada?"

"Not too bad. Just got back from offworld. The magic isn't affecting the tech here, is it?"

"No, thankfully. Apparently, this particular branch of Klathican technology isn't affected by the magic levels."

"There were people with implants from Klathica causing trouble in the Passages," I said, walking alongside her down the corridor.

"Ah, that's different, seeing as they're internal sources."

She didn't know *I* had an internal source. Amanda was Ms Weston's younger sister, so she was more aware of what was going on than most Alliance employees. But if the magic level on Earth kept climbing, how long before I was exposed for the unnatural magic-wielder I really was?

"So are the simulators," I said. "They change your thought patterns, right? Make you think you feel pain?"

I'd been hit a few times in simulation training, and it wasn't fun. Somehow, the sensations were exact enough to simulate actual pain, while you were hooked up to the visor. Lucky I'd not been killed in there, because that had to be a hell of a mind-trip. The pain felt real enough until you unplugged it.

"Yes, in a way. I imagine it's different on Klathica. Their latest simulators aren't entirely computer-controlled. They stimulate the brain so you create the virtual world yourself, using your own subconscious thoughts. It all appears real."

"Really?" I blinked. "Damn. That sounds like something my little brother would freak out over."

Amanda rearranged her blond ponytail. "It does have its advantages. But I can't say I'm keen on the idea of a machine controlling my mind."

"Ha." I shook my head. "That's so weird. The computer's in control, but it's working through people..." Like a god, magic, working through its subjects. What Mathran had said... was uncomfortably close to that. A shiver ran up my arms. "Yeah, I take it back. I think I'll stick to real life."

"I don't blame you," said Amanda.

We ended up sparring for a bit. It had been a while since I'd had a new training partner, and things were still awkward at home. Besides, I needed a friend. Even one who could kick my arse at hand-to-hand combat.

"Sorry, Ada," she said, as I sprawled on the floor of the training room yet again.

"Dammit." I lifted my head. "I almost got you that time. Where'd you learn to fight?"

"Danica insisted on signing me up for combat lessons when I was younger," she said, helping me to my feet. "I never thought I'd end up teaching novices here. I always assumed I'd be going offworld."

"What made you change your mind?" I asked.

She shrugged. "I decided Earth wasn't so bad after all. I still have my permit. It's nice to travel, but being stuck in meetings all the time isn't really my thing."

"It's not always meetings. Sometimes a giant three-headed bird randomly dive-bombs you on the side of a mountain." I grinned.

"Did you tell my sister about that?"

"Mentioned it," I said.

"Are you sure you want to get involved? It sounds a little intense for a first assignment. Not that I don't think you can handle it, but you can tell me anything."

I nodded. It had taken me a while to adjust to not snapping at anyone who offered me help. Maybe because of Nell's fiercely independent upbringing. But as Amanda had told me, I was far from the only Alliance employee suffering the aftereffects of the attack on Central, and admitting so wouldn't get me blacklisted from patrols.

"I'm sure." I checked my watch. "I should go and meet my brother."

Turned out my timing was pretty good, as I reached the entrance hall just as Jeth came downstairs from the tech office.

"Did I hear you went *offworld?*" he asked, immediately.

"Yeah. Who told you that?"

"This Ambassador came to the tech office. Iriel?" His forehead creased with worry. Though part of me knew why he was so concerned, I couldn't help but feel annoyed. My family knew the dangers of my new job. I hadn't signed up just to sit in an office.

"Yeah, we went there to check out something to do with what's happening on Earth. With magic acting up."

"You're okay, aren't you? It's dangerous out there."

I rolled my eyes. "You know I can take care of myself."

"Yes, but you're my little sister. I'm supposed to worry about you."

I gave him an abbreviated version of what had happened, concentrating on the details about Vey-Xanetha's gods rather than the potential dangers. The evening was chilly, and I was glad of my coat—it was a total contrast to Vey-Xanetha's tropical temperature. To Ambassadors, I wondered if all worlds were alien, even their own.

As we reached our house, I said, "I'm going out to the Blind Wyvern later."

"With him," said Jeth, a slight inflection in his voice. He unlocked the door.

I passed him and dropped my bag in the hallway. "Yeah, and Simon. Maybe some of the other Ambassadors. I need to revive my nonexistent social life. It's borderline embarrassing."

"You have me and the tech team." He opened the door to the kitchen and threw his coat over the back of a chair.

I rolled my eyes at him. "I need one of your translator earpieces to understand your tech talk."

"How were those, by the way? You tested them, right?"

"Yeah. I could understand every word. Kind of strange. It's set to modern English, isn't it?"

"Yeah, it doesn't really work with idioms and local phrases, but if you speak plain English, it'll translate. None of your gibberish."

I grinned at him. "Ha. I don't know how you come up with these ideas."

"The battery life's shit," said Jeth. "That's the one thing we never found a way around with the Chameleons, too."

"Oh yeah, how's your computer?"

"Still not responding. Wonder where Nell is?"

"On the moon." Alber appeared the top of the stairs. "Nah, she's at the other shelter. She'll be back soon."

"I'm heading out later." I shot a meaningful look at Jeth.

"Hey, I'm not going to stop you," he said. "You can make your own decisions."

"You're not the only person looking out for me."

Jeth sighed. "I doubt that's the first thing on his mind."

"I can guess who you're talking about," said Alber. "He finally made a play? Last time at the hover-port, I thought you two were gonna rip each other's clothes off right there in the back of one of those cars."

"Please say no more," I said. "Firstly, we're meeting friends. Secondly, I don't need to hear the phrase 'rip each other's clothes off' from my little brother."

"And *I* don't need the mental image," said Jeth. "I'm going to check on my computer."

"I'm going to change," I added, climbing the stairs. "Not a word," I added to Alber.

Nell still hadn't come back by the time I set off. The lights were off downstairs, so when Jeth appeared from the shadows in the hall, I jumped violently.

"Whoa, only me," he said. "You're not heading out alone, are you?"

"No, Kay's coming to pick me up." I peeked through the letterbox. I was early, but then, he always arrived dead on time. "I did say you weren't the only person looking out for me."

"Yeah, but I'm your family. He doesn't know you."

"He knows more about me than I've ever told anyone else," I said. "When are you going to let this go? Kay saved me. Saved Nell, and Alber, too. He got both of us jobs, and he's the one who stopped the Alliance arresting the people who run the shelters. He's probably the reason Nell can keep running her business. It came together way too fast to be coincidence."

"Because he wants to score with you," said Jeth. "Come on, he might be an Alliance guard, but he's also a guy. You can't think it's never crossed his mind. I don't want you getting hurt again."

I shook my head, though I wished he'd give it a rest. Okay, so I'd got close—both physically and emotionally—to a guy a couple of years ago, only for him to back off when it started getting serious. I was usually the one to do the back-ing-off, because of my once-secret double life sneaking around the Passages and helping Enzarians. So it had kind of hurt. A lot. Still, that was ancient history.

"He already turned me down," I said pointedly to Jeth.

"Oh." Jeth blinked. "Well, then he wants to make up for nearly getting us all killed."

"Jeth," I said. "He's not like that. At all. He doesn't have anything to gain by helping the shelters, but he's the one who stopped them going under. And he doesn't have any family. He has no one."

He sighed again. "All right. I'm here for you whatever, sister."

The sound of a motorcycle outside. My heart flipped over again.

Yeah. Maybe I needed a reality check.

Simon waited for us outside the bar. "Hey, Ada. Did I mention it's weird to skip time zones through the Passages? Reckon it counts as time travel?"

"Nah, not quite." Kay appeared to be avoiding my eyes. Seeing as I'd taken the time to dress nicely and put on makeup, it was kind of disappointing.

The general mood in the Blind Wyvern reminded me of a storm about to break. People glared and shouted and argued with the bar staff. And there were more offworlders here than before, I couldn't help noticing as we ordered drinks and sat at the table closest to the door.

When someone started a fight at the bar, Kay stood up to intervene.

"Don't bother," said Simon. "They've got it."

He sat down again, with another glance over his shoulder. "They're magic-wielders. If the magic level kicks up again, they might set this place on fire."

"Yeah, but it's not up now," said Simon. "It's not our job, either."

"The whole reason they're here is to complain to the Alliance," said Kay.

So that's it. Offworlders would have been the most affected by all the magic-related chaos.

"So they're hanging out here until Central sorts out their problems?" I asked.

"Same thing's happening in New York," said Simon. "When it comes to offworld district, there's a fifty-fifty chance of running into a brawl on every street. People are easily insulted," he added. "Earth people who don't know better will try and pin the blame for anything magic-related on them. Or on the Alliance. And they blame each other, of course. High-magic worlds take the blame usually."

"Whatever the problem is this time, it's bigger than our world," said Kay. "I don't understand how it could have such a major effect and then just vanish. No warning or anything."

"Eh, never mind," said Simon. "We can't deal with all their problems. Half of them aren't ours, anyway, they're Earth people who've bought something from offworld without checking the instructions and are looking for someone to blame."

"Yeah, I'd file those unicorn people into that category," said Kay, resting his elbows on the table. The scars on his left arm gleamed under the dim light.

"Unicorns?" asked Simon.

"Yeah, a family bought a unicorn thinking it was a fancy breed of horse," said Kay. "It went apeshit when the magic level rose, and ran off. We had to catch it."

"Epic," said Simon, cracking a grin. "I wish I'd seen."

"They still thought it was a horse," I said. "Even with the horn."

"Some people will believe anything," said Simon.

"Damn right." Kay looked over his shoulder, where the

bar staff had broken up the fight. "They didn't send you after that griffin?"

"No, I was in the Passages. Had to stop a bunch of teenagers with magic implants going crazy."

"Magic implants?" I echoed, a chill racing down my spine. I couldn't help meeting Kay's eyes then, but his expression didn't give anything away.

"Yeah," he said. "Klathica sells temporary enhancements. They're not supposed to work offworld, but a guy with one almost started a fight yesterday, too."

"But why would you even want that?" I said. "Magic implants? For what?"

Kay gave an offhand shrug, but by now, I could work out when he was faking casualness. Like whenever anyone mentioned magic. And he'd been on edge since we'd entered the bar.

"Super-speed, super-strength. That kind of thing. I dealt with some people on Klathica a few days ago selling them illegally. They're temporary, not like regular magic-wielders."

Not like us. Magic lived in our skin, a permanent part of us.

"That's what went wrong in the main Passage yesterday, right?" asked Simon, eying him curiously.

"Yeah. Idiots. Those boosts aren't even supposed to work if they leave Klathica."

"Damn," I said. "There go my plans for becoming a cyborg." Though I wasn't overly keen on the idea of any more questionable offworld substances being injected into me.

"It sounds like a cool idea until you set off every scanner or metal detector," Kay said. "I always wondered why you don't see many cyber-sorts in Valeria. Their security's too tight."

"I'd rather have magic." Simon grinned at Kay.

"It's overrated," said Kay.

Simon glanced at him, then at me. "Yeah, guess it is. Just saying why it'd appeal to other people. Anyway. I'm going to get another drink. You two up for that?"

"Aren't you supposed to be going back into the Passages in an hour?" said Kay.

"Lighten up," said Simon. "Ada, you need to get him to chill the hell out every once in a while. Your job isn't your whole life, you know. Even now."

"Yeah, but I hear Cethrax is having a pest problem again. They might set you after the latest rat outbreak."

"They'd better not," said Simon, with a slight shudder.

"Didn't you have to deal with that kind of thing at the Academy?" I asked.

"Only in final year," said Simon. "That was kinda intense. Somebody—" He raised an eyebrow at Kay— "decided to drag us through Cethrax's swamp."

"That same someone saved all our necks," said Kay.

Simon leaned back, rolling his eyes at him. "Lunatic."

A spark shot over our heads. Kay spun around and I immediately spotted the source of his attention. Markos the centaur stood in the middle of the floor, facing off against Evan, a guy around my age I vaguely recognised from the admin department as one of the asshats who'd found it amusing when I'd been arrested. The two squared up to one another, while everyone in the vicinity edged as far away from the centaur as possible. Markos's back feet kicked up.

"The door," said Markos, "is right there. If you'd like a close-up view, I'd be more than happy to arrange it."

Evan took a couple of steps towards him, hands curling into fists.

"You've got to be shitting me," said Kay.

"My money's on the centaur," said Simon.

"Not helping!" I shot an alarmed look at Kay. As I predicted, he moved in their direction.

"Get out of here," said Evan. "You're not welcome."

"I've been here longer than you have," Markos said to Evan. "And I have impeccable sense in style, which is more than I can say for you. Get out."

"Like hell. You and your offworlder sorts are who screwed up the magic here on Earth."

"Evan," Kay said, warningly. "I wouldn't do something you'll regret."

"Stay out of this, magic-wielder," Evan spat, anger twisting his face.

Oh shit. They knew each other, all right.

The gathered crowd muttered amongst themselves, and more than a few had left the pub.

"Tell him to leave," someone said.

"Shouldn't let their sort into here."

Centaur and human both turned on the crowd. And then Kay moved between them.

"Hold it," he said. "Who started it?"

Nobody answered. Evan glared at both Kay and Markos, while the centaur's expression could have frozen everyone on the spot.

Kay, however, looked unimpressed. "Either leave or stop arguing. Simple enough."

The centaur tapped a hoof, accidentally knocking several glasses over with his tail. "I was minding my own business until *he* started making personal comments."

Kay glared at the novice. To Markos, he said, "He's trying to wind you up. Leave it."

"It's a little too late for that, human," said the centaur, then looked around at the audience, which kept a safe distance from him. "But it seems I have outstayed my welcome."

He swept around and left, tail swishing. Evan dusted himself off with a rather self-satisfied expression on his face.

"Don't think you've won this," Kay said to him. "You'll be lucky to have a job by the end of the week."

Without giving the novice the chance to reply, he re-joined us.

"So some things haven't changed," Simon said, with a glance at Evan. "Jesus. He's still being a dick, then?"

"You know each other?" I asked.

"Yeah, he was one of Aric's cronies," said Kay, crouching to carefully move a piece of broken glass away from the nearest table. His aura of *don't mess with me* was so potent everyone edged away from him even though he hadn't used magic. The scars on his arm were warning enough.

"He's right about one thing, though. Magic *is* changing on Earth. I just wish I knew why."

I looked past him, at the worried crowd, the bar staff picking up more pieces of broken glass. "Me, too," I said.

7

KAY

There was a decidedly edgy atmosphere in Office Fifteen the following day. Evan scuttled around, shooting wary looks at Markos, who I gathered had 'accidentally' shoved him into the front doors of Central. And more reports were coming in from all over Earth of yet more magic-related disasters as the level kept rising and falling.

With no instructions, I returned to pacing the back of the office, and I sent a quick message to Simon: "Any more giant rats?"

Simon messaged me back telling me where to shove it. When we'd left the Blind Wyvern last night, he'd met the other New York Alliance members and gone back to the Passages. I'd got a message yelling at me about giant rat-creatures crawling up from the lower Passage again. Apparently, Cethrax was having issues. Like the Alliance needed anything else to worry about.

Right now, we were stuck in the office while Ms Weston tried to get in touch with Vey-Xanetha again. From what I gathered, they had some kind of computer at their base, but were having 'technical difficulties'. They weren't the only ones.

"Jeth blew up his computer," said Ada, who was as restless as me. She hovered near the window. "It has some sort of magi-tech in it—well, it did. It's in pieces now."

"Offworld tech?" There'd been a few similar reports in, I remembered, and wondered if it was a matter of time before something blew up *here*. "Which world?"

"He can't remember," she said. "Not helpful, I know."

"I was under the impression," said Markos, looking up from a mountain of papers at his standing desk, "that it was illegal to use non-Earth tech here without Alliance permission."

"Uh," said Ada. "He works here." She shot me a guilty look.

"The Alliance have bigger problems right now," I said. "At least it wasn't a flying car."

Markos snorted. "What is it with you humans and flying? I prefer to keep four feet on the ground, thank you very much."

"Huh." Good thing I hadn't bought the supersonic speed-enhancement a Valerian merchant had tried to sell me last time I'd been in Neo Greyle, which he promised would work on Earth motorcycles. I'd rather save that for a world where it wouldn't get me arrested *or* inconveniently explode.

Right now, the main Passage was locked down in case any other magic-creatures showed up, and only patrols were allowed in. Apparently, the lockdown had caused no end of contention for offworlders wanting to use it, judging by the number of people crowded around the Complaints Division downstairs. It looked like London's entire offworld community had come here, and Ms Weston wasn't happy about it. She had no patience for complainers.

"I don't see how they think Earth's Alliance can help," said

Ada. "Most people don't even understand how offworld tech works. Even my brother doesn't, and he built a computer out of it."

"We're a convenient target," I said. "Any idea where Raj and Iriel are?" The other Ambassadors normally worked in different offices. They might have been called in to deal with some of the chaos. If not for Vey-Xanetha, Ada and I would be chasing griffins around Westminster Abbey.

I'd rather be doing that than staying here, but judging by Earth's surging magic levels, offworld must be having a worse time of it than we were. I'd kept my communicator newsfeed on all night and every minute brought more chaotic reports. Now I regretted sacrificing sleep to keep up to date, though the constantly fluctuating magic level didn't help, waking me every few minutes like a mild electric shock. It was as persistent as magic burn, but less painful. Judging by the dark circles under Ada's eyes, she'd been tuned into it, too.

Magic was starting to really piss me off.

"No clue." Ada yawned. "I didn't see where Evan went, either."

"Hope something ate him," said Markos. "The dragon's supposed to be keeping an eye on him."

"Yeah, well," I said. "You're supposed to be setting an example. Not getting into fights with the staff."

"Don't you lecture me, human," said Markos. "The two of you have a history, don't you?"

Great. "He was one of Aric's henchmen at the Academy." And like hell would I let on that he and his buddy had beaten the crap out of me in the Passages two years ago. Before I'd accidentally blasted Aric with magic.

Iriel came into the office, looking frazzled. "Raj has been arrested," she said.

"What?" I turned to stare at her. "On Earth?"

"Yeah, he had to deal with an issue somewhere near Trafalgar Square. The regular police got involved, and wound up arresting him as well as the culprits."

"Damn," I said. "Don't tell me the idiot lost his Alliance ID again."

"Right in one," said Iriel. "He left it in the office. Has the dragon given you any instructions?"

"I can't believe everyone's calling her that now." Ada stifled a laugh.

Behind her, Ms Weston's raised voice came through her office, but too muffled to make out the words.

"Who's she yelling at, anyway?" asked Iriel.

"No clue," I said. "What exactly happened? Isn't Trafalgar Square in West Office's territory?"

"They're preoccupied with complaints," said Iriel. "Same as here. All their senior staff are dealing with offworlders coming in and kicking up a fuss about not being able to use the Passages."

What a total clusterfuck. "All right," I said. "I'll come down and—"

Crash.

Everyone jumped as the floor shook underneath our feet. And the ceiling and walls.

"The hell?" I ran out the office, looking up and down the corridor. People were coming out of the other offices, too.

"That was downstairs," said Ada, from behind me. "You don't think we're being attacked?"

"Considering we're unarmed, I hope not." But I made for the balcony outside Office Fourteen which overlooked the entrance hall.

A gigantic, feathery lion-bird hybrid flew past, colliding with the balcony in a rattling *crash*. Broken metal restraints hung from its wings and eagle-like feet, scraping against the walls.

"You have *got* to be shitting me," I said. "That's a full-grown Alvienne griffin."

"Who in the Multiverse brought it in here?" Iriel gaped at it.

"How unfortunate." Markos came out the office, looking amused. "Except for those of you hoping for a little action."

"Yeah, thanks, Markos," I said, already heading for the stairs, and the guard office. Not that a weapon would help if no one could catch the damn thing.

"Hang on." Iriel moved back as a curved beak hit the balcony, leaving a huge dent. Griffins tended to hate enclosed spaces and make for the nearest exit, if there was one. Except there wasn't. The griffin made high-pitched noises, its heavy body smacking into the walls.

"Screw it," I muttered, and ran downstairs, my steps punctuated by more crashing sounds from above.

"Wait." Ada caught up to me in the entrance hall. "You're not serious? Or do I even need to ask?"

"Someone has to do it," I said, and above, the huge feathered form of the griffin crashed into another balcony. People gathered on all five floors to see what the fuss was about. In the entrance hall, full-blown panic had erupted. People ran every which way, shouting at anyone who looked vaguely authoritarian or wore guard uniform. I made for the guard office before anyone waylaid me.

The office was locked. No sign of Carl. He'd have had this situation under control, but he must be out dealing with something else. Most of the guards were probably in the Passages or trying to stop complainers from overrunning the building.

Crash. Broken glass rained down on the shrieking crowd, and I kicked at the office door. I swore again when it didn't give. The weapons were stored in here, so they'd made the bloody door out of adamantine. Lucky I wore my guard boots, otherwise that'd have really hurt. *I don't have time for this.*

Magic sparked against my skin as Ada stepped forward. "Wait," I said, realising what she was about to do. "It's magicproof." Plus using magic in here broke a dozen rules.

Crash. More glass fell from above, along with red droplets. Blood. The griffin must have crashed into one of the glass lifts.

A red bolt hit the wall to our right, rebounding with another crash. *Someone used magic.*

"Shit," I said, and like everyone else, threw myself to the ground to avoid a waterfall of sparks. A claw-footed man shouted something in another language and hurled a handful of sparks up at the flailing griffin, which clawed at the ceiling high above. The reflective surface had probably confused the beast into thinking it was a way out.

Swearing, I got to my feet and said to Ada, "Back me up if this goes wrong."

"What're you—?"

This was stupidly risky and I'd never have done it under normal circumstances, but there wasn't a weapon in sight and a hundred-odd people were shielding themselves from the falling glass and rebounding magic sparks. If the magic level surged again, we'd be in a crapload of trouble.

The griffin let go of the ceiling and dived, and I made up my mind.

"Everyone move out of the way!" I shouted.

Most people had cleared aside already, and more than a few had left the building. Ada gaped at me. "You're not seriously going to—?"

As the griffin swooped down, and jumped. My arms locked around its feathered leg, propelling both of us into the air. The only weapon I had was the magic in my blood, and right now, it was the only way I could think of to stun the griffin before it hit anyone with those clawed talons.

Magic waited under the surface, enough for a first-level zap. It had no effect, and I cursed as the griffin's talons kicked at the crowd. Second level it was, then. I clambered higher, onto the griffin's feathered back, and released the magic through my fingertips.

The griffin screamed, legs jerking. I threw myself over its back as its heavy body hit the ground with a *thud.* It lay in the centre of the entrance hall, shuddering all over. I jumped and rolled on the ground, avoiding the broken glass.

Everyone stared, Ada included.

"Who's in charge of this thing?" I demanded of the shell-shocked crowd. "It'll recover in a few minutes, and I'm not catching it again. Someone could get hurt."

If I hadn't been sure of my aim, I'd never have used magic in the middle of Central. More than a few people were staring at me in open astonishment, though the majority were more scared of the griffin than the fact that I'd used magic.

The front doors slid open and several guards ran in, led by Carl.

"Good timing," I said, removing slivers of broken glass from my jacket sleeves.

"What the devil happened here?" He marched past the griffin, to the guard office, and unlocked it while I explained. Though how the damn creature had got loose in the first place was a mystery to me.

"You did *what?*" he said, from inside the office, where he'd opened a black-doored cabinet in which some of the weapons were held. "Used magic? In here?"

"We didn't exactly have a lot of options," I said, as he pulled out an Alliance-issued tranquiliser gun from beside a set of cuffs. "It smashed the lifts, there was broken glass everywhere. It was only a matter of time before someone got hurt. And other people were using magic, too," I added, shooting a glare at the claw-footed man. He froze, glancing shiftily towards the exit.

"Please tell me you at least asked a senior member of staff," said Carl.

"It was an emergency," Ada jumped in. "Our boss is… uh. Busy."

"That's no excuse—" He cut himself off, striding past us with the tranquiliser gun in hand. Ada jumped as he fired at the struggling griffin. The beast promptly collapsed, unconscious, its beak hitting the ground with a final trembling crash. "Absolutely no excuse. Kay, this is *Central.* I appreciate what you were trying to do, but—"

"You left the guard office locked," said Ada. "Nobody here was armed. That thing could have killed people. And there were others using magic, too."

"Who even let someone bring it in?" I added. "That's the part I don't get." I scanned the remaining complainers, who'd crowded the edges of the entrance hall.

"All right," said Carl, loudly. "Own up. Who owns the griffin?"

A pause. Most of the crowd looked like they weren't sure who to be more scared of, the griffin or the scarred, imposing head guard.

A couple of teenage girls wearing feathered hats, who'd been looking nervously towards the door, stepped forward. "It's ours," one of them said.

Carl muttered a curse. "I'll deal with this. Kay, I'm putting you in charge of telling the council *what* exactly happened here."

Great. I made for the stairs, seeing as the elevators were now reduced to a mess of broken glass. Good job no one had been in them at the time, I thought with a slight chill at the memory of my own narrow escape from a similar situation.

"Ada, you don't have to come," I said, as she hurried behind me.

"Like hell," she said. "They *can't* blame you for this. What else were you supposed to do?"

"Call the council? God knows." I could have put out a call on my communicator, of course, but apparently someone already had. I picked up the pace, irritated beyond belief, both with myself and the morons who'd brought a freaking *griffin* into Central. And the morons who'd *let* them.

"Who the bloody hell thought domesticating that thing was a good idea?" said Ada. "It can't be a house pet."

"Might be," I said. "You'd think most people would think twice before buying a two-ton griffin as a birthday present."

Ada laughed, then shot me a guilty look. "They're not going to yell at you, are they?"

"Ms Weston will," I said. "I'd stay away from her for the next century or so."

Mercifully, the council were in a meeting. Must have been an important one, because even with the racket outside, no one had even come out of their third-floor office. Then again, I remembered belatedly, the meeting room was sound-proofed.

"Great," I muttered, as we left through the reception area to the third floor. Ada paused, looking around her. She wouldn't have been on this floor before. The Law Division worked here, alongside councils from various worlds, which meant it was mostly empty meeting rooms. Except for the official Ambassador's office, empty now Ms Weston had moved down to the first floor.

"No way." Ada indicated a plaque on the back wall, extending across the corridor. "Over a hundred Ambassadors have been killed in action?"

Something twisted inside me. My mother's name was on that list. I'd never looked that way if I could help it, and now, I turned my back. "Come on. Ms Weston's going to be on the rampage already."

"Yay," she said.

Yeah. Pretty much.

As predicted, we found Ms Weston in raging thunder-cloud-mode. "Kay Walker!" she shouted, loud enough for everyone on the floor to hear. Like I hadn't drawn enough attention already.

"Yes?" I said in my most polite voice.

"In here," she said, beckoning me into her office with a sharp finger. "Now. Ada, you should inform your family you will be taking another trip to Vey-Xanetha."

"Oh, right," said Ada. Given how overprotective her older brother was, this might not turn out well. Though I wasn't overly keen on the idea of Ms Weston throwing Ada head-first into dangers only Ambassadors faced. Not at all. That goddamned plaque was a blazing reminder of the costs of this job.

Not now. I needed to focus on the issue at hand: a raging mad Ms Weston. Was I the first Ambassador to blatantly use magic inside Central? Probably.

"Are you going to explain to me what that ungodly racket was?"

For a brief moment, I was tempted to answer with *yes* again, but I wasn't that far beyond caring about getting another tongue-lashing. I summed up the situation, empha-sising that I wasn't the only person to use magic, and adding no one had yet found out who'd let people bring in a griffin in the first place.

"Yes," she said, packing enough venom into that one word to kill a small animal. "Evidently, *someone* hasn't been doing their job. But *you*, Kay. You of all people know the risks of using magic. Earth's levels are unstable. We've already contacted the media asking them to send out a public warning against using magic at all, now the level has climbed."

Goddammit, she was right. "I used the same level as a stunner," I said. "If I'd had one to hand, I'd have used it, but there was no other way to bring it down."

"If you'd *missed*, Kay, anyone could have been hit. You know the rules. I refuse to authorise this."

"I understand," I said. "I wouldn't have used it if I thought a chance of another person might get hit."

Ms Weston's lips were a thin line. "However perfected you think your skill at magic is," she said, "it's no excuse. If it wasn't for the circumstances, I'd have you placed immediately on probation—as it is, however, your presence is required on Vey-Xanetha once again."

I blinked. "It is? I thought the Passages were out of bounds."

"We don't have many options. It appears Earth is the only world being affected—us, and Vey-Xanetha. None of the other Alliances will volunteer Ambassadors to help."

"Seriously?" I asked.

"Yes, *seriously*, Kay," said Ms Weston, eyes narrowing. At least she wasn't yelling anymore. "As I'm sure you're aware, it takes a great deal of prompting to spur the Alliance to action, and as we were the ones who tracked the disturbance to Vey-Xanetha, the mission has been left to us. Or, specifically, to you and the other magic-wielding Ambassadors on Earth."

We're the only ones? No way.

"That's not enough people to search a whole world," I said, shaking my head. "Even taking into account that the whole continent of Vey-Xanetha's smaller than Europe—if the problem's even there, and not in the middle of the ocean or on an iceberg."

Ms Weston became dangerously still. "I am glad to hear you have at least read the research material," she said. "As a matter of fact, we *do* have another way." She placed an object flat on the desk. A gleaming black-coated metal rod.

"That's…"

"A world-key," she said. "To use the rather simplistic name. Carl's authorised this one for use anywhere in the Passages. It'd be downright suicidal to expect you to walk all the way to the door."

At least someone here had an iota of common sense.

"Authorised for who to use?" I asked.

"You, unfortunately," she said. "Before you saw fit to demonstrate our incompetence with a blatant display of magic."

Thanks. "At least the offworlders know we can handle griffins," I said. "Speaking of which, are there magic-wielders from other Alliances on Earth? There can't be so few of us." Especially considering Ada and Iriel weren't even *from* Earth. And I was no natural magic-wielder.

"Unfortunately, they are preoccupied at the present time. I've certainly made my opinions clear to the council members at other Alliance branches, but right now, we're the only branch with authorisation to send in a team. Mathran has requested you come and speak with him and the others at the base. And you should bear in mind, Kay, if I hear a whisper that you've used magic in Vey-Xanetha, you can consider your Ambassador's licence hereafter revoked."

An icy pit opened in my chest, but I met her eyes steadily. "I'm sure the person who brought the griffin into Central will be charged accordingly. As will the individual who used magic first." Or, they would if I had anything to do with it.

I wasn't naive enough to think I'd taken no risk in what I'd done. But god only knew the Alliance would be a laughing stock after this no matter what. At least no one had got hurt.

"I will see to it," said Ms Weston. "And as for these deities of theirs, the research team, even those not from Vey-Xanetha seem to be convinced they are real beings... I wouldn't concern yourself with them. Look for the evidence."

That figured. She might as well have "sceptic" tattooed on her forehead—not that I was one to talk. Still, if *magic* were involved, then that was something else entirely.

"You ready?" I asked the others, just inside the Passage entrance. Ada, Raj, and Iriel were behind me. I pressed the end of the world-key to the blank stretch of wall, nodding to Carl, who stood nearby, holding up his communicator screen with an image of the symbols I'd need to draw to open a doorway. He'd offered to do it himself, but I'd already committed them to memory. *Might as well get used to it,* I thought, tracing a horizontal line, then turning it into a sideways arrow. Besides each of the three points, I drew a small symbol, copied from the image. It wasn't any language I recognised. Probably an ancient one used by the earliest Alliance members. But it worked. The arrowhead became a handle, and the doorway spread floor to ceiling. Iriel sucked in a breath, and Raj stared openly. Ada was the only person who didn't look totally surprised. I knew Carl had used this device to open an emergency door to Aglaia when Ada needed to go and help stop the Conners. So this was how the senior Alliance members created doors to new worlds. Ordinarily, none of us would have been considered senior enough to access that information—but as Ms Weston said, this situation merited it.

I drew the last symbol above the handle, the one unique to Vey-Xanetha. Then I pushed on the door and it slid open.

Thick jungle blocked the view, and I shook my head. "That's nowhere near the base." I closed the door again. "I have to draw it again, right?"

"Just the world-symbol," said Carl. "It's the anchor. Keep drawing it, and sooner or later, you'll get the right place."

Encouraging. It was impossible to pinpoint exactly where a doorway would end up, so the Alliance closely investigated anything that might mean a new connection between a world and the Passages in case they ended up in empty space or the middle of the sea.

I drew the symbol again. And again. Each time, the doorway opened somewhere different, but I knew there was a limit—world-keys were designed to hone in on places with a high magic level, maybe because they were made of a source themselves. So we wouldn't end up too far from a habitable area. It still took over ten attempts before I recognised the stairs not far from the Passage door.

At least there were no three-headed birds or storms this time. I left the door open and we entered Vey-Xanetha again.

"I can't believe you used magic in Central," said Raj, who, of course, had found out about the whole griffin debacle once he'd got back to Central.

"I can't believe you got arrested again," I countered, and that shut him up. We climbed the stairs, even warier after what happened last time. At least we were armed, though Ms Weston's ban on using magic didn't do much to ease my misgivings.

"You're both idiots," said Iriel. "You should have asked someone who has experience dealing with large animals. And I don't mean the senior guards."

Raj snorted. "What, you can tame a griffin?"

"I've flown on one before, yes," she said. "On Alvienne. I realise nobody could have tamed it while it was panicking, but you might at least have waited for the guards to arrive."

"Yeah, but we had no weapons," I said. "What if one of the offworlders had turned hostile? Some of them have magical enhancements. And all of them had something to complain about."

"True," said Iriel. "It's a first-class disaster if I ever saw one. And now we get to deal with absentee gods and giant three-headed—"

"Did you have to mention that now?" said Raj, with a nervous glance at the sky. "I'm more of a diplomat than a fighter. Just so you know."

"You trained as an Alliance guard," said Iriel.

"You can't reason with a chalder vox."

We reached the top of the stairs. Mathran stood in the doorway to the base. We picked up the pace, very aware of the low-hanging red-tinted clouds which might hide anything.

Once inside the building, we gathered in the meeting room with Mathran and Avar, and explained how Earth got the worst of the backlash from whatever was happening here.

"I am sorry," he said. "I would not trouble the Alliance with our woes, but the continent has yet to move. The summoners have not come here, either."

"Summoners?" I said.

"You would call them… magic-wielders?"

My eyebrows shot up. "Are you one? A summoner?"

"Yes. I am a follower of Aktha."

"And can you use magic? How does that work here?" Ada leaned forward in her seat, as keen for answers as me.

"We use the craft only at the deities' direction."

I blinked at him. "What does that mean?"

"You call it… channelling magic?"

"What, something *tells* you to use it?" asked Ada. "Like, consciously?"

"Is this not how magic works for you?"

Ada glanced at me, but I didn't have a clue what he meant, either.

"Where we come from, magic obeys laws," I said. "There aren't any deities who control it. It's… a force."

He frowned. "Is that not the same as a… god?"

"A… what?" Ada's eyes widened. "You're saying 'force' and 'god' mean the same thing?"

"We use the word 'hathet'." He tapped on the spare communicator we'd brought. While we couldn't make calls from here, it had an application that worked as a translator, but in written form. He showed me the symbol, then hit the button that translated it to English.

"Looks like it," I said, but my heart started to beat faster. Magic in the Passages felt like a separate entity sometimes, but a *god?* If the deities directed the summoners, it sounded like an odd reversion of the way humans could pull on magic to make it do as they wanted. Magic gained consciousness? That was possible?

The image of the smoky red magic-creature in the Passages came to mind, and the building suddenly seemed confining. My skin prickled all over. A creature of pure magic. Unnatural. Like these deities—unheard of anywhere else in the Multiverse.

"When you use magic," I said, carefully, "if you were to use it to open that door…"

I hesitated, then checked to see if I could still feel magic. Just about. Curiosity rose, much as I tried to push it down.

Raj said, "Don't. It's not worth it."

Damn. A risk like that here would get me worse than a lecture from Ms Weston. "In other worlds with high-magic levels, you can throw a spark of energy—of magic—and knock the door open. But then the same reaction will come back at you."

"Like bouncing a rubber ball," said Ada, to another confused expression from Mathran. "Um. If you have those here…" She looked helplessly at the rest of us.

Raj shrugged. "I've got nothing. Anyone bring a physics textbook with them?"

"Never mind," I said. "We call it the backlash reaction, anyway. If you use magic, you or someone nearby can easily get hurt. Does that happen here?"

"Hurt?" Mathran shook his head, appearing even more baffled. "The deities would not do us harm."

There's no backlash? Impossible. Even in Aglaia, where the mages used magic for almost everything, the three rules held. They'd summon up a storm, and it'd cause a drought elsewhere or later on.

This world, though…

"It's possible," said Iriel, slowly. "If you use first level to do something subtle, the backlash is absorbed into the atmosphere. That's what happens on midlevel magic worlds like Valeria.

"It does?" asked Ada.

I nodded. "I think so. Can't say I know much about it. Like you can pick a lock or open a window, and the backlash will barely stir a breeze. It's in the application, and it depends on the world's magic level. I don't know how that would work here." If these deities supposedly governed all magic use, then probably not. But I couldn't count on that.

"Wow," said Ada. "I'd never thought of it like that. On Earth, the backlash is pretty noticeable."

"You use magic on Earth?" asked Iriel, curious.

"Uh." She flushed. "I used to. Before I found out…"

Before she found out how destructive it could be. She'd never used it to harm people before, even in the Passages. I shook my head to disperse the lingering guilt. I'd been at least partly responsible for breaking her trust in magic, even if it *was* about as safe as a rampaging wyvern.

"So, can you demonstrate?" I asked Mathran instead. That seemed a reasonable request given what he'd told us.

Mathran bowed his head. "Very well. We shall have to go outside."

He stood, and Raj and Iriel exchanged raised eyebrows. Guess none of us had expected him to say yes.

Several feet away from the base, Mathran paused, turning to face us. He adopted the same stance he'd used when we were being attacked.

"I will attempt to call Aktha," he said. "It's been so long, but he rewards those who follow him."

Magic made its presence known as he splayed his hands. The surface of the rock he stood on swirled, like an invisible hand drew on it, and a scraping sounded as it dug deeper into the rock. When Mathran lowered his hands, a symbol appeared etched at his feet, a complex glyph of swirling lines.

"Aktha," he whispered. "Why have you forsaken us?"

No response. The others stared at the symbol, too, but it gave us no answers.

"This is carved into our places of worship," he explained. "It's usually clearer... perhaps Aktha is weakening. That is the only explanation I can think of."

"You think the deities are losing their power?"

"I dare not suggest it, yet it seems one of few explanations that make sense. The trio have protected my people since we first arrived on this world. Now the world itself has changed... I need to talk to a friend," said Mathran, with a glance at Avar. "We lost contact."

"Contact? How did you communicate with them, exactly?" asked Iriel.

"Our technology no longer works," said Mathran. "We

used to keep contact with a group of... I suppose you would call them science-summoners?"

"Scientists," I said. So magic and science coexisted here?

"Yes... they have certain artefacts, certain information. It has been a long time, but if you have a way to cross the continent... you did not use the door?"

He worked with the Alliance, but I hesitated before pulling out the world-key. Ms Weston had said he'd seen that technology before, and it wasn't strictly an Earth Alliance secret.

"Yes," I said. "If you come with us into the Passages, I can open a door anywhere on the continent." Pity it didn't work like a tracker, which picked up on a particular person who'd used magic recently and could track their exact location—well, it worked on Earth, but not usually on high-magic worlds. Though, if I combined the two and amplified them, maybe *I* could. I'd never had reason to try...

Later, I told myself. I'd done enough magic-related meddling today already.

"Very well." Mathran gave the symbol on the ground one last, sad look, then walked around it, as though afraid to disturb the one tangible sign of his god left in the world.

For some reason, the thought sent an uncomfortable chill down my spine.

Outside the Passage door, an outline cut into the cliff-side, and Mathran regarded it warily.

"It's safe," said Raj.

Mathran nodded. "It's just a silly superstition... the Vey-Xanethans say if one person leaves this world, every other Vey-Xanethan will be forced to follow them or face destruction."

Raj and Iriel exchanged uneasy glances, while Ada chewed on her lower lip. Mathran's people had been forced to leave their world once already, and a legend like that didn't bode well. After all, if gods were real, all bets were off.

There *had* to be an explanation. I didn't think Mathran was lying. The people really believed it. And I'd seen no shortage of evidence for preternatural beings, creatures of pure magic. Might these deities be like that?

But whatever they were, I wasn't sure they were on our side.

8

ADA

Kay used the world-key device to open another doorway after closing the first one. Mathran scanned the Passages nervously, edgier than the rest of us put together. I couldn't exactly blame him. His eyes grew round as Kay opened the door, but the scene on the other side was empty sea, no land in sight.

Imagine using that world-key to travel anywhere on Earth. But it was set to Vey-Xanetha, according to Kay. Even Ms Weston didn't entirely understand how it worked. Yet another mystery only the higher-up members of the Alliance would understand. It kind of bugged me, seeing as *we* were the ones going into dangerous territory, but I wouldn't pass up the opportunity to explore. And possibly get answers about magic. I'd never heard of a world where 'force' and 'deity' meant the same thing... but Vey-Xanetha had had nothing to do with the Alliance for the past twenty-five years.

The view through the doorway looked more like a forest than a city, though a path carved its way through thick red-barked trees with roots taller than I was. A rainforest, with low-hanging clouds draped around the trees like curtains.

"This is close to the city," said Mathran.

The sweltering heat got to me immediately, and even though I knew this world was teeming with magic-related threats, I couldn't help but wish I wore something more suited to the weather than skin-tight, jet-back guard gear.

"I'm dying," Raj muttered. "Is there a fountain I can jump in? Or is that breaking some law?"

Mathran gave him a blank look, and I stifled a giggle.

"Where's this city, anyway?" asked Iriel. She had a point; the snaking path didn't seem to lead anywhere but deeper into thick forest. Bright flowers bloomed all around us, filling the air with unfamiliar scents, which combined with the heat, made it even more difficult to breathe. I'd never been to a rainforest on Earth, so I didn't have anything to compare it to, but I hadn't thought *walking* would become exhausting within minutes. And even with the track beneath our feet, thick vines draped across our path, and strange, bright-winged insects buzzed around us. My ear stung as something bit me, and spun around, swatting at it.

"Nothing's poisonous in here, is it?" I asked, warily. I really didn't want to die in the jungle on a distant world.

Mathran shook his head. "Not the insects, no, but I wouldn't touch the plants."

"And there went my plan to take some of those as a souvenir," said Raj, pointing at a cluster of vivid yellow mug-shaped flowers.

"Those are hideous," said Iriel. "And you're still doing that?"

"Still doing what?" I asked.

"He insists on taking 'tokens' from every world he goes to," said Iriel.

"Not tokens," said Raj. "Souvenirs. Only from Allianceapproved areas. Come on, I have to have something to show my girlfriend after I've been gallivanting off for a week."

"You have a girlfriend?" I asked.

"That was a joke," said Raj. "Non-Alliance members tend to tire of the excuses. Sorry, I can't come home tonight, I'm staying on Alvienne and there's a sixty per cent chance I'll be mauled by a griffin. Been there, done that."

Iriel burst out laughing. I couldn't help glancing sideways at Kay. Had *he* been thinking long-term, before I'd screwed everything up? Or had he even wanted a relationship at all? Sure, my family's general attitude towards him didn't help, but still. If not for the obvious total inappropriateness of the scenario, I almost wished for another glass of inhibition-killing wine so I could just *ask* him. And then I wondered if there wasn't the tiniest chance the heat had short-circuited my brain cells.

Right now, Kay was in Alliance-mode, closed-off and tense, though I'd sensed anger beneath the surface ever since he'd come out of Ms Weston's office. I'd heard her yelling at him in there, and I gathered she'd threatened to put him on probation for using magic in Central. I could hardly believe he'd actually done that. None of us had a weapon, but with Earth's magic levels going crazy, even I didn't dare use magic.

Still, he hadn't used it in a way that might have hurt anyone, no more than the damage the griffin caused. And Ms Weston had been in her office and the guards nowhere to be found. To be honest, a griffin in Central didn't seem like something the Alliance would allow at all, but Earth itself had gone absolutely insane over the past two days.

We really needed an explanation. Fast.

"We're here," said Mathran, stopping in the middle of the path.

"Here's... where?" asked Raj uncertainly. Thick tree roots enclosed the path like natural-made fences, and the trees themselves were as wide as houses... wait. I looked up at the canopy, convinced I'd seen movement. Yes—there were *people* up there, crossing the thick branches between the trees, some of which were hollow.

There were people living in the trees.

"Holy crap," I said, gaping as a figure jumped between two trees high above.

Mathran shook his head. "Xanet's followers."

"What is this place?" I asked. "Is the whole city up in the trees?"

"The trees *are* the city," said Mathran. "This is the main entrance," he added, leaving the path via a sort of alleyway between two curving tree roots. Alongside the tree lay what looked like a handmade pulley system supporting a cage of interlocked branches.

"This is how goods are carried in and out of the city," he said. "And people."

"You're kidding me," said Raj, mouth hanging open. "That doesn't look safe."

"It is perfectly safe," said Mathran, a touch of reproach in his voice. "Xanet's protection is in the branches."

Considering the deities were supposedly losing their power, this wasn't exactly reassuring. I glanced at Kay, whose frown suggested he'd had the same thought.

Once Mathran had demonstrated the platform was, however, pretty sturdy, and signalled to someone in the tree-building at the top to activate the system, we didn't have a lot of options other than to climb in.

"And there I was, thinking we were done with tree-climbing," I muttered, but didn't get a reaction. Kay's hands were clenched on the edges of the platform, like he wanted to jump out and climb instead.

"Lighten up," Iriel said to Raj, who looked equally uncomfortable. "This is hardly different from the Alliance's glass lifts."

"I thought a griffin smashed two of those to pieces today," said Raj, through clenched teeth.

"Thanks for the reminder," I said to him.

"Are there many people about?" Iriel asked Mathran.

"Few will leave their houses, given the circumstances," said Mathran. "Kevar is a summoner of Xanet. I would have also liked to introduce you to a Veyak summoner, too, as I am told the Alliance would like to hear all sides of the story."

"All three deities," said Kay. "You said this city pertains to... Xanet?"

"Xanet is our nature deity, so this is her natural home," he said. "Particularly gifted summoners take on the appearance of the forest itself. As followers of Aktha may develop certain aspects to their appearance, too." He tapped the side of the platform with a finger, creating a distinct, and unexpected, hollow sound. More like one rock striking another.

"You're made out of stone?" said Raj. "Um. Not literally. Right?"

"In a way, I take Aktha as part of myself."

Holy wow. This I'd *never* heard of, and I'd talked to people from so many worlds I'd lost count.

"And there's no chance we can talk to anyone else?" asked Iriel.

"None of you speak Vey-Xanethan," said Mathran. "That would not be wise."

"Yeah," said Kay. "I doubt we'll be able to convince many people to accept a piece of offworld tech. They'll have never met offworlders before."

Once the platform reached the top, Raj was the first out, while Kay climbed out the back way and, standing near the edge, peered through the branches at the view. The thick clouds masked the sky, and thin rays of sunlight lit up the reddish haze overhead.

"Kay, I wouldn't stand too close to the edge there," I said.

"Don't worry," he said. "Did you see anything odd?"

"See what?" I echoed, puzzled.

He shook his head. "Never mind. Probably a bird."

There *were* a lot of birds at this level, but not the bright-coloured ones I usually associated with images of the rain-forest. These were large, cat-sized, and the same burnt red colour as the trees themselves. I jumped as one flew directly overhead, but not a savage three-headed monster.

"The jekath don't live here," said Mathran. "The savage birds only live in the mountains. Xanet's protection lies over this part of the forest."

That's why the canopy's so thick. But had the forest always grown like this, or had people somehow changed it? Or the deities?

"Who *does* live here?" I asked, as Mathran led us up a staircase made of more interlaced branches. They looked more like they'd grown that way naturally than man-made constructions, and, as we reached the top, I saw the same was true of the narrow branched paths leading between each tree. This whole city lay thirty-odd feet in the air, and it gave me an odd feeling of unreality to see the deserted road below.

"More to the point, why?" asked Raj, head tilted up at the sky, probably to avoid looking down. "What if someone's born here who happens to be scared of heights?"

That comment earned him another blank stare from Mathran. I was starting to think Vey-Xanethans had a different idea of humour to Earth people. And Zanthan/Klathican people, I guessed, remembering Iriel. She examined a bright-red skein of flowers, her strange blank wired eye whirring.

"Pity about the non-disturbance rule," she said, poking a metallic-coloured plant with sharp bristles. "These would fit in at Central."

"Those are used to make weaponry here, as it happens," said Mathran, pulling out a metal stick like the one he'd thrown at the three-headed bird. Close up, it was identical to the plant's spines.

"Huh," said Raj. "Interesting."

"Xanet gives us what we need," said Mathran, pocketing the weapon. "Now, it's this way."

Like the platform, the bridges between the trees were sturdier than they appeared, but I hurried as fast as possible, like the others. We reached an intersection where a bunch of trees grew close enough together for their branches to form a wider platform, where the tallest of the trees towered far above the rest. Its tip disappeared into the clouds, giving the odd impression of a tower. Shadowy figures moved about inside, visible through the gaps in the bark. And those weren't the only people. A group of close-knit figures moved across a parallel platform, and as I stared, one looked right at me. A chill went through me, and Mathran hurried us across the bridge.

"Who were they?" I asked.

"Certain summoners patrol in the city, looking out for trouble. Those are aligned with Xanet."

"Like the police force?" I eyed the knotted bark, which did give the impression of barred windows. But Mathran didn't seem to know the word. *More communication difficulties.*

Mathran led us across the bridges, finally stopping at one which ended in a staircase spiralling down the inside of another hollow trunk. He rapped sharply on a wooden knob, which made a surprisingly loud echo.

A figure appeared on the stairs below, climbing to the top, a bald man with skin like rough, red bark, like the trees, in fact. His gnarled hands made the comparison even more distinct. His clothes were plain and pale-green-coloured, of some kind of soft cotton-like material, though his feet were bare and as burnt-red as the rest of him, curled around the platform like he was used to climbing high places. His eyes, however, were a startling dark green, more like an Earth-forest—it kind of surprised me how quickly I thought of Earth as just one other world, even though it was my home. Guess I was always going to leave it, really.

"This is Kevar," said Mathran. "He is... what you would call a science-expert?"

"Scientist," I said, nodding, as he introduced all of us.

We climbed down the trunk of the tree into a room. I couldn't help staring at the way everything appeared to have moulded to make it comfortable to live in.

Even with the earpieces, introductions were pretty awkward. A number of other men and women hurried around and several teenagers stared at us, wide-eyed. Appearance-wise, however, there were distinct variations. Some were red-skinned, like Kevar, but most had bronze colouring, like Mathran. One's skin looked so much like rock, I couldn't help but stare when his hand bumped against the table with a thudding sound as he offered us cups of water. I sipped it gratefully, glad of the hydration.

Rule one of an Ambassador: *don't stare.* Or Carl's version, which was "Don't stare if you want to keep your face the way it is". And I had enough experience of being gawked at by people on Earth to hold my tongue. That guy must be like Mathran, then.

We all gathered around the raised wooden table, Kevar at the head, in such rapid conversation with Mathran, even the earpiece couldn't catch every word from Mathran. Someone else offered us refreshments, odd tart-like things with sweet fruit I'd never tasted before. Kind of like strawberries.

As they paused in their conversation, Raj asked Mathran, "What exactly do they study here?"

Mathran spoke to Kevar, who turned to face us.

"I have met your kind before," said Kevar. "Many years ago. They came here to hear the story."

"Story?" I said.

"The story of how we came to find this world." Kevar and Mathran exchanged glances.

"Yes," said Mathran. "I think this would be relevant to your purpose here."

"Our old world was dying," said Kevar. "The stories say humanity had become the playthings of terrible monsters and were in danger of dying out. But one summoner, maybe the first, found a door in the wastelands. He and his companions followed the door through to another realm. When the creatures found out the humans were escaping, they were furious. Battles were fought, and the humans banded together, combined their magic in a way no one ever had before. The result tore open a great chasm between their old world and this one. The survivors were able to cross the chasm to a new world."

Whoa. I studied the others, who listened intently. I'd never heard of a world in the Multiverse were humans weren't the dominant species, even worlds they shared with other cross-humans, like Aglaia. The playthings of monsters?

Kevar continued, "But their new country was nothing like their previous home. The continents rearranged themselves every cycle, their old technology did not work here, and terrible things happened when they tried to exploit the planet's resources. Those who cut the stone were drawn into the earth, buried. Those who tried to cut the trees were taken by the creeper-vines."

Raj mouthed *holy crap,* while Iriel and Kay looked as taken aback as I'd ever seen them.

"And certain individuals," Kevar went on, "developed unusual talents. A small group found they could speak to the forces that governed their world, and through carvings, were able to interpret them. They found there were three forces which governed the world. Many, many people were aligned to one of them, and so, the summoners were formed."

I fidgeted, resisting the urge to take notes. This must be relevant to what was happening now, right? But I'd never heard of actively *speaking* to gods. Still, those magic-creatures came to mind when I thought about magic with consciousness...

"Xanet provided land for them," said Kevar, "and they were able to adapt their farming techniques from their old world. Aktha helped them build towns and villages, while the summoners of Veyak learned to adapt the weather and control the unpredictable storms. Gradually, humans and deities learned to live in harmony.

"But one summoner found a map, hidden in Aktha's first village. The map was drawn by the last inhabitants of Vey-Xanetha, and marked a certain mountain where they left further instructions. He and a group of others took a dangerous journey to find what lay under the mountain. And they found more carvings, and strange artefacts their predecessors left behind. The last people on this world left a record of the cycle of the seasons. Their birth and their downfall. Most people dismissed it, and it is not a widespread text. It has been adapted into story and myth, as most old legends are. But I cannot pretend it does not worry me..." He and Mathran exchanged dark looks. "There are some who take the carvings to be a prediction, who believe the chasm will open again. The downfall of our world begins then, and according to the last travellers to pass through the city, the chasm is already open."

"Damn," said Raj, in a low voice.

"Is it true?" Iriel asked Mathran. "Is that what you believe?"

Mathran shook his head. "Who would want to believe they are doomed to lose their world again? It may be a story. But there is often truth in myth."

Too true, if these living deities were anything to go by.

Kay turned to him. "What exactly is supposed to happen? Aside from the continents stopping, and this chasm?"

"There are too many variations of the story to tell," said Kevar. "Mathran has the original at the base."

"You do?" asked Kay, eyes narrowing slightly. "You didn't think to mention it before?"

"Kevar tells the story better than I do," said Mathran. "And I thought you would want to meet some of the people who would be affected if our world is destroyed."

I shifted. That sounded uncomfortably like guilt-tripping to me. It wasn't like we were just here for a holiday. We did mean to help these people. Somehow.

"We'll figure it out," said Kay, with more confidence than I felt.

"I hoped to introduce you to the summoners of Veyak," said Mathran, "but they are here no longer?" He directed the question at Kevar, who shook his head.

"They passed through, and left. It was they who told us that the chasm is open."

Several other people came into the room, and the quiet broke into general conversation. I shifted, uncomfortable, wondering how any of this would help us solve the problem. This was a world with rules I couldn't begin to understand.

"What do most people do for a living here, anyway?" Raj asked Mathran.

"Non-summoners mostly work the land," said Mathran. "Merchants who buy from them work the pulley system, bringing in food, water, and so forth, and taking it to the marketplace. Others perform necessary services, making things people need, gathering supplies, deliveries, travelling to the other cities to trade, ensuring our energy supplies are sufficient, and so on. And there is a large population of scholars, especially in the city."

"Wow," was all I could say. The people here weren't ignorant, not at all, and their world must have functioned like clockwork. Until everything had changed.

And I wanted to know why. These people shouldn't have to leave their whole world behind because of some inexplicable disaster. If we could do anything to help...

"You have Veyak's mark," said a voice, and I almost jumped out of my seat. A boy appeared behind me—probably around Alber's age. He stared openly at me, as though the others weren't there.

"I—what?" I said. And then remembered he wouldn't understand me because he didn't have an earpiece.

"Veyak has touched you." His hand reached out, and I automatically leaned out of the way. "Be careful." He walked past, and I stared after him, heart beating wildly. Maybe it was my imagination, but the air tingled with static. *Magic?* Of course. I'd become immune to its presence, but everything from the walls to the furniture had been made from the power of the deities here. From magic. I shivered.

"Ada?" said Kay, jolting my attention back to the present. He'd stood, and so did the others. "We're leaving now. Mathran is going to show us the carvings." He gave Mathran a look that suggested he wasn't pleased with the scholar for keeping the information from us before.

"Yes," said Mathran. "We should return to the base."

The chasm is already open, I couldn't help thinking, as we climbed into the rickety branch-cage again. But that made it sound like it was already too late.

9

KAY

Perhaps the world-key was tuned into the places it had already opened doorways to, because it took only three attempts to reach the base. Avar hovered outside, clawed feet shifting anxiously.

"There has been a... complication."

I glanced back at the others, all of whom seemed hesitant. But this was an Alliance base, technically. No danger to us. I took the lead and followed Mathran into the building, and through a door to a side room.

A couch lay in the centre of the room, and on it, a man. His face was wrapped in bloodstained bandages, as was one arm. Wild, scared eyes stared at us.

"It's all right," Mathran said, in Vey-Xanethan. "These people won't harm you. They work for the Inter-World Alliance, and they're here to help us."

If we can. Through the bandages, I glimpsed long lacerations that could only be claw-marks. The scars on my own arm seemed to tingle in response, a reminder.

Avar turned to us. "We should discuss this elsewhere."

He led us back to the meeting room.

"What happened?" asked Iriel. Of the others, she seemed the least spooked. Ada and Raj both hovered close to the door, neither taking a seat at the table.

Avar himself stood in front of the window and faced us. "He was attacked on the mountain. The entire group of merchants was, in fact. They were late midway through their passage when the continents stopped moving. We found him halfway up the path. Something attacked them. We've yet to investigate what exactly did. There were two hundred of them, and he was the only survivor."

"Did he say what attacked them?" I asked.

Everyone jumped as the door opened, but it was Mathran. "He used the word *verek*—abomination," he said. "I do not know to what he refers."

That might mean anything, as far as this world went. "And whatever it was killed everyone else?"

"Apparently so," said Mathran.

"Whereabouts?" I asked.

"Northwest of here. The other side of the mountain."

"You're not going out there alone!" said Ada, guessing my plan before I spoke. "Are you crazy?"

I checked the world-key. I barely felt the magic charge, which suggested it was running out. We didn't have long left. Maybe enough for one more use… after this one.

"We'll have to return to the base soon," I said. "The battery's running low on this, but we have another one on Earth."

"I see," said Mathran, forehead creased with worry. "I hope time does not run out for us. If such abominations have appeared, it may be that the reassembly of the world has begun."

"Uh," said Raj. "What exactly do you mean by that?"

"It's a belief held by some scholars," said Mathran. "And it is in my notes. I made it my life's mission to understand the few documents left by the people who lived on this world before we did, whoever they were. This is part of the reason we set up base here, because the carvings are inside caves in the mountain itself... but as I said, they spoke of a cataclysm, of their world reshaping itself. We have never found an efficient way of translating the words on the carvings, though we've taken imprints. An obscure people from an outlying world is not of interest to the Alliance, and precious few of Vey-Xanetha's own show an interest in the history of a species unknown to us."

So this happened before? "How long have your people lived on this world, exactly?" I asked.

"Approximately one thousand years, by your measurement. We ourselves have a more complicated system. We count years by multiples of cycles—three day-cycles to a moon-cycle, and fifteen of those to the turn of the first sun. When our world has completed its orbit and the trio of stars is visible, then comes the start of a new year."

Well, that wasn't complicated at all.

"And do you know how long passed between the last inhabitants leaving this world, and your people's arrival? How long they lived on this world for?"

"It's impossible to tell. They left nothing save for the carvings, and trinkets of metal. Whatever the metal is, we've been unable to determine. It has never been found on this world since."

"I see," I said slowly. "Do you have samples of this here at the base?"

"We do."

"Can you show us?"

He hesitated, then nodded, leading the way to another room two doors down, which contained a sort of computer. Not Earth tech, but not Vey-Xanethan, either. It resembled a block of glass, wires twisted inside and hooked up to a wall-sized projector screen.

Mathran manipulated the wires with hesitant hands. It was beyond me to figure out what he was doing, but after a moment, an image appeared on the projector screen. Three symbols surrounding a circle. The top one I recognised as the glyph he'd drawn in the rock.

"Your three deities?" I asked.

He pointed to the one on the left, then the right. "Veyak. Xanet. And Aktha."

"I can scan this and take it back to Central," I added, taking out my communicator. "Those are the only carvings you found?"

"No, there are others." He fiddled with the wires again, and more images flashed across the screen. Other symbols, glyphs. Unreadable, at least to me, with no resemblance to any language I knew.

"What does it say?"

He shook his head. "It's incomprehensible to me. It is not Vey-Xanethan as we know it. Wherever the previous inhabitants of this world went, they took their secrets with them.

"And you haven't been able to translate it here?" asked Raj. "I know the Alliance have translators."

"We have limited access here," said Mathran. "But you said you can record an image?"

"We can code it into our computers and work on a translation. If I can take a picture with this?" I held up my communicator, and he nodded. I swiped the touch screen and found the image-recording application. It even had an image-reader, but as I expected, the language and origin came up as unknown. Worth a try.

"Okay," I said. "What did you say about finding some metal the previous people who lived here left behind? Is that here, you said?"

"I will fetch it."

As he left the room, I turned to the rest of the group. Ada regarded the screen with a vaguely puzzled expression.

"That's odd," she said. "Those symbols look familiar—but I'm sure I haven't seen them before."

"Hmm." I studied them, but I couldn't say they looked like any I'd seen before, and I'd seen text from more than a dozen worlds. But Ada had had contact with worlds the Alliance didn't usually deal with. "I haven't. I'll scan them, though."

"I can do that," said Iriel, switching on her eye-scanner. "Hmm... this isn't coming up with anything. These are pre-Alliance, though."

"What, you can translate with that... eye?" said Ada, her expression a cross between revulsion and fascination.

"I used to be a code-breaker in the tech division on Klathica before I transferred to Earth," she said. "This comes in handy. But those glyphs don't match up with anything in our database. I might be able to do more with full access to Klathican technology. I bet I can wrangle some from the Embassy."

"Good luck," said Raj. "If *you* can't crack it, then Klathica's computers can't."

Iriel rolled her eyes—one considerably more intensely than the other. "I'll record this here anyway." As she recorded each image on her communicator's scanning device, I took out the other device I kept in my pocket, alongside the world-key. This particular piece of Alliance tech gleamed black, rectangular and palm-sized. A magic-scanner, or tracker.

It was a long shot, and if anything odd happened, I'd have a hell of a lot of explaining to do to the others. But as long as the battery kept running, I could use it in any world. Thanks to the amplifier.

And there were definitely traces here. More than one.

Now I'd practised, I could isolate a single magic trace. Like when I used the Chameleon's magic to become invisible, similar to tuning into a radio station. Except tracking magic signals was more like a tangle of radio waves at slightly different frequencies. Four... no, five. Four magic-wielders had recently been in this room, though there were others hidden beneath. And that included Ada, Iriel and Raj. Mathran was the other, and one came from the room next door.

It must belong to the surviving nomad. And if I amplified the tracker and focused on his signal, I could use it to find where he'd come from.

The question was: how to do that without giving away the nature of my abilities to the others? I hadn't used magic yet here, either. I'd have been a fool to risk it. Even more than using magic inside Central. The amplifier didn't count as it was an internal source, and I could even use it on Earth, to some extent.

Mathran returned, accompanied by Avar, who held three pieces of silvery-coloured metal.

"We believe one corresponds to each of the deities," said Avar, with a glance at Mathran. "Though, of course, we cannot be sure. But the symbols carved on the rocks match the other carvings inside the mountain caves."

The metal piece was roughly fist-sized and made up of hard planes engraved with swirling glyphs. When he passed it to me, it was lighter than I'd expected, like it was hollow on the inside. I turned it over. The same symbols marked each side. Six in total.

I passed it on to Ada, who regarded it with puzzlement, and examined the second. Though a different symbol was on each base, they were otherwise identical.

And the magic pulsed through them, enough that I didn't want to hold onto each one for too long. The static of the third in particular buzzed against my skin, like raw power waiting to be unleashed. These weren't dormant. They were alive.

Shaking off the uneasiness, I turned to Mathran. "Who found these originally?"

"The first settlers. There was a museum, at first, I believe, a collection of such objects as these. But with the reshaping of the continents, so much is lost that this particular historical detail was forgotten."

"I see," I said. Now I concentrated, I sensed the trail of magic from each rock like another radio station signal. Crap —the last thing I wanted was to get wrapped up in more strange magic I didn't understand. But once again, magic had the upper hand through the astounding lack of information, even here on this high-magic world.

So be it. "I think we should leave now. We'll be back later once we have another one of these." I drew the world-key. "There's one at the West Office branch of the Alliance. How long before night falls here?"

"Half an hour in your time."

"All right. That won't be enough time for us to find another one of these—" I indicated the world-key—"but I'll ask my supervisor if we can come back later."

"Then we are grateful, Ambassadors."

I couldn't help but feel the next step was to find these deities—whoever or whatever they were.

But we left the base, again, and I opened a door back to the Passages.

One return-trip left. I knew what I had to do. The tracker still responded, and I had a feeling this might work.

I turned to the others. "Right," I said. "We've one shot in here, not much, but I have an idea. I think I know how to check on those merchants."

"How?" said Raj. "Even if it's possible, something killed them. Horribly."

"And the details don't add up," I said. "It might not even work, but there's not enough charge left in this for a longer trip. Just give me a minute." I was eighty percent sure this would work, anyway. I held onto the magic trace, though it was a fragile thing, and I couldn't be fully certain I'd picked the right one. But if I did, the amplifier would mean I could follow the injured merchant's magic trace to the place he'd last been. The place everyone had died. I knew we wouldn't find anything good on the other side, but if there was a clue at the site of the killings, I had to be sure.

"Kay," said Ada. "You know what you're doing?"

I knew she must suspect how, exactly, I intended to follow the trail. I hoped the others wouldn't guess. More for their own safety than anything. What I could do was so uncommon as to be unbelievable, as far as magic-wielders went.

And no deity had granted me this power, I knew that much. Life had played its hand and I was stuck with the consequences. But I was damned if I wouldn't use it to try and solve this.

"Yeah," I said. "I'm sure. You guys don't have to come. I'll only be a minute. Less than that, if I can help it."

"I'm not letting you go out there alone," said Ada, moving to my side, as I pressed the doorway-opener to the wall once again. I could tell from the set of her jaw she wasn't budging.

Damn it all. The door opened, the magic-sense tugged at my veins, and the ground behind the door was dark with blood.

"You should stay back," I said to Ada, but she shook her head fiercely. Out of the corner of my eye, Raj hung back, muttering to Iriel.

I stepped through the door and down the slope, following

the trail of blood. Then I saw the first body, a woman's. Three long claw marks almost severed her body into three pieces, blood soaking into the rock.

I stared for a long moment, transfixed. Somehow, no matter how mentally prepared you were, whatever you expected to see, it never did justice to the reality.

A sound from behind as Ada stumbled over her feet, bringing me back to the present. "Oh, gods…"

"I told you not to come," I said to her. "I'm going to take a look down there."

"Are you mad?" Her eyes were round, horrified, her face deathly pale.

"I want to check on something." But I drew my weapon all the same and took one careful step after another, avoiding the thickening blood. Three bodies were heaped on top of one another. A woman shielding two children.

Rage ignited and my hand clenched on the dagger. Ada made a choked noise, and when I looked back at her, she'd pressed her hands over her eyes.

"Who would do this?" she whispered.

Monsters. Human ones or non-human, it didn't matter.

More bodies. This must be the centre of camp. People lay every which way, where they'd fallen over one another trying to escape. And in the centre, furrows marked the ground. Blood filled the gaps where a glyph had been carved.

A familiar symbol. Not Aktha's. I had to think for a moment. This belonged to one of the other gods. Veyak, the sky god.

Fury mingled with a cold, primal terror, and I froze to the spot. Magic sparked from my hands, though I hadn't consciously used it. The ground shifted under my feet, the rocks grating against one another, and the sky overhead darkened to a deeper red. I let the magic drop, stumbled forwards. An old man lay sprawled on the ground in front of me, eyes open, perpetual horror carved into his face.

I closed my eyes. "Come on." My voice sounded distant. "Let's go back."

Ada didn't need any encouragement. She shook all over as we headed to the still-open doorway, where the blue light from the Passages cast an odd glow to the blood-soaked rocks. I was one step from the door when a shadow moved in the corner of my eye. I spun on the spot, dagger slashing at —nothing.

Nothing was there. Nobody but the dead.

10

KAY

None of us spoke as we left the Passages and walked back to Central. Raj and Iriel had stayed long enough to see the first body. Ada walked apart from the group, not speaking to anyone. And try as I might to block it out, the image of the massacre was burned into my brain.

And that symbol. I could think of two possibilities, and neither meant good news.

First things first. We had to tell Ms Weston what we'd found out. And we needed to get hold of another tracker.

Never mind those carvings or Kevar's end-of-days prophecies. They had nothing to do with the here and now. They sure as hell didn't seem to have anything to do with the brutal slaughter of a hundred travellers. No. The monster, the killer, wasn't some vague myth. The gods were real, and present in Vey-Xanetha.

Magic surged, without warning, for the second time since we'd left the Passages. Must be acting up again. The swarming crowd in Central's entrance hall confirmed my suspicions. It looked as though every offworlder in London had come to complain to the Alliance. A group of claw-footed men like Avar had even bought a flock of multi-coloured birds, which flew around shrieking and shedding feathers over the crowd.

Ada flicked one out of her hair, staring. "Wow."

She appeared a little less dazed, at least. But I wished she'd stayed behind the door. Stupid, considering I knew full well she'd been helping people escape from war-torn worlds over half her life—but one look at her face and I knew she'd never seen anything like that close-up before.

Back to Ms Weston's office. She was less snappish with us than earlier, though I gathered from hearing Markos talking to a couple of novices that she'd taken her rage out on the unlucky guards who'd let the girls with the griffin into the entrance hall. Turned out they'd been new recruits and had panicked at the sight of the giant eagle-lion hybrid, and had no chance to reconsider the idiocy of letting it into Central before they'd been called into the Passages.

Still didn't mean they weren't morons.

Careful, I thought. How much to tell her? I decided against pushing my luck any further, and explained everything we'd heard, both in the town and from Mathran and Avar at the base. But I left out how I'd used magic to track the slaughtered merchants.

My suspicion that the deities were linked to the myth of the world coming to another cataclysm earned me raised eyebrows from Ms Weston.

"You'd put stock in superstitions?"

Exactly what I thought she'd say. I'd be the same, if I hadn't seen the magic with my own eyes and known Vey-Xanetha didn't operate on the rules we were used to.

"It's one possibility," I said—after all, most superstitions had some basis in reality, however distant.

"It fits with what we've heard," said Ada. She hadn't

expressed an opinion on my theory about the deity being involved in the merchants' deaths until now, and to be honest, I half-thought she'd dismiss it as superstition, too. Not that it worked for Ms Weston, even after I explained how Mathran made that symbol appear when he'd used magic.

"We told Mathran we would check the other villages." I handed her the world-key. "But this has run out of battery. Is there another one here at Central?"

"No, but West Office has one. Earth's other world-keys were used to track Vey-Xanetha down in the first place. They were recharging, but the magic level issues have forced us to switch off our offworld tech."

That figured. "Should we go back, then?" I asked. "If Kevar's story is to be believed, we don't have a lot of time. Superstition or not, is that really something we want to risk?"

As if to emphasise my words, another surge in the magic level made the hairs on my arms stand up, and a muffled shriek sounded from downstairs. Human, but I tensed all the same.

"That would depend upon whether you have a plan," she said, eyes flashing, in the way they did when she was incredibly displeased. "If time's as limited as you say, acting fast is our priority. We need to find what went wrong in the first place, ideally. Seek out the problem at its source."

Source. The word brought to mind the image of shining black rock, buried deep underground on Aglaia. Might there be something similar on Vey-Xanetha? The source of these gods? I didn't know if Ms Weston's choice of words was deliberate or not, but there was so little information.

"Right," I said. "Should I go to West Office?"

"Hold on," said Raj. "Mathran said the sun's about to go down, and the monsters come out at night. It's not safe."

"Is that so?" asked Ms Weston. "Their days run in short cycles, of course. When does the next begin?"

"Six hours after," I said. "It's a ten-hour cycle, more or less."

"Crazy," Raj commented. "How are we supposed to solve anything in that time?"

"Then you'll have to temporarily relocate to their base," said Ms Weston. "I believe the world-key at West Office is more equipped for long-term use than our last one, but I'd prefer not to over-use it. It's the best Earth has, and sad to say, none of the other worlds in the Multiverse are making any effort beyond their own worlds."

"They're not?" Iriel blinked in surprise. "None of them at all?"

"Magic levels have stabilised… everywhere except Earth."

I stared, as did the others. "What? How's that possible?"

"I thought it was high-magic worlds which would be the worst affected," said Raj. "Why Earth?"

"It was recently the seat of a magical disturbance," said Ms Weston. "The Balance must still be fragile. In any case, only Earth seems inclined to act, aside from those already based on Vey-Xanetha, of course."

Seriously? "And they aren't concerned about the Balance, at all?"

"They are," said Ms Weston, "but we have no conclusive answers. The council will act only upon evidence, and our tracking the world down in the first place was purely coincidental."

"Coincidence?" I frowned. "How's *that* possible? I thought the council actively went out *looking* for what caused the disturbance. Or, someone did."

"Actually… it's very strange. I didn't want to tell you any more without proof, but our scanners picked up on an odd magic signal. That's what led Carl to that particular door, and he crossed paths with Avar, who'd tried to relay a message to the Alliance but was attacked by one of those magic-creatures. The kimaros."

"A signal?" I said, thinking of the way using my own amplifying ability to tune into the tracker led me after any magic-wielder, and how much it was like crossing radio signals. I could track any magic-wielder, even those without an internal source. But I couldn't find a pure source by signal alone—could I?

Damn Earth's total lack of information. Ms Weston paused before answering my question. "A magic-trace, yes. I don't pretend to know in detail how magi-tech works, but in any case, it certainly led us to the probable source of the trouble. I don't know if other worlds with similar devices picked up on it, but we were the only people to act."

That seemed odd, given the level of the chaos the other day. But people tended to look out for their own first. Even the Alliance, especially as Vey-Xanetha wasn't a member and had little to offer in way of compensation. If this had happened on Valeria, one of the most important worlds in the Alliance, every guard this side of Cethrax would flock to help out in the hope of getting a massive paycheque for it. Even if we spread word across the Multiverse, few would want to risk their necks in a hostile world, without further proof. Proof we didn't have, not really.

"Then what next?" I asked. "There's no way we can risk leaving this be. Especially if it's affecting Earth like this. We're lucky nothing more serious has happened."

"I think the council, at least, are aware of the dilemma. With the level of risk, Mathran has agreed to act representative authority for Vey-Xanetha and temporarily upgrade its position in relation to the Alliance so you have permission to go back. I would advise you to hold by the Alliance's noninterference rules wherever possible, but in the event of a threat to the people of that world, you can step in as authority with Mathran's permission."

I blinked. He must really think we could deal with this.

"I'll have someone from West Office run over with the spare world-key."

As I left, she asked the others for written reports. Apparently, even with the Balance crumbling around our ears, Central needed to keep the paperwork up to date. *Like it matters,* I thought, the image of the slaughtered merchants flashing before my eyes again.

My fists clenched. I was damned if I did *nothing* about that.

"What's the plan?" asked Ada. "I was going to check on my brother. The Chameleons might come in handy if we're going back."

"Good idea," I said. I'd reluctantly handed mine in, but it wasn't much use with the battery drained anyway, and only the tech team had the resources to recharge it. Of course, Raj and Iriel didn't know my own invisibility worked even with the device switched off. Out of our group, only Ada did.

The tech office was predictably chaotic. I went to fetch the Chameleons from the store room—to suspicious looks from the rest of the department, like they expected me to steal their tech. Or maybe they'd heard about the griffin.

When I got back to the main tech room, Ada and the others gathered around a computer monitor, with the other staff looking on from the side lines.

"Well, it isn't Klathican," Iriel was saying. She leaned over the keyboard and typed one-handed while using her other hand to swipe the communicator's touch screen on the desk. "I swear it *looked* like it, for a moment, but I've never seen that script before. I studied ancient codes, maybe that's why."

Oh. They were checking the images on the carved spheres against the Alliance's records. Iriel had scanned the images into her communicator, and now they filled the computer screen. I squinted at them, frowning. They weren't remotely like any language I could read... so why did they give me a strange sense of familiarity?

"That's odd," said Ada, leaning forwards. "Because I swear I've seen something like it before."

I caught her eye over the desk, navigating my way around a tangle of wires to join them.

"I don't," said Raj. "Never seen it before in my life. It's got to be pre-Alliance, if the systems don't recognise it, but you'd think there'd be a record somewhere. Earth has experts in ancient languages."

"Not every world does," said Iriel. "Most Alliance worlds do, of course, but if a large-scale disaster wiped out the entire population of Vey-Xanetha, the newcomers wouldn't have known where to start."

Yeah. Unless there was something else at work. The Alliance had formed of worlds who wanted to learn from history, not erase it, but that wasn't the case on some of the outlying non-Alliance worlds. Not that the Vey-Xanethans were under any Orwellian totalitarian government, but maybe some kind of erasure had taken place. Or maybe it was the paranoia talking.

Maybe I wanted to distract myself from the other possibility—that the glyphs looked familiar to Iriel, Ada and me because we had internal magic sources. They had magic written all over them. I didn't need a translator to prove that.

"Were they definitely carved by a sentient species?" I asked, realising I hadn't been able to tell.

"That's another thing," said Iriel. "They weren't carved with any tool I'm familiar with, but it's possible the ancient civilisation's technology was lost in that—cataclysm, whatever it was."

"Hmm." It seemed unlikely that every single piece of

evidence had been wiped out—apart from those carvings and spheres, of course. And the entire world had rearranged itself. As though a sentient force controlled it…

Quit it. If I entertained the possibility of magic *living,* I'd never get anywhere. And like hell would I bring it up in here, with half the tech department listening in.

The others apparently didn't share my wariness.

"Something *did* happen a thousand years ago," said Iriel. "That was before the Passages were properly logged, so it *might* have been possible for a civilisation to cross from one world to another."

"Kevar said they walked across the chasm," said Raj. "See, that doesn't seem right, either. It might just be a story, but they came from *somewhere.* Then they adapted to the world's rules. Those gods… they can't possibly be living. They follow rules, so does nature. Natural laws aren't exactly human-friendly. You play with fire, you get burned."

"I was thinking artificial intelligence," said Iriel, bringing up another screen on her communicator. "The computer makes the rules, and the pattern repeats itself. Maybe they're like codes… but that suggests someone put them there. I don't think a *person* could have done it, but there are certainly other sentient species with the ability to use magic, and you can't always control the consequences. Look at the backlash rule."

Yeah. Use magic and the exact equal force would hit back. If humans had tried to control nature on a massive scale, maybe Vey-Xanetha's system wasn't *that* far out there, after all. But what was the nature of the catastrophe that drove the former inhabitants to leave? Cataclysms didn't happen for no reason. Every war or disaster in the history of the Multiverse had a cause, whether natural or unnatural.

Or both.

"I think we need to have another look at what, exactly, these deities are supposed to do," said Iriel.

"I think we should discuss it when we're back at the base," I said, with a meaningful glance over at the other computer desks.

"Relax, no one's going to go out and try and create living magical deities," said Iriel.

"Not even me," added Ada's brother.

"You'd better not," said Ada. "It's bad enough that your computers sometimes talk when you're not in the house."

I wasn't in the mood to argue the point. I didn't think any of the tech team would set out deliberately to pass that information around, but the more people knew, the more opportunity for error. It took one slip, one misguided comment to spark rumours, and considering Central sat on the brink of the Multiverse, those rumours could reach far. After Aglaia, anything that involved the words "magic" and "source" was a cause for suspicion. And to think in my first week at the Alliance, I'd left that bloodrock file lying around. Now I'd probably have padlocked it in a secure cabinet.

My communicator buzzed in my pocket.

"Looks like Carl's sent a call to the guards." Ada took out her own communicator.

"Why?" I flicked the touch screen. Blasted thing wouldn't sync into Earth's network after I'd repeatedly taken it out of range. "A monster. Just what we need."

"Rather you than me," said Raj.

"Great," I said. "Don't tell me Cethrax is pissed off again."

We don't have time to deal with this.

"Whatever it is, it's got away from the guards three times in the last hour," said Ada. "We have time before we have to go back. I'm going after it."

"I'll keep working on this," said Iriel, over her shoulder.

"Wonder what it is this time?" said Ada, as we hurried downstairs. "I got the Chameleon earpieces, by the way."

"Good," I said. "We'll need weapons, too." We'd handed them in when we'd come back to Central, for obvious reasons. Given there were dubious offworld creatures flying around the entrance hall and two lifts were out of order, this irritated me to no end.

"Yeah. I only got two earpieces, though. The other burnt out when the magic level went up."

I swore. "All right. We'll have to leave one behind if we want to contact Central. I'll hang onto the other. If I need to turn invisible for whatever reason, it might save our lives."

"The others don't know," said Ada, nodding, but some uncertainty remained in her expression. "All right. But I don't want you throwing yourself into danger."

"Considering we're working with a hostile world, I think it's safe to say the usual rules don't apply."

She half-laughed. "Yeah. Usual rules with you aren't the same as normal people's. When you opened that doorway, I thought…"

Ah, crap. "Yeah… I'm sorry. I didn't know it would be that bad." A lie. I always mentally prepared for the worst, even if it never took away the shock. There was nothing I could say to her, because if she wanted to be an Ambassador, she'd have to accept situations like that were sometimes unavoidable. Ambassadors saw the best and worst of humanity in all its forms. But did *she* know it? I didn't want to push her, far from it, but now we were at the centre of this, and she was still getting over the horror of what the Campbells did to her —not to mention the Conners kidnapping her family.

She shuddered. "It was just a shock. What could have killed people like that?"

"Let's hope we never meet it," I said grimly.

11

ADA

We met Carl in the entrance hall.

"I've just had a call from the guards in the Passages," he said, as we walked to the front doors. "Apparently some magic-creature's giving them trouble again. They're worried it might get through one of the doors. We've had fifteen magic burn injuries today already."

I fought back a flinch at the memory. I wasn't about to underestimate a magic-creature again.

"Whereabouts exactly is it?" asked Kay.

"That's the problem. It's incorporeal, like the other one."

Great—it might be anywhere. "We've fought those things before," I said.

"Weapons?" said Kay, and Carl handed us each two stunners. I pocketed them, and Carl hit the button to open Central's doors. "It's not on *Alliance* territory, is it?"

"Nah, we've got people at the gate."

Two guards waved us over. "It disappeared again. Must have got through the Passage door during patrol changeover.

Carl swore. "Crafty bastard. Okay, we'll have to split up."

"This way?" Kay said to me, pointing.

"Sure." My pulse started racing. Earth's magic level was higher than it should be. I knew how to control magic now, and I wasn't about to let a magic-creature run amok around London.

We headed out the back gate, past the wrecked houses from the wyvern attack. I felt *something,* but it might have been the residual disturbance from the magic levels going crazy. If there was one thing I hated, it was not being able to *see* the enemy.

A jolt of magic made every hair on my body stand on end. I spun on the spot, stunner ready, and sparks flew even though I didn't press the button.

And a shape materialised in the middle of the road. Shadows swirled, turning purple-red, and my mind struggled to comprehend the shape—vaguely defined, bear-sized, and spitting sparks from its fanged mouth.

Carl approached it warily, stunner at the ready, and Kay and I did likewise, so we surrounded it on three sides. I readied my finger over the stunner's switch.

As the creature solidified, growing at least a foot in height, I aimed the stunner and hit the button. A fork of reddish lightning speared the creature through the middle and it growled, writhing, its form becoming indistinct. Carl fired his own shot, the crackling lightning striking the monster, rising higher as the magic level heightened again. The air around us darkened, tinted reddish purple, the broken-down houses obscured. I couldn't even see Kay or Carl.

Sparks flared from the smoke. I leaped out of range, heart beating wildly. *It's not dead?* I ducked more sparks, backing away, not daring to fire my stunner in case I hit one of the others.

The smoke cleared, revealing... two monsters.

Oh, crap. It had split down the middle, but divided, two halves becoming separate creatures entirely. Identical fanged, smoky monsters bore down on us, two pairs of eyes flaring. The flash of a stunner, and a clawed hand swiped at me. I jumped back, acutely aware we had a limited number of stunner shots—what if it kept multiplying?

One way to find out. I fired my stunner first, and it had the exact effect I dreaded. Now there were *three* monsters—no, four. Kay had hit another of them with his own stunner.

"Fool me twice, shame on me," I muttered, my heart racing. How could we beat a monster that kept multiplying? And it was so close to Central. Like we needed over-curious tourists wandering over.

Carl swore under his breath, putting his stunner away and raising his hand. Magic sparked from his fingertips, and for an instant, I stared, mesmerised by how controlled the magic stream appeared to be compared to my own out-of-control magic. Kay stared for an instant, too, and then fired a bolt of magic at the ground beneath the monster. It shot upwards, and the beast reeled back.

I reached for the magic, wild and uncontained, and let it flow through my fingertips. The pavement shuddered as Carl's backlash hit it, and I released the charge. Second level, blazing bright as fire, not like lightning this time. The beast hissed, thrown back, only for the second one to jump forward at me, sparks flaring from its smoky red skin.

Stunners weren't strong enough, but with the higher magic level, *we* were stronger. But one wrong move and we'd cause more damage than the monsters.

The backlash of my attack ricocheted off the pavement and shot at the nearest house, burning a hole right through the brick. *No one lives there. You're all right.* But guilt stopped my hand all the same.

I dodged another swiping claw. The monster must have

been stronger than the last one, because the magic raging in the air didn't show any signs of burning out.

"Use the daggers!" said Carl, who used his as a shield to block the sparks flying from the monsters. *Good idea.* The adamantine blade absorbed magic.

Another monster faced me down, a shuddering mass of reddish smoke, clawed and menacing. I fired magic at it and didn't miss this time. Its face twisted in pain, and for a heart-stopping moment, it looked... human.

Two faces in a warehouse.

I froze.

No! I pulled on the magic, a cry building in my throat, and tugged, hard. The creature staggered, and I recalled the way magic had responded to me in Aglaia, when I'd worked with the council and mages alike to push the magic-creature through the doorway. I pushed against the creature, and Kay caught my eye, nodding. He'd worked out my plan.

My heart lifted, then slammed into my ribs just as swiftly when the creatures both divided again. I was forced to back into the wall, alongside Carl. But Kay ran at the creatures from behind, surrounded by a haze of magic. Splaying his palms, he shot pure energy at the monsters, sending them careening into one another in a bizarre domino effect. *How did he do that?* I copied him, and immediately felt the difference. Rather than a wild arc of lightning, magic was more of a pulse, a wave-motion that I could push on. Like on Aglaia, the bolstering sensation grew as my magic joined with Kay's.

"Do what I'm doing!" I said to Carl. "If you can, push it back!"

Carl nodded and did as I said.

Magic flooded my veins and I gasped, eyes burning as the power demanded to be released. Sweat dripped down my forehead. *Concentrate. Stay in control.* I pushed again, and Carl did likewise. The two enemies facing him collapsed into one another, becoming a single swirl of smoke, and I shuddered as the energy streamed into me, leached away from the monster. Another claw lashed out at Kay, but he'd already moved with a striking motion, using his dagger to block the magic strike as Carl did.

Carl himself said, "Keep doing that. I'll finish it!"

Sparks flew overhead as another two creatures collided. I held the magic, and gave it another push. The level surged higher, and a clap of thunder sounded, magic sparking off the house walls.

The remaining creatures slammed into one, shrinking. Carl marched over to it with his stunner in hand and levelled one final stunner-strike at it. A blue pulse blazed against my eyelids, and the creature was gone.

"Jesus Christ, Ada," said Kay. "Are you all right?" He crossed the still-smoking pavement and took my non-weapon hand, flipping it over. Not so much as a graze. I'd got lucky this time. Yet the shiver when Kay's hand brushed over mine caught my attention. I realised I was staring at him, and looked away, suddenly hyperaware of a tension in the air that had absolutely nothing to do with magic and everything to do with Kay.

"I'm fine. That was close."

"Tell me about it." He glanced at my hand as though just aware he still held it, and let it drop. To my disappointment. "Lucky it didn't do any more damage."

"Lucky it didn't get at Central." Carl grimaced. "God-damned magic burn."

"You got hit?" asked Kay.

Carl touched his reddening jaw, with a slight twitch despite his obvious attempt not to show pain. "Must have. You two are okay?"

"Yeah," I said.

"Good. There's no way I'm going off-duty, so don't mention it to Ms Weston."

"You don't have to do that if you're hurt," I protested.

"And there's no other head guard around." Carl looked stonily at the place where the creatures had been. "Accursed creatures. Someone has to deal with it."

"You both have a death wish," I said.

"I beg to differ," said Kay, turning back to Central. "Come on. Guess we have to report this, too."

Ms Weston was locked in her office, on the phone. Her raised voice came through the door, but I didn't recognise which language she spoke.

"What now?" I said, turning to Kay.

"God knows," he muttered, tapping his communicator screen. "We still have an hour."

"Not enough time for a hover-bike ride?" I tried a smile, but his eyes were on the screen. "Guess the Passages are still out of order."

"Yeah." He finally looked up. "I'm sorry about what happened over there. You don't have to come back later if you don't want to."

"What?" I stared at him. He thought I wanted to quit? "No way. I'm involved in this now."

"I can tell Ms Weston. We don't need all magic-wielders to be there." He paused. "These kinds of missions are usually reserved for Ambassadors with more experience dealing with conflict—"

"I've dealt with plenty, thanks," I said, and instantly regretted snapping at him. "Sorry. But you're forgetting I've been escorting people from hostile territory since I was eight."

Kay blinked. "I know. I just wanted to make sure you're all right."

Oh. I didn't really know how to respond. Part of me was a little annoyed, like when Jeth was fussing over me, but I got a totally different vibe when Kay did the same.

I wasn't completely dense. I knew a far-more-significant part of me *liked* that he worried about me—whether as a friend or something else, I didn't know—but I'd had first-hand experience with how quickly Kay could shut me out and I wasn't keen to repeat it by pressuring him to tell me why.

I dropped my gaze. "Yeah. I'm fine, Kay."

"Good." He paused. "You know Ambassadors get little in the way of compensation. It's not like when you were helping people in the Passages. Those were people who wanted to be saved, who had no choice but to depend on you. But we're from the Alliance, and some people are going to see us as an interference no matter what."

"Maybe," I said. "I'm amazed Mathran even wanted to work with us. And the people in the city."

"His world's falling apart, literally," said Kay. "Wouldn't you make an exception?"

"Fair point." I drew in a breath. "So what made *you* want to be an Ambassador? You could have seen the Multiverse on a permit, right? Or was someone you knew an Ambassador?"

I could picture him being in Carl's position as a senior guard, maybe. Definitely not in an office, though he knew the council and had worked with them before. But his family had founded the Alliance. All the Walkers had been council members, right? I didn't know for sure.

I watched him, convinced he wouldn't answer. Then he inclined his head. "Yeah."

"All right. Just curious." My deadly sin. And it'd be the

death of me, at this rate. Had his mother been an Ambassador?

"Nobody in my family's ever worked for the Alliance, have they?" I said, very aware of the growing silence. "You can't blame me for wanting to know why other people sign up. Apart from offworlders, that is."

"Earth people?" he said. "Raj is a magic-wielder. I don't know how he found out, but I'm guessing that factored into his decision. Ms Weston was born into it. The Westons have a history with Central, I think. And Carl wanted to fight monsters."

"That's the only reason?"

"It's what he said when someone asked," said Kay.

"Sorry. I've more curiosity than common sense. Guess that's why I asked Markos why he worked at Central."

"He did answer you and not trample you. He must like you."

"Ha ha." I shook my head. "I can deal with this, you know, Kay."

"I know you can. I just wanted to be sure."

"Right. I should go home and pack, anyway." And stop Nell freaking out about me going offworld. Stifling a sigh, I turned to Ms Weston's office. "Wonder what she's doing in there?"

"Terrifying someone," he said. "Carl will be on her case later about those idiot guards who let that creature slip past the doorway. Tomorrow Cethrax will be knocking on the door."

"Hope not," I said. "What even *was* that creature? I know they're made of residual magic, Carl told me."

"I did wonder," said Kay. "Residual magic—like living backlash. Hmm."

"Living?"

Like living deities? No, that couldn't be right. The magic-creatures were barely sentient, and didn't even have corporeal forms. Then again, the same could be said of some of Cethrax's monsters. But that place was a magic-free zone.

"Well, 'attacking'," said Kay. "If I had to guess, I'd say we beat it by outclassing its magic level, but we're in trouble if stunners don't work on it. There aren't enough magic-wielders on Earth."

"Damn. I guess I get why Carl didn't want to leave anyone else in charge." And the others didn't have internal sources. That creature was level two, at least. We really were in over our heads. All I knew was the magic-creatures came from somewhere in the Passages—which might literally mean any world.

Even Vey-Xanetha.

"Yeah, I'm gonna meet my brother and head home," I said. "I'll meet you back here in an hour, okay?"

"Sure," said Kay.

I went down to the entrance hall again, where I found Jeth waiting. Good timing.

"Hey, Ada. You done with that mission?"

"Er." Far from it. "We're staying over at the base tonight. I need to pack for a long trip."

"You are?"

"Yeah. The day runs in weird cycles, and it's night time over there now. Next day begins at midnight properly, but we want to get there early."

But if their carvings were to be believed, time was limited. I decided against mentioning that to my family. No reason to worry them half to death.

"I'm going shopping," said Jeth. "You need anything for wilderness survival?"

"We're staying at the base," I said. "Not camping. I have a sleeping bag, you know." Not that I'd ever been camping for real. Or on a holiday of any sort, seeing as Nell had never wanted to leave London and we'd always been strapped for cash. And busy. This was the closest to a holiday I'd had, I thought wryly. A one-way trip to the end of the world.

Cheerful, Ada.

At home, Nell waited in the living room, where she was practising combat moves. The furniture had been pushed against the walls and nobody else was in there. "I thought you were offworld," she said.

"I will be." I flopped on the sofa. "It's a longer mission, I have to go back in an hour. They have weird day-cycles, it's night-time over there now."

"When will you be back?"

"Tomorrow," I said, with more certainty than I felt. "Hopefully, if we solve this, all the craziness on Earth will stop."

"Good," said Nell. "The Knights are having difficulties, too. Offworlders are complaining to them about all kinds of things which are none of their business—the ones who don't trust the Alliance."

I should have guessed the other Enzarians would be affected by this. Which reminded me...

"Er, Nell," I said, hesitantly. I tried to avoid bringing up my homeworld if I could help it. "There's this legend on Vey-Xanetha about how they crossed between worlds using some kind of direct doorway. When you brought me to the Passages from Enzar, was it like that? Didn't we go through the Passages?"

A long pause. A tension took hold of Nell, one I recognised from whenever anyone spoke of Enzar and when she'd smuggled me from my homeworld. Her mouth became a flat line, and her hands, normally so steady, began to shake.

"I don't know. I can't pretend I remember much of that day, and at the time, I didn't understand how travel through the Passages worked. But I do remember the first time I saw the Passages. And I remember you staring around in wonderment. Somehow, even then, I knew you'd find your way back." She sighed. "I've done things you wouldn't be proud of, Ada. I killed a dozen people the night I escaped the palace. Maybe more. Once, they used me as their slave, their warrior. No more." She shook her head. "If the Alliance even attempts to use you for anything against your will…"

"I won't let them. Of course I won't." I got to my feet. "I'm going to pack."

Would they even have running water there? Stupid question. I knew they were self-sustaining. But given the state of the rest of the world…

And now I felt guilty on top of everything else, for worrying about being able to shower when their world might be ending. *At least I know I can deal with those kimaros now.* I could fight, if I knew who the enemy was. But the situation over on Vey-Xanetha was way more complicated than that.

I crawled out onto the roof with a nest of blankets, looking up at the sky. Our sky. Grey. Dependable. But for how long? What if magic altered this world permanently, too?

I remembered the one story Nell had told me from my homeworld. Though she hadn't read to me since I was young, the tale of Enzar's star-deities had stuck with me. That was why I'd painted stars on the ceiling of my old room. But I didn't know the legends, not in the same way I'd have done if they were part of my life. If I'd lived on Enzar before the Royals took over and burned every other culture to the ground. Even the Alliance hadn't been able to stop it.

Maybe we were trying to stop the inevitable.

I climbed back down to find Jeth had bought half a convenience store and dumped it on my bed.

"Jeth, you know they have food there, don't you?" I said. "And I don't need a tent!"

"Better to be prepared," he called up from the landing. "You did a wilderness survival course, right?"

"Yes, but not offworld!" I said. "Lighting a fire there brings down the wrath of the gods, and half the wildlife wants to eat us, not the other way around."

And like hell would I be camping in the jungle. Shaking my head, I sorted everything into two piles—necessary and unnecessary. Then I stopped and stared. Okay, Jeth was taking the protective older brother thing way too far. Condoms? Really?

"You have *got* to be kidding me," I said.

"What?"

"I'm not even—what do you think I'm going to, some kind of orgy?"

"Keep safe, Ada!"

I rolled my eyes, leaving the condoms in my desk drawer and trying not to think about how Kay and I would be in close proximity for the first time since... well, a while. Or that if I admitted it to myself, I'd spent more than one sleepless night reimagining the last time I'd made out with him.

"Priorities," I muttered to myself.

Zipping my bag, I knocked something off the bed with a clatter. Something invisible. "Jeth, I thought the other earpiece was broken."

"I fixed it," he said. "Well, don't tell the others. Thought you might want to keep in touch."

"You lied to Ms Weston?"

"She didn't ask."

I clipped the device to my ear. "You sure about this? Because we'll be there all night."

"I can live with it. Just as long as you're safe, sister."

I smiled. My family had my back.

My communicator buzzed.

Kay. *"I'm at Central now."*

I checked my watch. We were a bit early, but at least it meant it was still light outside. *"On my way,"* I replied, and set about gathering my things.

"I'm heading to Central," I called down the landing.

"Good luck!" said Jeth. "I'll keep the earpiece switched on, so if you find anything, let me know."

"Bring me a souvenir!" called Alber.

"Not allowed to carry offworld substances," I said, with a grin. "It's in the rulebook!"

This couldn't be goodbye. I'd be back tomorrow. They didn't need to know any more. Those legends might just be legends. Like doomsday theories on Earth.

Still…

I hurried down the road, not caring when people stared at the sight of a girl clad in black faux-leather running through the crowds of tourists. I had the feeling time was limited. For Vey-Xanetha—and Earth.

1 2

ADA

No magic-creatures awaited us in the Passages this time, but we moved quickly all the same. Kay led us to a deserted stretch of corridor around the corner from the doorway back to London. Everyone was on edge, and by the distant sound of voices, there were a lot of guards about, though this corridor had been blocked off for our use only. I couldn't help glancing at the old staircase to the hidden Passage, but there was definitely no activity down that way. Damn. Just as the Law Division had started properly putting a plan of action together to help the Enzarians get safely to the shelter, this magical chaos had thrown everything off.

"Right," said Kay, world-key in hand "I can take us through to the base, or open a door at random and try to find the villages. Anyone got any other ideas?"

"Find Mathran," I said. "And see if he's found anything else." There didn't seem to be much more we could do, short of using magic. Part of me was curious what would happen, of course, but maybe Kay's influence was rubbing off on me. Next I'd be challenging griffins.

"Yeah. He used magic," said Kay. "If he was channelling that deity, maybe we could do the same."

"What?" I said. "Seriously?" He couldn't seriously be considering tapping into magic on this world, especially after the stunt he'd pulled with that griffin. Did he *want* to get himself put on probation?

"Are you out of your mind?" said Raj. "I think pissing off a magical deity is a great way to get yourself dismembered."

"Just an idea."

I wondered what else he might be scheming. Using his invisibility power, maybe. He still hadn't told the others about being an amplifier. Probably, he didn't want Mathran or anyone else on Vey-Xanetha to know. It didn't hurt to be careful.

But I couldn't get Ms Weston's words out of my head —*seek out the problem at its source.*

Kay used the device to open a door, clipping the Chameleon earpiece to his ear. I wore the other one, though I hadn't told the others yet. Even Kay. Part of me was still irritated he'd even think I'd consider quitting, but I knew he was more concerned for my mental well-being. But like dealing with the nightmares, the only way I could think of to push what happened to those merchants from my mind was to take practical steps to figure out who—or what—was responsible.

The doorway opened less than a metre from the entrance to the base. We stepped through, and into a storm.

Lightning stabbed the sky, and Raj jumped back, cursing, even though it was nowhere near us.

"Doesn't look like a normal storm," I said. For one thing, no rain fell, and the magic level surged high with each fork of red-tinged lighting, making my skin buzz all over.

"Great," said Raj, and cursed as Kay ran the three metres

to the door, which opened. The rest of us joined him, and Mathran hurried us inside.

Lightning struck right behind us, accompanied with another thunderous clap like falling rocks.

"What in all universes is going on out there?" Raj demanded. "Is it safe for us to stay here?"

"Of course," said Mathran, not reacting to his outburst. "The storm is the first ordinary sign we have seen in days. It means the seasons may be returning to normal."

"Reassuring," Kay muttered from beside me.

The injured man lay in the other room, half-conscious on the sofa, watched over by an anxious-looking Avar.

"I've set up a link with Central," he said. "Our communication systems went out, but I used the backup system so you'll be able to send messages back, if you need to."

"At least there's that." Iriel exchanged glances with Raj.

"So what now?" I asked. "We have to wait here until it passes?" I glanced at Kay, who didn't look too pleased at the idea.

"That would be the wisest choice."

"I can work on translating those codes now, anyway," said Iriel, in an attempt to defuse the tension brewing in the air. "There's something else I wanted to do. Do you have a map?"

A flash lit up outside the window. Purple lightning raged, the sky burned red, even the clouds over the forest. To the people living below, it really would seem like the end of the world.

Mathran showed us upstairs. A number of rooms had been put aside for guests. An uncomfortable-looking metal-framed bed was the single piece of furniture, but I had an en-suite bathroom, even running water. But I couldn't suppress a pang for all the people out on Vey-Xanetha, enduring the storm.

I headed downstairs to find Iriel and Raj in the computer room, the latter surrounded by papers.

"Where are the others?" I asked.

"Mathran and Avar are talking to that injured guy," said Iriel. "And Kay's…" She shrugged.

"No clue," said Raj, throwing and catching a tennis ball. "I was trying to demonstrate the backlash rule," he explained. "Mathran still doesn't get it."

"Don't break anything." Iriel stacked papers on the table. She must have printed them on Earth. I joined her, flipping open a notepad. Logic wasn't my strong point, fighting was, but hey, maybe I could come up with something. Starting with the three gods. I divided the page into three columns and listed what we knew about each of them.

In the end, my list said:

Veyak: weather.

Aktha: machinery and buildings.

Xanet: nature and healing.

That suggested Veyak's power was the one causing the trouble, right? But it didn't explain *why.*

Chewing on the end of my pen, I debated. It felt oddly like tempting fate to write down what *I* could do, but I couldn't help thinking there might be some kind of connection. Vey-Xanetha's sources were external, but did some summoners have internal sources, too, if magic could alter their appearance? I wished I'd asked Kevar how that worked, but the language barrier was a problem. If they had no term for third level or backlash, they didn't see magic in the same way that I did. And I couldn't claim I completely understood my own magic. The only records were on my homeworld—

Wait a minute. It had totally slipped my mind. There *was* a record… in Ms Weston's office. The file that showed my real identity. *How* could I have forgotten about it?

"What are you doing?" asked Iriel curiously. I wondered what my facial expression had shown.

I shrugged. "Thinking. Trying to figure out about these gods. Different magic types. Like if there's a reason one works and the others don't."

"It's all alien to me," said Raj, tossing the tennis ball into the air again.

At that moment, Mathran came back in.

"Hey," I said to him. "Er. I've been writing down what each of the gods can do. I thought it'd help if we knew. Is there any way to tell if the same thing's happening to everyone who has Aktha's power? Or Xanet?"

He hesitated. "I have been unable to make contact with anywhere, but I can think of a village which is sustained by Aktha's power."

"And there might be answers there?"

I took his silence as *maybe*. But walking out into the storm wasn't a wise move.

"It was the summoners' destination."

Oh. I glanced at Raj and Iriel, who looked equally uneasy at the prospect of facing whatever force killed those merchants.

"I will assist you, if need be," said Mathran. "This is the sixth day since the gods left, and if all is as they say in the carvings, the village will soon fall."

"Wait, what?" said Raj, his eyes widening. "The carvings predicted this?"

"We have never been able to translate the text, but the pictorial form is well-known." He returned to the computer-like glass box in the corner, and manipulated a series of wires. A sequence of images flashed on the screen.

"The first image shows the continents stopping their motion."

It looked like a meaningless jumble of lines to me, but I had no clue about ancient Vey-Xanethan art styles.

"The next image shows the fall of Aktha's village."

This time, I made out the image amongst the lines, of buildings falling in pieces.

"And the next?" Iriel prompted.

"A great chasm opens in the world's centre, and our world unravelling, one piece at a time. Our cities fall, the forests return to the earth, the mountains are levelled, and the skies rain down upon the land, flooding it. As the floods clear, the gods have departed for good, leaving nothing but barren wasteland. Then the land rebuilds itself. But the image shows no people. Presumably, they die when the chasm opens—most accounts say all life is sacrificed to the abyss."

I gaped at him. "And you didn't tell us this before?"

"It's a scare story, right?" said Raj, shifting on the sofa, away from the images.

"I didn't want to alarm you. Your supervisor said you would see these tales as... scare stories, as you put it."

"Let's hope so," said Raj. "Iriel, please tell me those symbols of yours don't say that."

"Haven't a clue." Iriel seemed calmer, so I guessed she didn't believe it was true. She'd been an Ambassador the longest, and they had to deal with false alarms all the time. This wasn't any different. Right?

Iriel lifted a piece of paper, the map she'd been working on, where she'd drawn a few dots. "I put some calculations through the computer at Central. Based on that, I've figured out the exact place where the changes started, based on what Mathran told us." She nodded to him.

"Wow," I said. This was more concrete than an old story about the apocalypse.

"She's a genius," said Raj. "I think your computer analogy was pretty apt. The changes start over here." He tapped a spot on the map. "Only it stopped… at this point." He tapped somewhere else. "Problem is, we'd need to get to the exact spot. The doorways are too random for that."

"Oh," I said, thinking of all the times the world-key had landed us in the middle of nowhere.

"That appears to be beside the village," said Mathran, frowning. "I will have to see if it's possible for us to get there after this storm."

The storm showed no signs of abating and as it was past one in the morning on Earth, I found myself dozing off on the arm of the chair. I jolted awake when someone said my name.

"You were talking to yourself," said Iriel.

"Oops." At least I wasn't screaming. Or drooling, for that matter.

"The storm's calmed now. Mathran says we might be able to leave."

"Might?" I asked, rubbing sleep from my eyes. "To go to the village?"

"He got a message from Kevar saying a traveller arrived from the village—he called it Aktha's village. Apparently something weird's happened there. Everyone's vanished."

"Huh?"

"That's what he said. And Aktha's village is near where the continent shift is supposed to start. Do you know where Kay is?"

I shook my head. "I'll check upstairs."

Probably beating up invisible monsters. Or trying out a new magic trick. Not that he'd use actual magic here… at least, I hoped not. I found Kay's room with the door shut, and knocked. Then knocked again. No answer. I pushed the door open a fraction, and froze. Kay lay on the bed, his jacket slung over the edge. At first he didn't appear to be asleep, considering his hands were clenched at his sides, but he didn't move when I knocked again.

"Kay?"

No response.

I crept closer, my guard boots making no sound on the floor. Even in sleep, the muscles in his arms were tensed, though I couldn't help remembering how nice it felt to have those strong arms wrapped around *me*. And that for my own sake, I should probably back off.

Heart beating so loud I thought it might wake him, I crouched down, and reached to touch his shoulder—

His entire body went rigid, then he rolled out the way and was on his feet in a second. I caught myself before I lost my balance.

"Whoa!" I said. "It's only me."

"Sorry," he said. His eyes were wide open, not at all like he'd been asleep a second before. He ran a hand through his hair, glancing over his shoulder as though he expected monsters to attack.

I backed away, my face heating up. "Sorry. I know a thing or two about nightmares."

"When are we leaving?"

"Soon. The storm's stopped."

"Sure."

I left the room. *You handled that well.* I guess it freaked me out to see *him* freaked out. I glanced over my shoulder at the slightest noise, half afraid the storm would come back and leave us stranded here. The sooner we got outside, the better.

I found Mathran pacing the hallway.

"Are we heading to Aktha's village?" I asked.

He nodded. "I fear we may not like what we find there. If the carvings are to be believed, its fall signals the doom of our world."

Very dramatic. "I thought the chasm wasn't supposed to come first? But Kevar said it was already here."

"There is no specified order in which one must interpret the carvings," said Mathran, unhelpfully.

Great. We were stranded on an unfamiliar world with someone who'd given up hope. *Cheeriest sleepover ever.*

"I got the computer working," said Raj. "Avar worked some magic—not actual magic, just technology. Central have been in touch, they have some people pulling all-nighters over there to figure out what's wrong in the Passages. Turns out they think there's a leak."

"A what?" I said, blankly.

"Whatever it is, it's causing magic to leak out into the Passages."

"Huh? Is that even possible?"

"Could be. There's a ton of residual magic in there already"

"So what does that have to do with Vey-Xanetha?"

"No clue, but at least that's something. If they can stop what's happening on Earth…"

I thought of Mathran, of the people in the city.

We have to help them, too.

13

KAY

Aktha's village was apparently in the middle of a canyon, in a place which sounded suspiciously close to that chasm. I didn't want to voice my suspicion that the village might not even exist anymore, so I followed Mathran's instructions and used the world-key on the Passage wall until we found the right place.

Dry ground spread out before us under a burnished red sky. We moved into a guard formation unconsciously as we passed through the doorway. My gaze immediately snapped to the sky, but there weren't any birds above. Nothing here but dry ground, and the distant shape of a town. Or a collection of buildings, anyway. We took off, treading carefully on the uneven, red-scorched ground.

The faint smell of burning was the first indication of trouble. Mathran had told us it was considered disrespectful to the deities to burn wood, and the flicker of flames on the horizon looked too big to be deliberate. As we drew closer to the cluster of buildings, it became apparent the flames came from the tallest structure. Smoke poured from the windows, and flames flared behind the glass, visible even from here. Not normal flames, judging by the white sparks.

But the houses surrounding the tower—made of the same red stone as every other building there—appeared to be deserted. No one ran screaming in the streets. Doors were open, lights gleamed in the windows—not electric, but these odd light-box-type devices—but no one was home.

"Creepy," Raj commented in an undertone.

"It's a ghost town," said Ada. "Is there really no one here?" She moved towards one of the houses. I turned in that direction, hand already straying to my weapon.

The house's door lay closed, but a faint sound came from inside. The only noise apart from the crackling flames.

"Should we knock?" asked Ada.

I pressed the heel of my boot to the door, which gave a little. One sharp kick, and it crumbled.

"…or you could kick the door down," said Ada.

"Quickest way." I kicked the remains of the door out the way. Except given by the way it crumbled, it wasn't sturdy at all. Either it wasn't usually used as a door, or something was wrong. *No shit, Kay.* Everything *about* this world was wrong.

I led the way into the dark hallway. A faint light in the adjacent room drew my attention. It gleamed blue, one of those light boxes set into the ceiling. As we watched, it moved slightly, the bulb, or whatever powered it, cracking down the middle. It fell in two halves, glass walls breaking away and scattering onto the floor.

"What did that?" Ada asked, behind me.

As if in answer, a piece of rock fell from the ceiling where the light had been. I took a step back.

"Better get out," I said.

Not a moment too soon. We all but ran from the building as the ceiling caved in, bringing the room above crashing into it. Swearing, we ran out of a haze of red dust, turning to see the house just... wasn't there anymore. A heap of red rubble lay in its place.

Before we could move, a rumbling sound like distant thunder filled the air. Another building fell, the seemingly-solid construction collapsing like the foundations had been knocked out from underneath. Rubble spilled over the way we'd come into the village, red rock breaking into smaller fragments and filling the air with thick dust. Coughing, we edged out of the way, and right into the path of the—

"Shit," I said. "The tower's going to fall."

Blinking dust from my eyes, I spotted Mathran frantically beckoning from the side.

We ran, feet pounding on the cracked ground. A chunk of red concrete fell, landing with an earth-shaking rumble not a metre from where we'd been standing. Another followed, and more, until the sound of breaking rock assailed us. I overtook Mathran, searching for the Passage doorway—it had to be somewhere close.

"Kay." Ada grabbed my arm, pointing frantically.

The doorway was still there, but shrinking by the second. I made sure the others were behind me then pelted for it, readying the world-key.

We made it. Just. I pelted through, skidded to a halt on the Passage floor. Ada leaned on the wall, gasping for breath.

"Remind me never to buy a house there," said Raj, in a similar condition. "What in the Multiverse was that?"

"Magical decay," said Iriel. "I think."

"Their habitations were sustained by magic," I said.

"So with Aktha not responding to them, everything's collapsing?" asked Ada.

"I was afraid of this," Mathran said, gravely. "The carvings say Aktha's village falls, the world will follow." His expression didn't give away whether he actually thought that would happen.

"Ever the optimist," Raj muttered.

Nothing to do but open a doorway to the base again. We had only an hour before night fell on Vey-Xanetha again, but on Earth, it was nearly four in the morning.

"Ms Weston's asking for an update," I said, as we gathered in the base's approximation of a sitting room. "Again. I figure if we haven't solved anything by nightfall... or dawn, whichever... it'd be more worth our while to go back to Earth."

"All right," said Raj. "I just want to sleep, to be honest, but at least Earth's storms aren't deadly. Well, compared to here."

"Don't speak too soon," I muttered, as Mathran re-entered the room—he'd been checking on Avar and the injured man. "Mathran," I said, a tad hesitant to share my theory until I was absolutely sure, "Do you know if it's possible for one deity to take power from another?"

Mathran gave me a blank look, while Raj and Iriel just seemed puzzled. Only Ada knew what I was thinking.

"The trio have always coexisted," said Mathran. "We do not think of them in such crude terms as power."

"That may be," I said. "But doesn't it seem suspicious to you that Aktha and Xanet are losing power, but not Veyak?"

At least, I didn't think so. What about that symbol where the merchants had been slaughtered?

"I do not... I do not know how that would be possible." Mathran shifted from one foot to the other, clearly uncomfortable. "There is no contest between the three, and there never has been."

"But could someone else have done it?" asked Ada. "Can a person take power from them?"

Or an object? Adamantine... Adamantine could absorb magic.

What were those strange pieces of metal made of?

It seemed a waste of time us even staying there. Plainly, even on a high-magic world like Vey-Xanetha, nobody knew anything about magic sources. The three deities were pure magic, forces of nature. The magic-creatures in the Passages were scaled-down versions. But if two deities were losing their power, then either the other must be responsible... or a person, gathering power.

It didn't take a genius to know that chasm was somehow connected to it. A gap in the middle of the earth had 'unnatural' written all over it, even in a world like Vey-Xanetha.

"Did you finish translating all those carvings?" I asked Iriel, as we gathered in the computer room again.

"The ones I could." Iriel shook her head. "It's obscure, most of it. Doesn't even match up with a hiero-code."

"I gave up trying to understand what she means an hour ago," said Raj.

"Like the Rosetta Stone, maybe?" I said. "Anyway, I wondered what it says about that chasm. Where it comes from. The earth doesn't split apart and then put itself back together again for no reason."

"True," said Iriel, "but the carvings don't show it putting itself back together."

"Huh?" said Raj. "A gaping hole in the middle of the earth? I think people would notice if it stuck around for a thousand years."

"It did only appear recently, right?" I turned to ask Mathran, and realised he was no longer in the room. Must be with the injured man next door.

"Yeah, it must have," said Ada. "Kevar said, remember?"

"Definitely doesn't add up," I muttered. "But then again, we haven't seen the chasm, have we?"

"Great, we'll add it to the list of tourist attractions," said Raj. "Under 'collapsing village' and 'death by lightning'."

Ada laughed. "As long as we don't add 'Armageddon' to that list."

14

ADA

Morning found us back on Earth, with no more answers than before. Ms Weston had called us back to report, and seeing as Vey-Xanetha's temperamental weather showed no signs of abating, we managed to sneak back between thunderstorms.

"I've no idea what she wants with us this time," Kay muttered. "Unless the tech team's designed angry-god-proof umbrellas."

Raj snorted. "I'm in favour of not going back until we have more of a clue what to do," he said. "A village crashed down on us and nearly killed us, and we *still* don't have answers."

At least Ms Weston didn't ask for written reports this time. She seemed preoccupied herself, her office desk stacked with papers.

But I wanted to ask Ms Weston something else. Something I'd almost forgotten about, even though I'd been at Central for weeks now. I couldn't get that file out of my head. Maybe the answers *were* here on Earth.

I waited for the others to leave first. Kay glanced back at

me, but didn't say anything. And then Ms Weston and I were alone.

"Is there a problem, Ada?" she asked, from behind a small mountain of paper.

"Not with the mission," I said. *Apart from the inevitable Armageddon and the living gods, that is.* "I wondered if you had that file. The one with my name in it."

"The Royals' records?"

Again, it felt utterly alien to hear the word coming from her. *Royal.* It didn't sound like it belonged to me at all.

"Yeah. I think I have the right to see it." I hadn't realised how angry I was with everything until now, but it came searing back. "You knew what the Royals did to me before even *I* knew. You know what I can do, you've known since the medical division examined my blood. Shouldn't I be able to access that information?"

"Certainly, you can see the file," said Ms Weston. "I assumed you would ask that question as soon as you arrived here."

I flushed. I *should* have, but I'd been preoccupied at the time, not to mention trying to avoid anything to do with magic.

"It's in the medical division, right?"

"As a matter of fact, I have it myself." She opened a drawer in her desk.

What?

Handing me the file, she said, "I requested Saki give me this, as well as the details from her examination, on the grounds that it would be safe from prying eyes in here."

"She knows?" I asked, turning the file over in my hands. "How many people..."

"The medical staff are strictly sworn to confidentiality," she said.

But the others might have told anyone, I thought, opening the file before I lost my nerve.

The list of impersonal details could have belonged to anyone. A bunch of meaningless ticked boxes. And a name: Adamantine. Parentage unknown. The Royals were an extended family, and even they didn't know exactly how they were interrelated. That was all the Alliance knew about me. I should have been relieved. But in the end, there was nothing in this file that I didn't know already. It was almost a disappointment. And it didn't give me any more answers about my magic, and how it might relate to Vey-Xanetha's.

"You're sure no one else knows?" I asked. "The Conners didn't, they went after my family for another reason." Markos knew. I hadn't told anyone else here.

"I am sure. I am not in the habit of discussing confidential subjects outside of the office, Ada. That is in part why I have yet to select an assistant to help me with this. Markos has proven himself trustworthy."

"You're... looking for something? In the archives?"

Her gaze dropped to the desk. "I am. But as for that file, Ada, it is yours by right. The medical division has no claim on it. I would know, since I once interned in the department. None of the information will have got out."

"Like the experiments," I said, before I could stop myself.

Ms Weston's shoulders stiffened. "What do you know of that?"

My heartbeat kicked up. "Skyla was out for revenge because of what they did to her, and those kids who attacked me. They worked with Delta—with the Campbell family. They were being used as weapons." *Like I would be, if I'd stayed on Enzar.* Goosebumps prickled my arms.

"And?" Ms Weston prompted. But she didn't meet my eyes. Uncharacteristic.

"There... there was a council member involved. The twins told me."

"Lawrence Walker."

I swallowed. The air seemed thicker, somehow, with the tension around that name.

"Kay's father?" I asked. "He started the whole thing, right?"

She bowed her head. "I saw it."

For a moment, I thought I'd misheard. "What?"

Her eyes flashed at my tone, more like herself. "I was an intern at the time. In the medical division."

I stared. Ms Weston had been there?

"They injected kids with dangerous magic-based substances," I said, my voice shaky. "Surely... surely you knew that was illegal?"

Her eyes flashed again. Now I'd really done it. I braced myself for the blow.

It never came. The life seemed to drain out of her, and she sagged against the back of her chair. "No. It's not illegal, technically. They found a loophole in Klathica's laws, as far as I know," she said. "It's common enough practice in other worlds, and isn't dangerous if you know what you're doing as those scientists did. I found out later," she added. "I wasn't even supposed to be there at the time. I didn't know about it when I saw Walker brought his son in."

I fought to untangle the questions in my mind. "You didn't think it was unusual?"

"He never talked about his family, or so the rest of the staff at the time said," said Ms Weston. "His wife was an Ambassador. I never met her. She... she died, not long before." Her jaw tightened, like she was fighting an unpleasant memory. "And his son—never a word. Until that day."

Oh, god. "She died?" I asked, in a small voice. I knew it already, but somehow it seemed the right question to ask.

"Failed offworld mission," said Ms Weston, the tightness in her voice clashing with her attempt at nonchalance. "Unfortunate, but these things happen. In any case, that's irrelevant. I put it out of mind, and nobody realised the far-reaching consequences of the experiment. Until now."

I swallowed. "You know what Kay can do."

"I know he is lying to me," she said. "He hides it well enough—learned that habit from his father, I don't doubt."

"His father isn't on Earth, right?"

"No, he and several other council members left for a distant world a few years ago. I can't pretend I know all the details. Those are confidential. Like…"

"Like the experiment. He—Kay didn't know. Not until he first went into the Passages, I don't think."

"Magical ability often only manifests offworld," she said. "It's not uncommon knowledge here at the Alliance, but thirteen years ago, it was less well-known on Earth. The age-restrictions on offworld permits meant no one thought the children's abilities might only work if they went offworld, and in any case, Walker had long since lost interest in the experiment."

I stared. "How could he do that? He wrecked those kids' lives."

"Kay told you nothing about his father?"

I shook my head. "I didn't want to ask. If he volunteered his son as an *experiment…*"

"Yes. Walker was—is—one of the most powerful figures in the Alliance, in the entire Multiverse, in fact. I can't forget that day. It was plain to see Kay wasn't here by choice. He was eight years old at the time, I think. When Walker wasn't looking at him, it was obvious to me he was scared half to death."

My heart twisted. "Why are you telling *me* this?"

"Because if Kay does something dangerous, I'm counting on you to stop him."

"What? What's he planning?"

She shook her head. "It's beyond me to tell. He's reckless, and if he isn't careful, he's going to end up making a terrible error that will cost him his life."

My insides pitched down into darkness at the thought of the narrow escapes we'd already had. I couldn't begin to guess what Kay might be planning.

I nodded. "I'll talk to him, I'll stop him." *If I can.*

"That's all I can ask of you."

"Well," I said, hesitantly, "I can't predict what he's going to do. Not always. Sometimes I think I know him, but…"

"I certainly didn't know what to expect when the Academy sent me his report," said Ms Weston, half to herself. "Aside from his grades, his tutor explained he had a track record of helping the other students. It certainly didn't compare to the accounts I heard about Walker." She shook her head. "But now he's openly using magic, there's a strong chance he's going to get himself into a lot of trouble."

I didn't even know what to think right now. Except if Kay had a plan, I wasn't sure I *could* stop him.

"I'll talk to him," I said. "But I think we're all in over our heads. Is it absolutely essential we go back? Not just me," I added hastily. "I've read the Ambassadors' mandate and there's specifically a clause about necessary risks, isn't there? Is the base safe?"

Ms Weston looked more like her old self as she glowered at me. "I am aware of the rulebook, Ada Fletcher. And I will tell you what I told the others: stay at the base unless absolutely necessary. It's protected by the Alliance."

Except maybe from the apocalypse. And given what I'd

seen in Aktha's village, I wasn't sure it was just a legend anymore.

"I don't understand why the doorways can only open to the Passages," I said, voicing a question I'd wondered about for a while. "Can't we open one straight to Earth?"

Ms Weston went still. "That is not possible," she said. "The interactions of substances from different worlds can provoke dangerous reactions, and most would react violently. The world-key is designed to work through the Passages, which are laced with thousands of years of protection. Used *directly*, you're effectively tearing the universe itself apart."

My heart lurched. "But—the Conners did that. How?"

"My guess is, they stole a source," Ms Weston. "As far as I understand it, there's a certain substance within the world-key which resonates with a particular frequency, and can be tuned into one world at a time. It's an energy source. In some worlds, that energy is present in the atmosphere. I can think of one which is rumoured to be riddled with doorways."

The emphasis she put on the word *one* made me tense, and a chilling certainty pressed on me. "Enzar," I said. "Was it Enzar?"

A pause. Then Ms Weston gave a tight nod. "Enzar was cut off twenty years ago, long before I started working here, but I've recently become curious about the methods by which the people at the transition points between worlds smuggled refugees from Enzar's war zones. According to reports from the offworld-aid department of the Law Division, the only way it would be possible for anyone to be smuggled out is if a doorway existed directly between Enzar and a different world, one linked to the Passages."

I stared. "The Passages? That's how Nell got me out."

"I suspected as much. The war laid waste to most of the planet," said Ms Weston. "I confess I cannot imagine the scale. For anyone to be smuggled out at all, the door to the Passages must be well-hidden, otherwise we might have been looking at a cross-world invasion. I don't doubt this was one of the reasons the doorways were mostly closed off by the Alliance, and the noninterference stance issued."

She was talking about *my* homeworld. And yet... I'd never been there, not really. Being born there didn't count. I didn't remember a thing, even if I'd put a picture together from the snippets of information the Enzarians we'd helped had told me over the years.

I fought to get back to the point at hand. "So you think high-magic worlds contain the energy to make doorways?" *Could Kay do it?* He was an amplifier... and he had control of the world-key.

Holy crap. *No. He wouldn't do anything that risky.* But could I know for sure?

"I honestly don't know. In the meantime, it is your job to help Vey-Xanetha. If, of course, you are willing."

"I... there are four of us," I said. "How can we save a whole world? What happens if we fail? What about Earth?"

She shook her head. "If it seems likely to fail, we have an emergency unit in place to permanently seal the doorway to Vey-Xanetha."

I stared. "No way."

"The Alliance's safety comes first, Ada," said Ms Weston, and for the first time since I'd met her, she appeared truly, genuinely tired.

"Could they not evacuate?" I said, desperately. "There has to be a way."

"There is one permanent doorway on that world, Ada, and you know where it is."

On the mountain. Cut off from the rest of the continent. I shook my head fiercely. No way was I abandoning those people. This was exactly what Ambassadors risked every single time they travelled offworld. And who else did Vey-Xanetha have? Someone had to do it. Just like helping the refugees from Enzar.

"If you can avoid unnecessary risks, your safety will not be in question."

Avoid unnecessary risks? In a world where the deities themselves seemed to be going mad? Either Ms Weston had more faith in us than I'd thought, or she was deluding herself.

One of the communicators on her desk buzzed, and she glanced down. "Do me a favour and find the others, Ada. It sounds like the storm's slowing down."

"Sure."

I left Ms Weston's office and absently walked to Office Fifteen. I nearly jumped out of my skin when I found Kay waiting there. Ms Weston's words replayed in my head as I imagined him as a kid—the same age I'd been when I'd first gone into the Passages, with Nell at my side. Tears burned my eyes, and I threw my arms around him.

"Jesus, Ada." He stepped back, eyes widening. "Not that this isn't nice or anything, but I'm gonna spill this coffee any second now."

"*And* you got me coffee?" I half-sniffled, but let go of him.

"Are you okay?" His expression was a mixture of *why's this crazy woman throwing herself at me* and genuine concern.

Dammit. "Am *I* okay?" I blinked furiously.

"What? Did I miss something?"

I took the coffee before I embarrassed myself further and sipped it, even though it was boiling hot. Apparently realising he wasn't getting an answer, Kay retreated to the window, chewing on a breakfast bar. I went to grab a snack from my bag and joined him, watching the sun rise over the city and paint the sky in streaks of pink and orange. Sometimes I forgot how beautiful this world could be.

Kay eyed me, puzzled. "What was that about?"

"It's nothing," I said through a mouthful of squashed nutri-grain bar—most things I'd put in my bag had taken a battering when we'd run through the storm. "We need to find the others. Storm's slowing down, apparently."

"Thought so." He took out his communicator. "I'll message them if Ms Weston hasn't already."

I looked out the window again at the now-greyish sky. "She probably has. They won't have gone offworld, will they?"

"Nah, the Passages are closed to almost everywhere right now."

"Bet that's causing chaos."

"Sounds like half Valeria's staging a protest," he said. "I might have gone there if we didn't have to go back right now."

"Thought you said it was out of bounds. Oh, wait." I tilted my head. "Invisibility, right."

"Why not?"

"Hmm." My eyes followed the crowds of people moving through the streets outside, commuters heading for the tube stations. It sure didn't look like magical chaos had been all over the city for the past week. I watched the shape of the river curving through the heart of the city... and a huge, dark shape under the surface, momentarily breaking out with a spray of water before ducking under again.

I stared. "What in the world was that?"

"Not our business," said Kay. "Don't tell me someone bought a sea dragon, or..."

"The Loch Ness monster." I grinned.

"Pretty sure that's a myth."

"Yeah, right. Least it wasn't a chalder vox," I said.

"Those don't count as household pets," said Kay. "No one

would be stupid enough to try bringing one of them to Earth."

"*Has* anyone tried?" I asked, now curious. "Seeing as you know all the Alliance's history?"

"Not everything," he said. "And as far as I know, all reports from old missions to speak to the Vox leaders on Cethrax say, 'Survived with limbs intact. Never again.'"

I laughed. "Please tell me that's not an occupational hazard of being an Ambassador."

"Nah, the staff turnover would be too high. They haven't sent anyone into Cethrax itself in years."

"Good." But at least Cethrax was a known quantity. Did we really know what we were up against on Vey-Xanetha? Even watching Kay out of the corner of my eye, he gave nothing away about what he might be scheming. What Ms Weston had told me was a reminder: Kay didn't volunteer information easily. Would that even extend to information about the gods of Vey-Xanetha? Or magic?

"You never went there, did you? Back in the Passages?"

I turned to him. "No. why?"

"No reason. Just I figured those hidden tunnels are right near the swamp."

"Yeah." I flashed him a smile. "But I didn't need to go into Cethrax for the monsters to find me."

"You figured your way around on your own, without a map?"

"I had help. *Is* there a map?"

"Only of the main areas. It's on your communicator, along with one of Central."

Oh. I ducked my head, kind of embarrassed I'd never checked. "Didn't know about that one, either."

"Really?" His eyebrow quirked. "If I'd known, I could have trolled you about the pest control department."

"That's not a thing?"

"It'd probably come in handy right now, but no."

I laughed. My communicator buzzed and I jumped, narrowly avoiding spilling coffee on myself. *Smooth, Ada.*

"They're outside," said Kay, putting his own communicator away. "Looks like we're heading back."

∼

Another storm raged on Vey-Xanetha. Bolts of lightning seared the air, and the sky appeared clearer than usual, blood-red and cloudless. As lightning struck the mountainside, only metres away, everyone in the meeting room jumped.

Mathran seemed more agitated than before, understandably. "We cannot leave," he murmured to himself. "But for how long can we stay?"

"One of the mysteries of the bloody Multiverse," Raj muttered irritably.

I sighed. Kay had wandered upstairs, and I debated following him. With the sound of the storm raging outside, I didn't feel entirely safe even in here. Iriel and Raj had got out their notes again, mostly copies of the Vey-Xanethan symbols.

"There's really no similarities with any other world?" I asked Iriel.

"Maybe Klathican," said Iriel. "But they're considered to have the most ancient script in the Multiverse. No one knows for certain, of course. But that would mean Klathican computers should have been able to translate it."

"That's weird," I said. I didn't know much about Klathica, except on that world, injecting humans with magic was considered normal.

"Yeah, it had the first *computer* language," said Raj, not

looking particularly impressed. "But that doesn't mean pre-Alliance, does it?"

"That's it," said Iriel. "The whole mystery of this place is that it seems to have avoided classification. It's nothing like any world we have access to."

"Any world *we* have access to," I repeated, a certain file coming to mind. A world logged as 'dangerous'. There were others. Hundreds of them. "Wait. You've been running comparisons with other worlds, right? What about things other than languages? Like the wildlife? There's got to be some crossover if it used to be linked to another world."

And the magic level? But the classifications were too vague. And no other allied world had sentient magical forces.

No other *allied* world.

Goosebumps sprang up on my arms. "Does anyone even know which world the kimaros came from? They weren't always running amok around the Passages, right?"

"No..." said Raj slowly. "First time we found one was at the same time as Aglaia, but they didn't come from that world."

Because the Conners opened a doorway. But they weren't born, or created, in the Passages. If they didn't come from here, then where? *Magical backlash given life...*

"Good point," said Iriel. "There's so little in the information file."

"Yeah," said Raj. "Maybe we need to ask Ms Weston. She was in the archives, right?"

"Maybe *she* was looking for something..." I trailed off. Frustration swirled below the surface, like the answer hovered out of reach. So this world had nothing in common with other worlds in the Alliance. That didn't mean it was alone in the Multiverse. Given how it *had* definitely been linked to at least one other world in the past, it couldn't be.

And what happened to that world?

One person to ask. I didn't *think* Kay would withhold information if it meant the difference between life and death. But maybe he had a theory. Or we could figure it out together.

Upstairs, his door lay open, but he wasn't in there. A stairway at the end of the hall caught my attention. I hadn't been up there before.

It turned out to lead to a large, deserted room, in the attic, judging by the support beams on the ceiling. Metal, not wood. And Kay sat on one of them, against the wall, feet dangling over the edge.

"Kay? How'd you get up there?"

"There are hand-holds." He didn't appear surprised to see me here.

I'll take that as an invitation. I made for the wall and pulled myself up, then grabbed for the nearest beam. I misjudged the jump and hung upside-down, my top riding up halfway. *Great,* I thought, flipping over the right way. Tugging my top down so I was decent, I sat with my legs dangling over the edge, right next to Kay, who regarded me with one eyebrow raised.

"Whatever I did right, tell me so I can keep doing it."

"Uh…" I stammered, my face heating up.

"Eloquent," he said.

"Quit it," I said, acutely aware of the inches separating us. "Jesus. It's freaking hot in here."

"Not the only thing."

I tilted my head sideways at him, thinking he was just messing with me, but his expression was serious. "Very funny. So what're you doing up here? Thinking?"

He shrugged. "Waiting for the storm to die down. Anything happen?"

"We thought of something," I said. I summarised our discussion. Kay listened, his face expressionless.

"So this world *was* linked to at least one other, but it's either destroyed or cut off." He nodded. "That makes sense. I reckon the three deities are some kind of backlash. Like the kimaros."

"You do?"

"Yeah. Well, the storm god, at least. Magical backlash given sentience. Sure, it's not familiar to us, but like you said, there might be other similar worlds out there."

"Yeah, not sure things worked out for them, though," I said, unable to help it. Enzar. I didn't know the details of the magic which ravaged that world. I'd thought it was third level, but after learning what the Royals had done to me, injecting me with pure antimagic, I knew magic went way beyond what I could imagine.

I glanced at Kay instead. He held a palm-sized rectangular metal device in both hands, one I'd seen before.

"I *knew* you used a tracker," I said. "When you found those merchants."

"Yeah, I'm surprised no one brought that up."

"You weren't planning to tell the others." It wasn't a question. Hell, if he hadn't been forced to use the amplifier on the tracker to help me save Alber from the Conners, he'd probably never have told me, either. I'd once asked him if he trusted me, and he hadn't answered. From what Ms Weston had told me, I was starting to understand why.

I indicated the tracker. "So that can pick up on my signal? What does it feel like, anyway?"

"Your signal?" He frowned. "I'm not sure there's a way to describe it to someone who hasn't felt it."

"I did," I reminded him. "When we went after Alber. It was like a radio signal. Like music only I could hear."

"Yeah... if I concentrate, I can tell one person's from another."

"What do I sound like, Valerian train-crash music?" I asked, flashing him a grin.

He smiled back, but it didn't reach his eyes. "No, of course not." A pause. "Like a rabid chalder vox."

"You!" I swiped at him, and he caught my arm.

"Not the safest place for a fight," he said, indicating the not-insignificant drop. "I bet I could take a vox-kind up here."

"Of course you could." I rolled my eyes. "You could decapitate a wyvern from that roof beam."

"Is that a challenge?"

"Seriously?" I said, as he started to edge along the roof beam. "I forgot you're a ninja-finishing-school dropout. Huh."

Kay's eyebrows lifted when I tightrope-walked across a particularly precarious area.

"Hell, yeah." I sat down on the edge, over the centre of the room. "Bet you can't do that."

"Challenge accepted." He joined me within seconds. For a moment, I felt like a kid running around over the roofs again, and not for the first time, I wondered what Kay had been like when he was younger. Even as a teenager. All I knew was he'd been arrested for arson and almost killing Aric when he'd accidentally used magic. And I wasn't even supposed to know.

"I don't get it," I said, perching on the beam. "You said the last thing I needed was to be around someone like you. But you're okay with being friends. That's kind of mixed signals, you know?"

He looked down, no longer smiling. "Sorry," he said. "I wanted to give you the option. You know what I am. What I've done."

"Hello? I almost destroyed the *Earth*."

"You weren't in control. You acted in self-defence. With

Aric's cousins—I wanted to kill them. I scared you. No," he said, cutting off my response. "I did, and I'm sorry."

"I don't care if you're a killer. You said what I did wasn't my fault. Why not cut your*self* some slack for once?" I edged along the beam, my heart beating faster. "Kay, you're the one person I trust outside of my family."

"You shouldn't." He shook his head. "I'm a Walker. We're not exactly known for keeping our word."

What else had his father done? "It's not all you are. I'm a freaking *Royal*. My parents have killed whole planets, probably. Blood isn't everything. Besides, I was raised by a killer, and she's one of the best people I know."

"Your guardian?"

I hesitated, torn between the instinct to keep Nell's secrets and the need to make him understand. "She was the Royals' servant, so yes. I don't know how many of them she killed when she smuggled me to Earth. If anyone had betrayed us on Earth, she'd have killed them, too. *I* might have. Would that make you think less of *me?*"

He shook his head. "Ada, that's not the point—"

"When you were torturing those men, the Conners, you didn't look like *you*. That's what scared me. Because it's not the person I know."

Kay studied the floor below. "Maybe you don't know me."

"Bullshit." I glared at him. "And if I don't, then I *want* to know you. I don't judge. You forget, I've spent most of my life keeping people's secrets. Even—"

My voice caught. Delta. Skyla. Old Ada wouldn't be here, talking to him. She'd never have taken the job offer. Old Ada didn't trust anyone outside her family—but that wasn't true. I'd let Delta and Skyla in, and they'd betrayed me. And now here I was trying to get through to someone who'd told me I'd be better off if I stayed away from him.

"Something up?"

"Nothing," I said quickly. "Just—" Oh, dammit. "I just thought about my friend from Valeria. Or, he used to be." Before I killed him. Would this ever get easier?

He nodded, getting it, but didn't say anything.

"Sorry," I muttered, suddenly uncomfortable with the silence. "I know you probably don't want to hear. Amanda said I should talk about it, that it'll help... after what happened. I guess I've been acting weird, huh."

"No, it's normal." He paused as if thinking, a frown pulling at his mouth. "I meant normal for what happened to you."

"Uh-huh." *Say something intelligent, Ada.* "See, I do know you. You keep trying to shut me out, but it's not gonna work anymore."

"Ada..." he said. "God only knows I keep getting this wrong. But it's a dangerous job we're in. And even the council might have taken advantage if they knew about your magic. I never told them—only a few people at Central know what's in your blood. I said you used magic, and that was all the explanation they needed."

So he didn't tell them what I did when I killed the Campbells?

"Like Ms Weston? *She* knows."

"She must have guessed," he said, frowning. "Good point. I know she's been involved in med-tech before."

My heart twisted. I spoke carefully. "And she knows..."

"About the experiment?" He spoke casually, like it was no big deal, but his expression darkened at the words. "Yeah, she knows. I don't know what her game is, but she's not out to report either of us to the council."

No. She just feels guilty. But I couldn't say it.

"I don't know how she thinks we can solve this problem," I said, my words punctuated by another well-timed clap of thunder. "Anyway, I never even told my family you were a magic-wielder," I added. "Or anything else."

His eyes narrowed a fraction, like he was trying to figure out what I meant by *anything else,* and I was glad he couldn't read my mind. I easily forgot how little he'd actually told me about himself. Nell had adopted a policy of 'don't ask unnecessary questions' and the same applied to her own life, but I'd never had a friend get close enough to bring down the boundaries. And I'd never been interested enough in another person to know how to do the same for them.

Mostly, I was terrified to say the wrong thing again and drive him away. I didn't try to repeatedly run myself into heartbreak, at least, not deliberately. But with Kay, it was different.

Maybe that was why it scared me. I wasn't used to caring so much about someone outside my family. I wasn't used to opening my own heart.

So I didn't say anything. I moved closer to him. Close enough that my arm brushed against his. I looked down, unable to help it, at the wyvern-scars on either side of his forearm—in fact, close up, they were far from the only marks. Other faint scars covered his knuckles. Looked like he'd broken bones at least once.

"It looked worse when they stitched me up," he said, making me jump.

"Um. You said you can't feel pain... there?" I tentatively poked the scar.

"No... depends on the angle." He flipped his hand palm-down to show where the most recent, pinkish scar overlapped the twin jagged marks, where Aric's sister cut him with her knife.

I sucked in a breath. "Damn." Heart beating fast, I ran my fingers along the scar on his arm. I felt him stiffen, and before I could lose my nerve, rested my hand on top of his. He blinked in surprise, but didn't pull away. Just in this one moment, we weren't Ambassadors with the fate of the Multiverse on our shoulders. We were us. If there *was* an 'us'. He tilted his head. Our faces were inches apart.

"Kay," I said, my voice little more than a breath, and this time, I let my lips brush against his, gently.

Thud.

"That," said Raj, "is a terrible make-out spot. Did you plan to fall to your deaths?"

I jerked back and Kay grabbed my arm to steady me in case I actually did fall off. My face lit up like a traffic light. Raj stood at the top of the stairs, staring up at us incredulously.

"Thanks a lot," I called down to Raj. "You have the most epic sense of bad timing in the history of the Multiverse."

Kay laughed, slightly unsteadily, I thought. "Yeah, you really do."

"The world's kind of ending out there. In case you two forgot." Raj left, and Kay shifted along the beam.

"He has a point," he said. "I reckon we should brave the storm and open a door. If we stay in the Passages, it can't hit us, and it's better than sitting around here."

Rolling my eyes, I followed him back down. Once our feet were safely on the ground, I crept up behind him and whispered, "This isn't over."

Kay glanced back over his shoulder, the corner of his mouth lifted in a smirk. *Oh, we'll pick up where we left off later.* I had no intention of letting him slip away again.

Focus, Ada. Apocalypse happening outside, remember?

Yeah. No big deal. The world might be ending, and I'm pretty sure I'm falling in love with Kay Walker.

We found Mathran and the others back in the room. Iriel winked at me, and Raj grinned at both of us, but their expressions turned serious as Mathran cleared his throat to speak.

"I have another suggestion," said Mathran. "The storm

appears to only be affecting this area, and there is another town at the far end of the jungle which might be far enough away from the storm to risk a trip. The town is devoted to Xanet, like Sekth, and from there, we might be able to discern if this effect is widespread."

"And if it is?" I said.

Mathran didn't need to answer: his face said enough.

15

KAY

I closed the door behind us in the Passages and opened another one. Trees obscured the view, and no path was in sight, the sky blotted out by branches.

"The forest," said Mathran, frowning. "No, this is not near the town."

All-too-conscious of the ticking clock, I opened several other doorways, one after another, while Mathran inspected them and shook his head each time. Finally, he indicated for me to stop.

"This is near the town."

It looked like another part of the forest to me, but I put the world-key back in my pocket and we followed him back into Vey-Xanetha. I noted he carried several of those stick-like metal weapons he'd had before, threaded into his belt, and kept his hand on one. The others, too, were prepared to draw a stunner or dagger at a second's notice in case something appeared and attacked us again.

Unfamiliar, thick-branched trees surrounded us, roots criss-crossing the ground every which way. There was no clearly defined path, but the shapes of narrow buildings were visible through gaps in the trees. Mathran led the way, expertly stepping over roots and vivid red-coloured plants with snaking vines. Careful not to touch anything, we followed. Everything smelled like decay. Like death.

"There should be a path here," he said, in a low voice. "Xanet controls the trees, and it looks as though it has grown wild. And some of it is dying."

That explained the decay-like smell. The air was thick with it, all the more because of the warmth. And there didn't seem to be any wildlife, not so much as a bird's call.

Mathran led us around a thick tree and past a broken-down building. The city had merged with the forest itself, judging by the vines and tree roots wrapped around so many of the houses and forming a thick canopy above, like a protective dome. Taller shapes stood amongst the trees, including a central tower. Nothing appeared to be collapsing. Yet.

And it was so quiet here. Nobody seemed to be about, at least not at first, but I glimpsed faces in some of the windows. The buildings were made of the same rock as the others, but the central tower, now I looked closer, was a hollowed-out tree trunk.

A shadow passed behind us. I whipped around, pulling my dagger.

"What's that?" asked Ada.

I shook my head. Maybe I was jumping at shadows, but this was the third time. And my belief in coincidence disappeared by the second.

I turned back, following Mathran. Now we were in the city proper, houses on either side, but still, there were no people. Not outside, anyway. Except...

People moved inside the tower. Robed figures, in green cloaks. Summoners? The tower belonged to Xanet, I remembered Mathran saying.

"He is gone," Mathran whispered, watching the tower.

"Huh?" Ada gave him a quizzical look.

"Xanet sustains life, and the tower with it. It should be alive."

And it clearly wasn't, judging by the dead, grey colour. Even the plants growing alongside it had withered.

Along with the bodies.

I couldn't believe I hadn't spotted them before, but they lay amongst the tree roots dressed in robes the same colour as the forest—grey and dead-looking. Ada made a choked noise when she spotted a man lying close to her feet and backed away, hand on her weapon. Raj and Iriel reacted the same. But I kept moving forward, trying to figure out if they were dead or unconscious. No. Their eyes were open, sightlessly reflecting the branches above.

My feet knocked a limp hand, and a faint spark winked into existence, then out. A white-red spark.

Magic. They were killed by magic.

"What... who are they?" Ada asked in a faint whisper.

"Xanet upholds the law here," said Mathran, his tanned face paling. "They are—were—his messengers, the police of this village. This—this means something terrible has already happened."

Mathran muttered something in Vey-Xanethan under his breath and indicated that we stay back. The wooden door opened, and two summoners came out, then another two.

A rustling behind us. My hand rested on my dagger, but a short, ragged-looking man wearing an expression of pure terror peered from behind a tree. Behind him, others came out the houses, too. A couple cast frightened glances at us, but most were fixated on the tower.

A group of children followed, all under the age of ten or so. Summoners surrounded them on both sides.

A chill went down my spine.

The summoners were speaking, but I couldn't hear most of the words at this distance. Except one. *Veyak.*

The group turned, forming a circle around the children, and started to walk in our direction. Mathran indicated for us to move out of the way, like we needed any encouragement, slipping into the shadowy alcove between a large tree and several houses.

They walked past, and I kept my hand on the heel of my dagger. *This is wrong.*

"I was afraid of this," Mathran said, softly. "This village has always been an outlier, and without Xanet, every magic-wielder will have lost their power... except for one small group. But I never would have thought they'd go as far as to commit this atrocity." He indicated the bodies.

They killed their entire police force? *Shit.* If the police relied on magic, and an insurgent group gained power right when everyone else lost the ability to use magic at all... I could guess what had happened.

Enough to know we were in a shitload of trouble.

"The trio were originally rivals, in our first mythology," he said. "They never worked together, but weren't outright enemies, though there is a school of thought who believe they were. Those are summoners of Veyak, and they believe their deity is superior to the others. Ridiculous, of course, because we all rely on all three. But that particular group—it doesn't surprise me that they would take advantage of this situation..."

"And do what?" I asked, staring at the kids in the middle of the group. My voice sounded distant, and my muscles locked in place as one summoner sharply prodded a kid who stepped out of line with a stick similar to Mathran's weapon. "Where the hell are they taking those kids?"

"To the chasm," said Mathran, and his eyes were closed.

"They believe that in order to pacify their deity, a sacrifice has to be made."

ADA

Shock gripped me all over. They were going to kill those children? No. I glanced at the others. Raj and Iriel looked on in outraged horror, and Kay had stopped dead, pale as a ghost.

I took a step forwards, raising my weapon with shaking hands.

Kay seemed to come back to life. "Ada, we can't interfere," he said, but his voice shook. "It isn't Alliance business. We're in their territory now."

I clenched my fists and glared at him, even though I knew he was right. "Dammit," I said. "Damn them all. They're not seriously going to…"

Raj cursed under his breath, while Iriel turned away, her hands shaking.

"There is nothing we can do here," said Mathran. "If I were to challenge them, they would strike me down like they did their law enforcement. The invokers of Xanet were some of the most powerful magic-wielders on our world."

"No kidding." Raj stared. "You're seriously gonna lie down and let that happen?"

"We're outnumbered, and Aktha is gone along with Xanet. You'll die if you intervene." Despair lined every inch of his face. But no… I couldn't let this go. I knew the Alliance's mandate as well as anyone, but there were some things I just wouldn't lie down and watch.

"Fuck that," I said.

"Ada." Kay grabbed my arm as I took another step forwards.

You can't save everyone, Nell had always told me. I'd always known it. But I'd never really accepted it. As long as I could walk, as long as I could fight, as long as my heart still beat, I'd always try to help.

I wouldn't let this go. No way in hell.

I pulled my hand away from Kay and followed after the group. He cursed. "Dammit, Ada." Footsteps sounded behind me.

"Don't you dare try to stop me," I hissed, aware that someone would hear us if we got any closer to the group of robed figures—and that they were heading the way we'd come. We couldn't get back to the doorway without passing within sight of them.

From here, I could count ten summoners, and almost twice as many children. Shuffling movements caught my attention, and out of the corner of my eye, I saw someone move in the window of a nearby house. A woman, crying. She caught my eye, and even though I didn't speak the language, I could see the words in her eyes: *help them.*

That did it for me. I broke into a swift walk, skirting tree roots, reaching for the magic I knew must be present here. I could go to third level...

And so could they.

Red smoke rushed towards us even though I hadn't consciously meant to draw on so much. *Stop!*

Too late. The summoners turned around, and all eyes fixed on me.

All of them spoke at once. One word, in a chilling monotone.

"Veyak."

Next thing I knew, they were kneeling in the dirt.

I stared at them. Did they call me by the name of their deity?

Kay swore. He was right behind me, and his hand brushed against mine, somehow calming the raging static against my skin. Did they think *I* was a summoner?

Crap. I didn't have a clue what to say. I looked pleadingly at Mathran, just behind Kay. Must have come to try and stop me. Too late.

"What are they saying?" I asked in a hoarse whisper.

"They believe you called upon Veyak. And as it happens, they are right."

My heart thudded. "What?"

The summoners knelt amongst the tangled tree roots, the children in a terrified huddle behind them.

"Well, that's what they believe."

My throat dried up. "Tell them—no, tell them to let the children go. Please."

Mathran shook his head. "Veyak is the strongest of the gods. You cannot challenge them and hope to survive it. If I could, I would, but with Veyak on their side…"

"Then tell *me* how to say it. Please." We were breaking Alliance code. Majorly. No interference. Except the handbook didn't lay down rules on what to do when faced with a local cult with magic acting up. But Vey-Xanetha was connected, however distantly, to the Alliance. They were breaking the laws of their *own* world, and had killed their entire police force to boot. I couldn't stop to think about what the Alliance would say to us about intervening with those kids standing right there.

Kay moved closer to me, fixing Mathran with his stone-cold Alliance guard stare. "Do it."

Fear flashed in Mathran's eyes, but he shook his head again, frantically. Behind, Raj and Iriel stood with their weapons out, but both looked more prepared to run away than to fight. They knew the rules, too, and the first order would always be to save our own necks. But if I really could do something… I couldn't sit down and accept defeat.

Kay muttered a curse, and spoke aloud. "Release them."

I stared for a moment, then remembered the earpiece. Did he speak Vey-Xanethan?

The blood drained from Mathran's face.

A summoner looked up, at Kay, then me. *Whoa.* His eyes were luminous laser-red, with no pupils. "This is the order of Veyak?" he said, in a low, buzzing monotone.

Holy shit. They really did think I was some kind of messenger. I cursed myself for not taking the time to at least learn a couple of phrases. Kay must have done so. Though he had the advantage of a genius memory.

"Yes."

"This one is *verek.*" He pointed to me. Abomination. "We will take her to the chasm."

I shook my head.

"No," said Kay.

"It is Veyak's wish." Every one of them stood. "We do not disobey."

Lightning crackled over *their* heads, this time. The magic charge built in the air, growing stronger and raising the hairs on my arms. The sky boiled red, clouds swirling in response.

Aimed at me.

Nowhere to run, so I threw myself behind the nearest tree root. A blast shook the earth inches from where I'd been standing, sending me flying back. I slammed into Kay and the two of us were flung into the dilapidated remains of an abandoned house. My head struck the wall and stars winked before my eyes. I slid to the ground, the summoners blurring. Shivers ran up my arms from the static. *I just absorbed—* second level at least.

Crap. The others. I twisted around and saw Kay slumped

a few feet away. For an instant my heart stopped, but then he tilted his head. Our eyes met, and he inched over to me. "You okay?" He spoke in a whisper.

"Yeah." My voice was more of a croak, my heart slamming against my ribs. *Holy shit.* I shook my head fiercely to quell the panic rising in my chest. If I hadn't been standing in front of Kay, he might have—

"Stay down. They think you're dead."

I glanced back over the giant tree root and saw the summoners had disappeared into the surrounding jungle. That was enough to snap me back to attention. Cursing, I pushed to my feet.

"Ada—"

I yanked my hand away from Kay. "I'm fine," I said, ignoring the throbbing lump forming on the back of my head. The summoners were leaving, taking those kids with them—and they were heading right where we'd opened the doorway. "I'm going after them."

"Hold on," he said. "You can't go running out there without a plan. They're magic-wielders, and those kids are right in the way."

"Then we'll get them *out* of the way," I said. "No question."

Kay nodded, and I knew I shouldn't have doubted him. Except I couldn't see the others anywhere. The aftermath of magic hung in the air, a red haze over everything, and my skin tingled again. *How much did I absorb?*

I couldn't worry about that now. Climbing over the tree roots, I saw the robed figures herding the children down a side-path between houses and amongst the thick-trunked trees. I cursed under my breath. How to use magic without drawing attention—strike them down without hurting any of the children *or* getting ourselves blown to pieces?

Magic swirled around my palm, as though in response to my thoughts. The charge built, demanding to be released, but

I couldn't attack them with all those kids in the way. I aimed carefully, playing out the scenario in my mind's eye. If I hit the summoners just so, nobody else would be in danger of getting caught in the blast.

A screech echoed from ahead, and the group drew closer together. Lightning split the sky above them and a heavy shape crashed through the trees. A winged shape. *Holy hell.* It might have been one of those three-headed birds from earlier. The summoners had killed it without even looking up.

Again, lightning flashed, and the static in the air rose. Kay swore behind me.

"Third level," he hissed. "There's no backlash."

No. That's what was missing. No backlash. Just like when Mathran had demonstrated magic.

The three laws didn't apply here.

I raised my hand, took aim, and the world burst apart in white light. My ears rang, a metallic taste rose on my tongue, and every nerve in my body lit up. I blinked repeatedly, trying to clear my eyes—trying to push away the feeling I wasn't entirely in control of my own movements—

"Ada!"

Kay's shout brought me back to the present. I staggered and almost fell over the edge of a crater which hadn't been in front of us before.

Where had it come from? When I'd used magic...

Crap, what had I done? I blinked, the white light clearing from my vision. The summoners were gone. The crater had hit the spot where the back of their line had been following those kids, but no people were about.

No! I ran towards the jungle, leaping tree roots like hurdles. My feet caught on something. Not a tree root. A body. Two summoners were splayed across the ground, unmoving. No blood. No visible injury.

I clapped a hand to my mouth. "Did I...?"

Kay clambered over the tree root behind me. "Ada, stop."

"Did I kill them? Where did the rest go?"

"The kids ran away in the jungle, but the summoners went after them—"

"Shit!" I ran, ignoring the shakiness in my legs and the magic buzzing against my skin. I racked my memory, but came up blank after that flash of light. I'd hit two, which meant...

A sharp stick whizzed past, burying itself in a tree root. Kay swore and raised his dagger in time to deflect a second projectile, which disappeared into the bushes nearby. They were hiding somewhere amongst the houses? Lightning flashed overhead and I jumped, thinking I'd done it—but Kay raised his non-weapon hand, sparks jumping from his skin. Eyes gleaming black.

My heart stopped.

I looked back at the roots snaking around the house we'd stopped in front of, the place the weapon had come from.

"Ada. Let's move." Kay's hand closed around mine, and I jumped as the sparks flying from his palm met the static in my own hand. He let go just as quickly. "Shit. I didn't hurt you, did I?"

I shook my head, scanning the trees for the others. No sign of them. We had to move.

I took his hand again and we turned invisible. I'd anticipated it a split-second before it happened, but barely caught myself before I stumbled over another tree root. This was a bad time to try this, but if it helped us avoid more attacks...

And helped us kill them...

I shook the thought away, disquieted by the way magic stirred around me as I imagined calling on it again. *The children. We have to rescue the children.*

"Where did they...?"

Kay guided my steps to stop me tripping over the roots with my invisible feet. Ordinarily I'd have protested when he went as far as to lift me over a particularly tall tree root, but the faster we caught those summoners—*how* had they moved so quickly?

I stopped dead. Stared.

A doorway lay open, cutting the forest in two. Not the doorway we'd come through. A new one.

Impossible. On the other side of the opening was what looked like a canyon. Burned red ground, no plants, no life, red cliffs rising on either side and cupping the sun, at the centre point of the purplish-red sky.

"What the hell?" I whispered.

"Shit," Kay said. "That must be the chasm they mentioned."

I hadn't heard. But now... *hell.* What I'd taken for the horizon behind the doorway was the edge of a cliff. My skin prickled all over.

Figures emerged from behind the trees on our side of the doorway, and I froze, breathing quietly. I counted six of them. *Where are those kids?*

The answer came when the final summoner said one word, and lightning flashed. Immediately, a number of smaller figures ran out from behind trees, behind roots, clearly terrified out of their wits but drawn by the magic. Scared of the magic, and what it could do.

Horror hit my heart.

Stop. Please.

The summoners beckoned the children from the canyon until they'd formed a group again, and they all stepped through the doorway. Except one summoner, who lay at the edge, unmoving, his coat fanning out. Magic sparked from his skin.

"He sacrificed himself to open the door." Kay's tone was flat, quiet. "Or, they sacrificed him."

"What..." I whispered, staring through the door, an impossibility merging two scenes together seamlessly. "Is that place even *this* world?"

Kay cursed under his breath. One of the summoners had turned our way, and raised his hand to the sky—as if to strike us down as easily as that bird.

No way.

I pulled my dagger. Magic rushed through my fingers, sparked into the dagger's hilt, and I let go.

The dagger sank into a summoner's back and he went down, choking on a scream. I'd got him right in the spine, a fatal shot Nell had taught me. He'd be dead in seconds.

The others saw, and chaos erupted around us. Magic-wielders moved towards us as though they could see us, ignoring their captives, and several weapons flew wide. Kay dragged me behind a tree as one came dangerously close. I pulled my second dagger and squeezed his hand. *Trust me.*

Three summoners had come back into the forest, into range. I let magic flow towards me, and it sparked from my hands, giving my location away—but it was too late for them. Anger surged in my veins, in tandem with the raging magic, and lightning speared the sky, striking all three of them down. Screams sounded from behind the doorway and my heart plunged. I ran past the dead summoners, ignoring the lingering magic sparking at my skin. Two behind the door had fallen, too, their throats cut. Only three remained, and one raised a hand to the sky.

Lightning exploded across my vision. I gasped, and when I blinked my eyes clear, I saw Kay blocking a knife blow from a summoner, swiping with his own dagger.

Two others moved towards me, blinking rapidly. They'd

been dazzled, too, but quickly recovered. And the invisibility had dropped at some point when I'd used magic.

I lashed out with a kick, sending magic through the heel of my foot to propel the man backwards with second level magic. *Bastard.* They were child-killers and vicious monsters. I bared my teeth, pure rage taking control as the second enemy raised a hand to send magic at me. I dodged and slashed with my dagger, barely noticing as blood spattered my face. The enemy fell. It wasn't enough. I wasn't going to leave any of them alive. A voice seemed to whisper in my ear, urging me on, feeding into the blazing white lightning around my hands.

Magic flared. The last summoner dropped to the ground, dead.

Silence. Breathing heavily, I stepped back. My dagger slipped in my sweaty grip, blood glistening on the blade. Kay, crouched on the ground, stared at me. Like I was a stranger.

I felt sick, and swayed on the spot as the adrenaline drained away. Kay stepped over the fallen summoners towards me, and an odd impulse seized me, to tell him to stay back. Even though the monsters were gone. But I was...

It's over. They're dead. "Kay," I said shakily. "Did I get all of them?"

He nodded. "Every one. Come on, we can't stay here." He took my hand, though I didn't need it to become invisible, but the support stopped me from sinking to the ground in horror. I squeezed his hand back, and a sharp pain shot up my wrist. I hadn't even felt when I got cut, but now blood seeped down my wrist and my face stung, too.

I stopped dead. The children hid behind the trees. They'd fled from the fighting. I swallowed. Wondered what, even if we spoke the same language, I could possibly say now. They probably thought we were monsters.

A little girl hesitantly approached us, head bowed. She

wore pale cotton-like garments, like the others, her bright-yellow hair a splash of colour. Kay stiffened as she reached to touch my bloodstained hand with the end of an odd, stick-like object. A weapon? It might have been. She pressed it to the cut on my arm, and I was the one to go still.

Small, twisting vines emerged from the end of the stick. I stared, mouth falling open, as they touched my skin, causing magic to spark to life again. The vines withdrew as swiftly as they'd arrived, like a flower petal folding into itself.

The cut on my arm wasn't there anymore.

"How… how?" I glanced at Kay, who looked as astonished as I felt.

"Xanet," the girl whispered, and touched my face with the stick, in the place where it stung.

Again, magic sparked. The cut healed.

Xanet was the deity of life. One of the deities was on our side.

Despite everything, I smiled at the girl, and tears pricked my eyes. "Thank you," I said. And she seemed to understand.

16

KAY

Ada appeared to be in a state of shock, walking mechanically as I guided her back into the city, small tremors running through her body. Maybe magical aftershock. I wasn't feeling too steady myself. Especially when I pictured the shadow that had fallen over Ada when she'd used magic.

A familiar shadow. It wasn't an aftereffect of the magic. And there had been no backlash, not even when she'd hit third level.

I hadn't pieced it together when I'd first seen the carving, or the symbol. But I remembered too clearly. And now it hit me: the symbol and the deity were one and the same, and one that had appeared behind Ada when she'd used magic. Veyak.

And it was too similar, far too similar, to those magic-creatures we'd fought in the Passages.

I couldn't even begin to think what it might mean. Except we were in way, way over our heads.

"What the *devil* were you thinking?" Raj stepped out from behind a tree root, grey-faced with panic and rage. "Did you both want to get yourselves killed?"

"You were about to let those summoners sacrifice those kids?" I said, with a glance at Ada. "It wasn't deliberate—the magic, that is. She somehow channelled the deity."

"She *what?*" Raj gaped at us. "We were trying to get a jump on those magic-wielders, but they moved too fast. No way could we get close to that magic. What were you doing out there, burning the forest down?"

"Never mind that," I said. "Where's Mathran?"

"Here." Mathran appeared from the doorway of a house. A frightened-looking woman withdrew into the shadows inside the hall as she saw us—and two of the kids. "They ran from the magic."

Well, at least he was doing something more useful than hiding.

"Iriel?" I asked Raj.

"She went after you," he said, through gritted teeth. "She's not with you?"

Shit. "I didn't see her." But we about-turned and followed the path back into the forest all the same. It wasn't hard to track down where we'd fought. Crater-like holes in the ground marked the spots where Ada had used magic. She seemed reluctant to go near them, tugging her hand out of mine to walk alone.

As someone appeared from behind a tree, four hands drew weapons—and Iriel stared at all of us.

"What?" she said. "I thought we were all running madly into the unknown jungle."

Raj walked over to her and shoved her in the shoulder. "You're all *mental*," he said. "Where the hell did you go?"

"To look at the trail of destruction," she said. "Ada, when you channelled the deity—don't look at me like that, Raj, you know that's what happened—it left marks." She pointed.

Damn, she was right. The area around where the lightning had struck had been torn up, the ground split… in the shape of a symbol.

Veyak. Again.

Ada crouched to examine the markings. Her eyes were wild, and blood streaked her face from the healed cut. She tilted her head up to face me, swallowed, and said, "The doorway. Has it closed?"

I turned around. This part of the jungle appeared unfamiliar, but we'd fought the summoners right here. The doorway had closed, leaving nothing but thick trees and torn-up ground in the spot where the summoners had opened it. The only trace of the doorway was the haze of magic hovering around the body of the summoner who lay in the spot where, just minutes before, a canyon had been visible.

"Doorway?" Iriel wore a faintly puzzled expression. "Isn't our door over there?" She pointed.

"Let's get out," said Raj.

Ada climbed over the cratered ground, declining my offer of help. "How did they do it?" She stared at the spot where the doorway had been. "Did they really sacrifice someone to open the door?"

"We must leave," said Mathran. "This is not our path. And the sky darkens."

He was right. "I thought it was day time?"

"The cycles become shorter." He shook his head. "Another sign of the end… of the chasm…"

The door the summoners had opened, the gaping hole on the other side of the canyon…Was *that* the chasm from the legend? We'd been too far away to see. But a cliff didn't appear out of nowhere.

A beam of light cut through the trees, striking the ground in front of us. I immediately went for my weapon, and the others followed suit. What the hell now?

"It's happening," Mathran said. "Veyak's storm is back."

Purple bolts of lightning crackled overhead with bursts of thunder, emphasising his words. Not like natural lightning, not at all like Earth.

More like magic.

Ada gasped. "Did I do that?"

"Of course not." But if the static buzzing in my fingertips was any indication, there might be a real danger of us creating a storm of our own soon.

"We must move!" shouted Mathran.

Lucky I remembered the way back to the doorway. As we ran, more lightning lit the trees, and thunder boomed so loudly, the ground shook under our feet and the trees trembled to the roots. Mathran muttered to himself, almost chanting, so rapidly I couldn't catch the words.

Finally, the doorway appeared in front of us, mercifully untouched. I waited to make sure everyone else got safely through before closing it behind us. After the level of magic on Vey-Xanetha, I barely felt the buzz of the Passages.

"You're not seriously going back!" said Iriel, as Mathran made for the door back to the base, which I'd left open on the opposite wall.

"I cannot stay here," he said. "I cannot leave my world."

"Dammit." I checked the door. The storm didn't seem to have reached the base yet, but given how unpredictable the deities were, we couldn't count on it.

Mathran had already crossed the threshold. The base's entrance was only a metre away. Raj and Iriel exchanged glances, clearly weighing the odds, then followed after Mathran.

Ada hung back, staring at the doorway, her eyes glazed.

"Ada," I said. "We have to go."

"I know. I can't believe—can't believe they took those kids. They were going to…"

"Things like that happen on Earth," I said, my voice sounding distant even to me. "Like every world."

"I know that. I…" She swayed on the spot. "What I did to those summoners. It's exactly what the Royals did. They—they walked onto every world they could get at, rounded up the natives, and…"

Shit. "It wasn't the same," I said, ineffectually.

"I don't *regret* killing them," said Ada. "Maybe I should regret blowing the Alliance's rules to pieces, but I'd rather resign as an Ambassador than watch shit like that happen."

"You didn't break the law," I said. "Mathran showed me the agreement Vey-Xanetha has with the Alliance. He was acting authority, since the police were dead…" I trailed off. I'd been far from thinking of the law when I'd gone after her. Maybe neither of us could be trusted to act rationally in the face of a situation like that.

"The mandate." She laughed hollowly. "Yeah. That really helped my homeworld. Enzar's authority figures are walking around slaughtering everyone over there." She rubbed her eyes. "Now I've just proven I'm no better."

"That's bullshit, Ada. You know it is." Anger on her behalf burned beneath the surface. We'd saved those kids, but how many more lives would be lost before we figured out what the god was doing? Giving up went against every instinct, but right now, my only weapon was powerless rage.

I struck the wall, hard. Sharp pain jolted in my knuckles and Ada flinched away from me.

That flinch undid me. I turned my back to check all the other doorway entrances were closed. "Go, Ada."

"Wait—Kay."

And the way she said my goddamned name. My jaw clenched, and I wondered how in hell I'd managed to let her get under my skin like this.

"Come on," I said, pacing to the doorway near the base.

The others were inside. "We have to figure out how to deal with this."

Veyak was clearly some kind of magic-creature, a super-powered version of the ones in the Passages. But pure magic didn't come out of nowhere. We were missing something. If Veyak had fixated on Ada, it clearly had to do with the level of power, tied to its source.

Veyak was a living source. I was almost sure of it. But how to prove it? If someone was controlling the deity, there was no way to tell *where* they were. Unless I searched every inch of the continent. And that was just one theory. The person—if they were a person—who'd opened the chasm might not even still be on this world, anyway. If lives really did have to be sacrificed to open it... but that couldn't be right either. I didn't know a whole lot about the theory behind doorways, but surely it'd have been on record if anything similar had happened on other high-magic worlds. Right?

Maybe I was headed in completely the wrong direction. But the thing I least wanted was for anyone to end up acci-dentally getting hurt or killed by this unstable magical force.

Looked like I had to make a new plan.

17

ADA

I headed for my room alone, fighting tears. Shock and horror warred within me. I'd channelled magic in a way I hadn't since I'd killed the Campbells, and this time, I'd...

Don't think about that. Not now. Not ever. I'd channelled one of the deities. I was sure of it. The heady rush of power, the way a voice had seemed to whisper in my ear... I'd never felt anything quite like it. But it was no deity. It was a natural magical force, like the force contained in my blood. It felt exactly the same. And there hadn't been any backlash. I must have absorbed it, except I hadn't fallen into a coma this time.

Whatever Kay had said, I knew beyond all shadow of a doubt he'd been as bothered by what those summoners did as I was. The look on his face when he'd seen those kids. *Oh, no.*

To distract myself, I tapped the earpiece.

"You around, Jeth?"

"Ada?" The voice definitely wasn't my brother. It was *Ms Weston.*

"Uhh…"

"I thought it would be wise to have a reliable way to contact you. Your brother generously donated this earpiece."

"Um." I had no idea of the time on Earth, but Ms Weston probably slept at Central. Unless she really was a cyborg.

"What happened?"

"Ah…" Dammit. She knew what I could do, she'd known all along. "I think," I said, hesitantly, "I might have accidentally channelled one of the deities. That's what the Vey-Xanethans seemed to believe, anyway."

A pause. "And do *you* believe this is true?"

"I'm sure those deities of theirs are like… magic with consciousness," I said. "Three of them, for some reason. I only channelled one of them, but it was like when magic was out of control, when the Campbells tried to…"

When I'd used third level magic, amplified to the max. Because I was no normal magic-wielder. Pure magic was in my blood. Was it the same here? Could I interact with the deity because the magic inside me matched the summoners of Veyak? Could the summoners have magic in their blood, too?

From what I'd learned, it couldn't be the same as mine— adamantine had been artificially put inside me, after all. The summoners were born with an affinity for magic. But magic lived in their blood. Maybe they didn't know that. Only a handful of Alliance worlds knew, and Vey-Xanetha had been cut off from that knowledge. Vey-Xanetha didn't have technology like the Alliance, or bloodrock, or any knowledge of the different types of sources. They could only use what they had. But that meant they were part of the source…

"Magic gained consciousness? An interesting theory."

"Is it more believable than living deities?" I countered. "I don't know what to think, but it was *dangerous*. Really dangerous. And I don't know if it's going to affect me again. Magic doesn't come with a rulebook," I added, echoing something else Kay had said to me once.

"No," she said, "I suppose it doesn't. You are certainly an unusual case, Ada. I would advise you to refrain from using magic again until you know where the problem lies."

"Right." Except I had the sinking feeling *we* were part of the problem. The way magic had reacted to me... it was like it consciously wanted me to kill those summoners. The anger wasn't all mine, and I wasn't sure I could fight it again.

Maybe it wasn't Kay she needed to worry about.

Maybe it was me.

~

KAY

I couldn't settle. Nor could I discuss my theories with the others. I paced the downstairs corridor, turning over the pendant I'd taken from the summoner in my hand. I didn't think Ada had noticed I'd picked it up. She'd disappeared upstairs wearing an expression that clearly said she wanted to be left alone. Not that I knew what to say.

Maybe she hadn't even noticed the summoners had been wearing the pendants, but I sure had, and when I'd picked one up, I'd seen the symbol for Veyak carved into it. So I'd brought it with me. Why, I didn't know, but Veyak's symbol kept appearing. The ground where those other summoners had died had been marked with the same symbol. And those were worshippers of Aktha. Was one deity killing off people who served the others, or did it just seem that way?

Or was Veyak *taking power* from the others, in the same way those magic-creatures fed on magic? If the deities were forces, powerful magical forces, it was a possibility. Of course. And I'd be a fool to ignore it.

So the balance had tipped. Aktha moved the continents, at least, I guessed it did, as the earth deity. Aktha had lost power first. Xanet... sustained life. And still functioned, but not enough for the police of that village to be able to stand up to the summoners.

Veyak was the deity of storms, weather... and power. Its symbol meant power, and magic itself *was* power. Somehow, on this world, people could channel it in other forms, through the other two deities.

But Veyak was unrestrained magic. Who knew, maybe it *had* been restrained, once, before whatever went wrong here.

Third level magic. I was almost certain it had to do with third level magic. Ada had used it, and a shadow had fallen over her. A familiar shadow. I knew where I'd seen it before —when Ada had used third level magic to take out the Campbells. When she'd drawn all that power into herself, and unleashed it. Even considering the state I'd been in at the time, it wasn't an image I'd forget in a hurry. But that cloud... hadn't looked like pure magic. Even though I'd been half-blinded by the glare when she'd unleashed that energy at the summoners, I'd been almost positive the shadow had looked familiar for another reason, too.

Like Veyak itself hovered over her.

Was Veyak... third level magic, but locked into a living form? Or had I jumped to the wrong conclusion entirely? I knew what I'd seen, but you could never entirely trust your own judgment as far as magic went.

One thing I *did* have to go by was the crater I'd seen through that doorway the summoners had opened. Everything had started with the chasm, according to the legends. A massive crater in the earth had to be a part of the reason everything had gone wrong here. But checking that out meant leaving the others, and going out into the storm.

I turned invisible, climbed out the window and dropped to the ground in front of the entrance, dodging another fork of lightning. Damn storm.

Running to the cliff wall, I used the world-key to open a doorway. Once in the Passages, I activated the tracker and concentrated on the magic trace I'd picked up from the summoner along with the pendant. I could amplify the tracker and use it to trace where the summoner had last been —right next to the chasm.

Using the signal as a pointer, I opened a doorway in the blank Passage wall. I'd expected it to take me to the place we'd killed the summoners, in the middle of the lifeless canyon.

Instead, the doorway opened into... nothingness. White fog obscured the view, and when I looked down, it was pretty clear no ground lay underneath it.

The edge of the chasm I'd seen through that doorway didn't lead to a gaping hole in the centre of the earth. There was just... nothing there. I thought I saw shapes moving on the other side, but it was too far away to see.

"Seriously, universe?" I muttered. Maybe I was hallucinating. Doorways couldn't lead *nowhere*. I might not know all the laws around creating doors, but I did know there had to be an anchor on the other side, which empty space just didn't have. I was no expert, but it must be to do with magic, and even on a world like Vey-Xanetha, magic couldn't anchor itself to a gaping hole in the universe.

There was clearly *something* on the other side, but from here, everything blurred, and I wasn't idiot enough to walk into the chasm. I hovered on the edge of the blue-lit corridor, leaning as far as I dared over the edge, and jerked back, heart beating fast. Even from here I knew there was no oxygen in there. The chasm definitely wasn't survivable. If I stepped over the edge, I'd have no way back.

"The hell?" I muttered. Was this the world-key's default setting? If it didn't anchor to one world, did it open into empty space? I couldn't even begin to figure it out. Unless...

I turned the world-key over in my hand. You needed a symbol to open a doorway to a certain world. So did that mean the signal wasn't coming from Vey-Xanetha, but somewhere else? A world I didn't know the symbol for?

How many people knew, anyway? The Conners had torn open a doorway directly between Valeria and Aglaia. But they'd also torn open doors to the Passages, too, to let the kimaros out.

Was *that* what caused this insanity? It hadn't been long since the attacks, and if the Conners had ripped the Multiverse itself apart, what if they'd done permanent damage? It didn't seem likely the council would have let that slide, even if they were pushing this whole situation onto Earth. If the whole Balance was concerned, they'd all have to get involved sooner or later.

I turned it over in my mind as I closed the doorway and went back to the base, climbing in the first-floor window again. I touched down on the landing, world-key still in my hand.

"Kay!" Ada jumped back. She must have been walking around the corridor. "What in the world were you doing?"

"Following traces."

"You went outside." She took a couple of uncertain steps towards me, her hand dropping from her ear. Had she been talking to her brother through the earpiece?

"Only for a second," I said. "I went in the Passages. I picked up a magic trace from those summoners when the magic was amplified, and I figured it'd take me to where they were hiding."

"Seriously?" Ada's eyes rounded. "You weren't planning to take them on alone!"

"No, I just wanted to check on that chasm. I didn't get a good look at it from the forest, but I figured they were somewhere nearby. But when I opened the door, there was nothing there. It was like empty space."

"Empty space?" Ada gaped at me.

"The trace from the summoner should have led back to Vey-Xanetha, but it didn't."

"Uh… you opened a door into a bottomless pit." Ada shook her head. "I don't think the storm's going to stop. If we wait, it might be too late. And if I channelled the deity once, maybe I can do it again. Maybe there's a way for me to talk to it, somehow."

That's what I'm afraid of.

"Yeah," I said. "The deity controls the storms, and he's seriously pissed off."

"The sky-god," said Ada. "The weather-god. That symbol keeps appearing. He's like a gigantic kimaros, like a living…"

"Source." I pulled a chain from my pocket, engraved with the same symbol. "I took this from one of the summoners. They were all wearing them, I think, and I can feel… some kind of magic. It's not friendly. I wouldn't try amplifying it."

"Good!" said Ada. "You can't go using your power on any unknown object you come across."

"Well, if I'm right, Veyak is pure magic, the magic in the atmosphere itself. You noticed how only the people who serve Xanet and Aktha have a physical difference in their appearance?"

She hesitated, then nodded. "The summoners of Veyak…

I thought about it, and I think they must have internal sources, if they can interact with magic itself."

"Yeah," I said. "I thought the others wouldn't be so quick to jump on board with that theory. On the surface, it looks like all magic is the same."

"But it isn't," said Ada. "What about the deities themselves, though? I've thought, and I can't tell what's supposed to be wrong with Veyak. If anything, he, it, whatever, seems *more* powerful, not less. Judging by what I felt." She shivered. "Did you feel it?"

"Yeah." I'd felt it, all right—felt anger that wasn't mine stir when she'd channelled the magic. "We need to figure this out. Maybe my amplifier can help."

"Just don't take unnecessary risks," she said.

I'd heard *that* one before. "You talked to the dragon."

"And managed not to get burned," she said, with a rather forced smile.

"Don't worry. I'm not planning on amplifying an already-pissed-off lightning deity."

"You think it's conscious, then? For sure?"

"Veyak's mark keeps appearing, of its own accord," I said. "Either there's an angry god out there murdering people, or someone's killing in Veyak's name. Either way, I'm intending to stop them."

This whole situation became odder and odder the more I thought about it. Why was Mathran the only person on Vey-Xanetha who seemed to have the slightest inclination to stop whatever was happening? The population was small, true, but they appeared intelligent. At least, Kevar and the others in the city were. They believed their deities were real because all the evidence was there, and they'd experienced it them-selves. Only those summoners had seemed out of it, and the way they'd acted had been unusual, even for this world.

Had the deity been *possessing* them? I'd thought I might

find some of the summoners when I'd followed the trace. Instead, it had led me to the abyss. A literal dead end. Still, when I thought of those gleaming red eyes, red like magic… the way magic acted like a living force in the Passages…

"Then I'm in," said Ada. "What's the plan?"

"Those spheres," I said. "If I can pick up a trace from the summoner's pendant, I reckon I can follow the trace from the spheres Mathran has. They were here when the Vey-Xanethans first came to this world. That's got to be a clue, right?"

"If you say so." Ada's forehead creased in doubt. "You said you won't amplify those sources."

"The tracker doesn't count."

She raised her eyebrows.

"It's true," I said. "I don't need to actually be touching a source to pick up the trace, just nearby. I can sense *your* magic right now. And the others'."

"You can?" Her hand twitched, like she wanted to see if it would transfer over to her.

"Yeah. This place amps up our magic-senses. I guess." I glanced downstairs, to check no one listened below. "All right. I'm gonna take those spheres. Can you divert their attention while I turn invisible and sneak in there?"

"You don't trust the others."

"I don't trust them not to stop us," I said. "And I don't want Mathran to know I can amplify the tracker. What he told us doesn't add up." I peered down the landing. "Come on."

I switched on the invisibility and slipped into the room, behind Ada. None of the others were even paying attention to the spheres, which lay on the table in the corner where Mathran had obviously left them after he'd shown us. No one turned around when we came in. They all watched the screen, which showed a series of glyphic images again.

While Ada struck up a brief conversation with the others, I crossed the room quickly and retrieved the three spheres from the corner, pocketing two of them. Then I returned to the empty meeting room, switching off the invisibility as soon as Ada came in and shut the door behind her.

"I don't know about this..." she said as I turned the sphere over.

Unconsciously, I'd picked Veyak. The metal buzzed against my hands. The trail of magic was easy to pick up on, and as I laid out the other two, I detected three signals. One considerably stronger than the others.

"Wait," I said, in a low voice. "I think they're all tied together, somehow. This one has the strongest signal." Veyak. Of course.

"What're you going to do? You can't go chasing after a random magic signal. And what about the Alliance's rules against taking offworld substances into the Passages?"

"Yeah, I know," I said. Taking the pendant was technically illegal, too. But I didn't want to leave it lying around in here.

"I can follow the signal without touching it," I said. "All right. You go and put those back in there. Just say you wanted to have a look, if they catch you."

"If you say so." She bit her lip, and her hands shook as they connected with Veyak's sphere. "This feels... wrong."

"I know," I said. "I hope we can sort this out soon."

And I felt like the biggest liar in the Multiverse, and like the deities themselves might strike me down for betraying her like this.

I didn't want to drag Ada after me. Even though she was on my side. She'd said she wanted to *know* me. And part of me froze in terror at the very idea. She knew I was a killer, but not the extent of it. She'd been born to secrecy, like me, but I'd never told anyone how fucked-up my life before the

Academy had been. Maybe even now, I physically couldn't. The words just weren't there.

Coward.

And I hated myself even more for lying to her. We had to stop Veyak, somehow, and letting emotions get in the way was the last thing I needed to do.

Which meant I had to try my last-ditch plan, and contact the deities. Alone.

Once she'd taken the spheres out of the room, I turned invisible, slipped around the corner and out the front door. Still following the signal, I crossed the doorway into the Passages and used the world-key to open another doorway, keeping at a distance.

But it didn't lead into the abyss. Instead, the doorway opened onto the canyon I'd seen from a distance through the other door in the jungle. The sides of the canyon climbed into the sky, and burnt red ground extended towards the horizon where it disappeared into fog.

Or, what I'd thought was the horizon. Up close, though, the fog-wreathed edge of the world stretched from one side of the canyon to the other. It didn't cover the whole conti-nent, and it wasn't a chasm, at all. It was another, giant doorway.

I stared for a moment, stunned. Someone had opened a doorway right here in the canyon, a good fifteen feet across. But it wasn't a hole in the centre of the universe. It looked like it led nowhere because the doorway was at a side-angle, and the world on the other side was wreathed in fog. But it must lead to another world. *Which world?*

The magic signal pulsed stronger. And it didn't come from the doorway itself, but from a spot to the right of it. An encampment had been set up, and figures moved around, too distant for me to see what they were doing.

I crept closer. All figures wore indistinct robes—the

summoners of Veyak came to mind immediately. And the signal was definitely Veyak. From here, I could still feel the three signals overlapping, and as the magic in the air heightened, it became clear Veyak's power emanated from the abyss—or the doorway.

The same place the other two signals disappeared. Through my almost-sixth-sense tuned into magic, the difference was so unmistakable I couldn't believe I'd never felt it before. From here, I could almost see the thin tendrils of power being drawn towards the abyss, at the same time as Veyak's power grew stronger, more heightened. To hold open a doorway like that, the world on the other side must be high-magic... or there must be a source nearby.

Walking into the middle of that camp wasn't the best option right now. But I'd planned to contact Veyak myself. Maybe...

I backed through my own door into the Passages again, and opened another one after closing the first. Thick jungle crowded the view. I closed the door and I opened another, repeatedly, until I found another part of the plain, out of sight of the group. The chasm was even closer from here. I must be on the other side of it. So it wasn't a hole in the middle of the earth but a doorway opened through Vey-Xanetha itself, connecting one source to another. From this side, a faint gleaming line divided it from the ground. The source must be there somewhere.

Maybe I could stop it.

Magic pulsed below the surface of the atmosphere, making my skin hum all over. When I tapped into it, the buzzing sense all but rushed towards me, lighting the world in red and violet.

The deity's presence flooded me. I gasped, eyes widening as light burned before my eyes, raging blood-red before it pulsed white, into colours the human eye couldn't see—

I couldn't control the magic pulsing to the heavens, vibrating in my bones. My mind blanked out. I was supposed to be doing something—to be...

A furious hum echoed through my head, a voice amplified, and not human. One word, over and over. And it came from my own mouth, too.

Veyak.

18

ADA

"Kay!" I shouted, throwing myself through the doorway. He stood outlined in red light, eyes black and gleaming. *Holy crap.* I'd seen him heading outside, but I hadn't thought he'd actually go after the god.

He didn't react when I called his name. In the sky overhead, lightning crackled, and each pulse brought a jolt of magic. Over and over, each bolt brighter, each jolt more intense.

A deep, horrible voice echoed in the back of my head, and at the same time, Kay said: *Veyak.*

Except it wasn't his voice. I took a step towards him, and the magic shook along with it.

There was so much magic here, the slightest movement disturbed it. Just like when the level had been out of control on Earth. The Balance...

Kay's hand raised, his eyes gleaming. Lightning surged down.

I threw myself at him, and my hands grabbed his as the

magic hit. I gasped, the world exploding in blinding white light, but I held on tight. *I'm adamantine, unbreakable. We can't break. Please!*

"Veyak," I gasped. "Stop!"

I blinked rapidly to clear my vision, not daring to let go of Kay's hands, hoping with everything I had that I'd got here in time to save him.

The ground trembled violently, knocking both of us off our feet. My back slammed into the ground and my hands dropped Kay's.

The whiteness cleared from my vision, penetrated by the red-purple haze ever-present here. And Kay…

He lay still. Eyes closed.

"No," I whispered. I shook him, hard. "Kay!"

His heartbeat fluttered against my hands, but though he was breathing, his eyes remained closed. Pure, ice-cold fear lodged itself in my heart.

"Kay, wake *up*!"

"Ow." He twitched one hand.

I fell off him with a shriek. "Holy shit, Kay. You're alive." And I collapsed onto my side, half-laughing, half-crying with relief.

"Whoa there," said Kay, his hand on my arm. "We should get out of here."

I shifted upright and hit him on the arm. "You total asshat," I said, swatting him with my other hand. "You moronic *imbecile!* You—"

"Save the insults for later." He pushed himself to his feet, not even flinching.

I joined him, placed my hands on his shoulders and looked into his eyes. They were clear, steady. "Are you sure you don't have a concussion?"

"Absolutely sure," he said, pulling away from me. "I didn't get knocked out, I just got dazzled for a bit. I'm fine."

"You scared me to *death!*" I spluttered, anger and relief warring within me. What the hell had he done, tried to *talk* to the deity?

"Come on." He moved towards the doorway to the Passages, and I followed, fuming.

Once in the Passages, he made to step through the door to the base, but I barred the way.

"I don't know what you were doing out there," I said, "but I *really* don't care for this martyr complex thing you've got going on."

"Martyr complex?" He frowned. "Ada, that's not what happened."

"Yeah? Could have fooled me. What the *hell* were you trying to prove? Or do you think your life doesn't matter? Maybe you do have a death wish."

Kay blinked, mouth pulled down in confusion. "I didn't know. I wanted to see where the deity's power was focused. I blacked out. What happened?"

"You said *Veyak.*" I shuddered. "And you were going to call on third level magic. You were totally out of it. I thought—"

"Damn," he said. "I'm sorry, Ada. I didn't know. I'm not about to die anytime soon."

"You are if you keep doing stupid things like that!" I glared at him. "You know what? I've changed my mind. I *don't* trust you. I don't trust you not to put your life on the line for some *stupid* reason—" I moved to hit him, but he didn't block me, and I ended up hugging him instead. I buried my head in the front of his jacket, breathed in the tangible scent of magic surrounding both of us and something underneath that, something uniquely him.

"Screw this," I muttered. "It's nearly the end of the world." And I kissed him.

Kay went completely still for a moment, then responded, kissing me back. Right then, lightning might have struck right next to us and I'd have hardly noticed. The heady combination of adrenaline and longing made me sway on my feet.

With difficulty, I broke away, flushed and breathless. "You're an idiot of the highest order. If we survive this, you're gonna get the lecture of a lifetime."

"I'll hold you to that," Kay said, in a similar condition, and half-smiled at me. "Right. I was going to head back to the base. Did you see the light around the chasm?"

"What?" I gave him an incredulous look. "Did you think I was looking at that? You almost died, you idiot."

"Okay, okay," he said. "I've seen it before. The chasm isn't this world at all. If it really was a gaping hole in the universe, there wouldn't be anything of Vey-Xanetha left."

"Well, what is it, then?"

"It's a doorway," he said. "Which means someone must have opened it. Where it leads, I've no idea. But that's no chasm. Someone's playing games with us."

"Yeah. I thought so. But the others… they don't know."

"We have to warn them," said Kay, and I heard the unspoken words, *before it's too late.*

KAY

At first, the base looked as we'd left it, the stone structure grown out of the cliff itself. Then a bone-shaking thud shook the ground as a huge chunk of rock fell from the building's side. Bronze rock-fragments already scattered across the cliff top.

No way.

Behind me, Ada gasped. "God, no."

"The others," I said, and sprinted through the doorway and uphill. *Damn.* Raj and Iriel had been there, with Mathran, and...

How could this have happened so fast?

That symbol—carved into the ground, splitting the stone, like it had been gouged there by a gigantic hand.

"Kay, wait!" Ada grabbed my arm, and I stopped as another piece of bronze rock fell, smashing to pieces less than a metre away from us.

"Shit," I said, backing out the doorway again. "Okay, Ada, you stay out the way. I'm going to try and stop it."

"The hell you are!" she yelled in my ear, over the sound of falling rubble.

"Trust me," I said, and pulled on the magic—not from Vey-Xanetha, but from the Passages. Ada stopped tugging my arm, understanding, and faced the rubble, too.

Magic from the Passages was wild, unrestrained by nature, but right now, I'd take that over a mad deity. I used the magic to pull on a piece of rock as it fell, so instead of crushing what remained of the building, it tumbled over the mountainside. I sensed Ada supporting me, too, her power adding to mine, which amplified it. The crumbling rock slowed enough for us to move pieces away from the danger zone. Sweat beaded on my forehead as the momentum rocked me on the spot, but I held my ground.

I didn't dare think it might already be too late.

Between us, Ada and I steadied the collapsing building, moved fragments of falling rock aside and onto safer ground. Just as abruptly as it had started, the tremor stopped.

Nothing remained of the base but a heap of rubble. The sky burned an angry red, clouds swirling low, and the ground felt unsteady under my feet. *They can't be dead. They can't be.*

Then I saw the limp hand peeking out from under the rubble.

Fuck. I ran over, and shoved the crumbling rock off... the body of the man who'd survived the attack on the summoners of Aktha. I didn't need to check for a pulse. His skull was caved in. But there were no signs of the others. I climbed over rock, shoving boulder-sized pieces aside, until I came to the remains of the computer room. The computer itself was reduced to a tangle of lifeless wires and crushed metal. But Mathran and the others were nowhere to be found.

A coughing sounded, and I whirled around. Ada stood, eyes wide, next to a heap of rubble. A clawed foot protruded from underneath.

"He's alive," she said, pushing at the rock. "I can't move this..."

I hurried over. The rock had crushed Avar's leg, but his eyes were open. A whimper escaped him.

"I... am truly sorry," whispered Avar. "They're gone—they took them."

"They?" I echoed.

Avar coughed, blood spattering the ground. "The summoners... I have to tell you something. Mathran told me, before he left. Veyak is a living shadow. Veyak is the shadow of magic gone horribly, horribly wrong. The worst. When someone uses magic past its limits, to kill."

"Third level?" I asked, heart beating fast.

"Yes. Every use of what you call third level... it casts a shadow. If enough power can be gathered in one vessel, then it continually builds up, feeding on all magic used in its presence."

"Because there's no backlash," I said. "But what do you mean by vessel? Not like a person, right?"

"Whatever animals the deities once were before magic enslaved them, I don't think they were ever human." Avar coughed again.

"Animals." Had *people,* the previous inhabitants of this world, stored the magic in living creatures, like in sources? Like—

Don't think about that now. No—he'd said the vessel continually fed on magic. So did that mean…?

"No backlash," I said. "Goddammit, I should have realised. Veyak feeds on *all* the backlash, not just third level. Whenever anyone uses magic. But when someone uses third level, it raises the magic level everywhere." Which meant every life sacrificed was more fuel for the angry deity.

"Holy shit," Ada whispered. "It has thousands of years' worth of power to feed on."

"Damn," I said. "But this happened recently. Right?"

Avar coughed uncontrollably, eyes glazed with pain. "They came here," he said hoarsely. "The summoners. They gathered a small power and opened a doorway. They came to this base, they demanded to see the carvings. And they took the spheres. To use as energy."

"To keep the doorway open." I remembered how the Conners had done the same in Aglaia. "The spheres Mathran showed us were fakes."

"Mathran told me he had no choice. I didn't know."

The lying old bastard could at least have given us a clue. Or maybe he had.

"The spheres—too unstable. You have to close the door. I couldn't…"

"Don't talk," said Ada. "We have to help him."

"I'll carry him through the doorway," I said, cursing the

Multiverse. "We have to find the others. If they were taken, I can follow the traces." *The summoners opened a doorway. They must have.*

"Shit!" I yelled, leaping aside as a heavy, feathery body dropped from the sky, three beaks snapping, claws slashing and tearing at the ground. I rolled over in the dust and pulled my dagger. One mad bird-head stabbed at Ada but she dodged and struck back with her own blade, sending a spray of blood over the rubble. The bird screeched and whirled around to meet the side of my dagger as I cut the tendon in one of its delicate wings, spinning to plunge the blade into the underside of its clawed foot.

Screams rent the air. The bird faltered back, landing on its non-injured foot in the ruins, and its sharp beak found the prone form of Avar. The magic level climbed, making my skin buzz so intensely I almost dropped the blade.

Damn. Clouds of magic roiled above and the presence of the deity pushed at me, insistent. I shook it aside and climbed over the rocks towards the bird, which tore at Avar's limp body.

"You stay away from him!" yelled Ada, running forwards before I could shout out a warning. The bird dropped Avar and stabbed at Ada with its bloodied beak, driving her back, towards the ledge.

Oh no, you don't. I drew my second dagger and hurled it at the bird, getting it in the eye. As the head slumped, Ada used the opportunity to gain the upper hand, driving the creature back with quick slashing motions. I climbed onto a heap of rubble, relying on Ada to keep both remaining heads busy while I sneaked up behind it. Balancing on a rock, I took aim, and threw my second weapon.

The dagger pierced it right through the spine.

The bird didn't die right away, but its legs gave out with a spasm. All three heads screamed deafeningly. I jumped down from the rock and retrieved the dagger as Ada stabbed one bird-head, then the other, putting it out of its misery. She pulled my dagger out of the third one's eye with a shaking hand. Blood soaked her face and hands, but her eyes were shining.

"I thought..." She swallowed. "I could feel him. Veyak. I didn't dare use magic."

"Me neither," I said. "Avar..."

The bird had torn one of his arms off, and he lay cold. Dead.

No time to waste. I searched below the surface for traces of magic and found more than one, tangled together around a spot not ten metres away. This must be where they opened the doorway. And I wasn't stupid enough to do the same. But the door to the Passages was open.

"Can—can you trace them?" She took my hand, after wiping the blood on her jacket. "God. That's..."

"Come on," I said. ""Might as well close the door here. There's nothing left now."

Lightning crackled overhead. A warning, or a sign.

Back in the Passages, I picked up the trace, and held onto it as I opened another doorway.

"You did a better job resisting the deity than I did," I said, sketching the last symbol. "If I get possessed, or whatever it was, like last time..."

"I won't let it happen again. Never."

I shook my head. She sounded so certain. How could she have faith in me, knowing what I'd done already? But self-delusion was all we had left at this point. Raj and Iriel might already be dead. And sacrificing magic-wielders... the whole Balance would feel the consequences.

"They're not dead," said Ada. "We'd have felt a power surge, I'm sure of it."

It had only been minutes, but I didn't dare hope. Hope

was too easily dashed to pieces. And this world's time was running out. If we didn't close that doorway, we'd die along with everyone else on Vey-Xanetha.

"Right." I let the door open slowly, despite the screaming urgency of the situation, to make sure we weren't going to run ourselves into a trap.

The plains. The encampment remained beside the abyss—no, the doorway. Clouds cloaked the world on the other side, but from here, I saw the slanted angle, and the gleaming ribbon of light around the edge. The source must be somewhere under there.

We had to get it out.

I froze. Three summoners passed b, dragging two people between them. Raj and Iriel. Mathran walked behind them.

"The traitorous bastard," I whispered.

One of the summoners stopped, shouted a warning—he'd spotted the doorway I'd opened. I swore and jumped over the threshold, releasing a bolt of magic right at the summoner. He dropped, convulsing. I'd hit him with second level. I didn't dare risk third.

As the other two approached, I grabbed for my dagger. Ada moved to my side, and I spun and pressed the world-key to the door, sealing it before any of this wild magic reached the Passages.

Climbing over their fallen brother, the two summoners said, in unison, "*Veyak.*"

Lightning speared the sky, and Ada and I moved to avoid it. Good job I'd closed the door, because a bolt of magic struck the ground on that exact spot. Who knew what effect it would have on a doorway?

Third level magic would kill either of us as surely as anyone else. We were magic-wielders, true, but also outnumbered, and it was pretty clear that deity was on no one's side. Like magic itself, amplified a hundredfold.

Better hope the Multiverse is on my side this time, I thought, as the summoners took one step forward in unison, then another. Completely under the control of the raging deity.

I held out my hand, Ada took it, and in unison, we raised our other palms to the sky.

19

ADA

I didn't even have a plan. I was half-terrified out of my mind, but we had to do our best for the others. The sight of Mathran on the enemy's side lit a fire in me. I wouldn't let anyone else die.

I let magic flow into the palm of my left hand, grasping Kay's with my right. Now we were both caught in an adamantine shield, and neither of us could be harmed by magic. As long as it held, maybe we could stand against the mad deity.

Lightning flashed above the summoners, meeting my own attack in a flare that lit up the sky. The two lights extinguished one another, but the summoners staggered back, rubbing their eyes. When they looked up, their eyes were blanked out and red. Like the others'.

"Veyak serves us," they hissed in terrifying unison, nothing human in their voices.

The deity possessed both of them. I was sure of it.

One summoner shouted in Vey-Xanethan to the others at the encampment, where some of them walked towards the chasm—or doorway. But more importantly, Raj and Iriel both lay unconscious on the ground, near Mathran.

The bastard. I gathered magic into my palm again, letting the level build higher. *Kill the traitor*, a voice whispered in my ear—a voice that didn't sound like me at all.

"Ada." Kay tugged my hand, jolting me back to the more present threat. The two magic-wielders staggered towards us, heads lolling, eyes vacant. Like puppets. Were they *dead?* Was the deity using them even now?

I redirected the magic at a spot in front of the summoners as Kay fired a shot of his own. The summoners walked right into it, and once again, the sky came alive in rays of violet and blood-red. This time, they fell, crumpling as if a hand had reached from the sky and struck them down.

Kay swore and stepped forward. Mathran had dragged Raj upright and held a knife to his throat. Raj's eyes fluttered, and he groaned.

"I cannot let you fight them," said Mathran, gripping the back of Raj's jacket. "I am truly sorry, but my loyalty always belongs to the trio. Even Veyak, whatever He has done."

"Even if your world is destroyed?" asked Kay, watching him steadily. I could tell by his stance that he was ready to fight, but didn't dare risk Raj's life. "You must know it's your own deity which is doing it. Veyak is absorbing the power of the other two, as well as the sacrifices of the summoners."

Mathran shook his head, the blade at Raj's neck trembling. "You have it wrong," he whispered. "Veyak would never seek to harm us."

"What about the evidence?" Kay indicated the fallen magic-wielders. "They were possessed by the deity themselves. They took your sources and opened the doorway. Avar told us. You can't hide from the truth, Mathran."

"Give it up." I pulled my hand free of Kay's and took

another step towards Mathran. "You've lost this fight. You're in the wrong. Let them go."

Mathran shook his head. "I will not." Blood beaded on Raj's neck. I stopped walking.

"We're both magic-wielders," I said desperately. "We can outclass you, Mathran."

"And you would risk your friend's life?"

"What do you want us to do? Leave?" *We can bring backup. We have the world-key.* But we'd have to move fast enough to outrun the possessed summoners and their crazy god, and the last thing we needed was that kind of power having free run of the Passages. That's what the Alliance guard part of me thought anyway—the other was more concerned with Raj and Iriel. Unless I got that knife away from him, we'd never make it out before he killed them.

Mathran's mouth twisted. "I can't have you telling our secrets to the Alliance. I am sorry, but you will serve Veyak."

Lightning crackled above. A warning. *Shit. Is he a vessel for Veyak, too?* Maybe everyone on this world was, seeing as Veyak was magic itself personified. Veyak was the wild craziness of magic in the Passages, tugging at my veins, demanding to be released, multiplied by a thousand. I shook my head, more certain than ever the voice whispering in my ear wasn't me. But out of the corner of my eye, Iriel moved, dragging herself to her feet behind Mathran.

"Magic's not stable!" I said. "As long as that doorway's open, this world's going to be in danger of tipping over the edge. Even with no Balance, your world won't survive it. You'll all die."

Crack. Mathran collapsed onto his face as Iriel delivered a kick to the back of his head.

"Ugh," she said, shuddering. "My head feels worse than a hangover from Aglaian wine. What did I miss?"

"The potential end of the world," said Kay, walking over

and nudging Mathran's body with his foot. "Out cold. Good shot. Except I'm pretty sure he was going to give us a clue."

Raj groaned, pushing himself up onto his elbows. "About those summoners?" He waved a hand vaguely towards the encampment.

None of the summoners had approached us, because they were fixated on the doorway. A small group approached the shimmering line dividing the chasm from the ground.

"Oh hell," I said. "If they sacrifice themselves, Veyak gains power."

"We have to knock them out first," said Kay. "If they're even alive."

With the others it had been hard to tell. *Kill them,* a voice whispered in my ear. The same voice had urged me to kill those other summoners, before. *Veyak.* The god didn't care *who* died. It just wanted death and destruction. Magic swarmed below my palms before I even called it—and stopped as it reached the hand I'd interlaced with Kay's.

His eyes widened. "Did you feel that?"

"Yeah. The deity's pissed off."

"I'll say it is," Raj murmured, sinking back to the ground. "What's with that chasm?"

"It's not a chasm," said Kay. "It's a doorway. Someone opened a doorway."

"To where?" asked Iriel.

"Not Earth." Raj scrambled back. "Oh, shit. Not those weirdos again."

I looked where he pointed, and saw a red, smoky shape moving from the doorway. Like an animal. *Animals,* Kay had said. So someone had put magic in a living creature. A conscious one? Considering the fury I'd felt—still felt—I'd say the creature was well aware of what had happened to it. And angry enough to take it out on every magic-wielder it could find.

"Kimaros," I said. "Shit. I knew they had something to do with this place."

It prowled like a cat, but that was where the similarities ended. Red smoke swirled, masking its pit-like shadowy eyes. Swearing in a language I recognised as Klathican, Iriel staggered towards it. She gathered magic in her palm, and a warning rose in my throat—too late.

The bolt reached its mark, to my surprise, without intervention from the god, but the kimaros split in two. Just like the one in London. Two smokelike monsters split to either side, circling our group. I moved forward, ready to attack, but the deity's presence pressed against me. Crap. Everything was unstable, and as long as it was, we had no chance of using magic to break down the kimaros like last time.

Magic surged high, again, the rising level prickling at my skin, vibrating in my bones. The whisper—more of a feeling than a whisper—promised me power, if only I'd unleash it. I shook my head angrily. I might not be able to out-magic the god—yet—but I wasn't about to let it break me like it did those summoners.

Speaking of… they'd divided into smaller groups. Two held another up between them and cut his throat. The summoner didn't even flinch before his life was extinguished.

And the kimaros grew, like it fed off the magic thick in the air. Both beasts dissolved into smoke and reformed as lion-sized creatures, blurring too quickly for me to get an opening to attack.

Raj pushed himself to his feet and shot a bolt of lightning at one of the beasts.

The beast divided, again, so now we faced *three* enemies. Three swirling smokelike clouds of rage. I could only assume Veyak hadn't struck Raj or Iriel down because it was more fixated on the summoners. Or on Kay and me.

"Well, that's bloody fantastic," said Raj, sinking to the ground, cross-eyed. "This is the way the world ends. Not with a bang but with a raging mad god hell-bent on destruction and his hellhounds of doom."

"That's one way of putting it," I said, glancing sideways at Kay... but he'd disappeared. *Crap.* Had he turned invisible? The deity had almost killed him already. Veyak had picked him as a target.

I couldn't it turn him into a puppet like those summoners.

I called on magic, abandoning all reason, but as the deity's power rushed towards me, it also swirled around the kimaros—all three of them. They grew even bigger, sparks flaring from their smoky skin, dark eyes gleaming.

They were pure magic, all right. They *were* Veyak. The deity was a living magic source.

We had to kill it. But if Veyak *was* magic, how could we...?

Swearing, I pulled on magic like I had last time, feet braced on the rock-hard soil. Hands clenched around the purple-red streams, I directed the magic, trying to force the creatures back into one form like I had on Earth. I'd rather face one super-powered deity than three.

The three kimaros hissed, switching from smoke-form to creatures once again. Raj backed closer to Iriel, who'd moved as far from Mathran's prone form as possible. Kay had reappeared and now stood in an attacking stance, and I could tell it was killing him to hold back—but he'd already seen what the deity could do to him. And every time we struck, the creature grew more powerful.

Except for me. I stepped forward, placing myself between the monster and the others—movement behind me told me Kay had caught onto my plan. My senses seemed to be in overdrive, enhanced by the magic—footfalls on the ground, the static noise of the creatures as they reformed around the energy swirling in the air, the shiver-like aftereffect of the magic we'd already used. Those whispers grew, engulfing my senses—taste, smell, touch—but Kay's hand on my arm steadied me back to reality. One look at his dilated pupils and I knew the god was having a similar effect on him.

A surge of determination rushed through me. I grabbed Kay's hand, so tight my nails dug into his palm. "Fight it, Kay," I whispered. "Fight it."

For us. I knew what I wanted, and it wasn't the power of a mad deity.

I reached out with my free hand, and tugged.

One kimaros tumbled into the other with a hissing screech. They dissolved in a yowling mess, but didn't disappear entirely. The third dived at me, but I hit back with the magical equivalent of a sucker-punch. Kay shook his head, coming to his senses in time to join me in another attack. Together, we pulled the magic from the two remaining creatures until they crashed into one another in an explosion of white light. White light. The magic had come from me, not from Veyak.

That's what I'd use to fight the deity.

Magic flared again, and at the same time, a figure dropped to the ground over by the doorway.

The summoners were sacrificing each other one by one, and as the latest fell, the kimaros roared.

The ground buckled under my feet, jerking me off-balance and knocking Kay's hand out of mine. The world flipped over, red sky flying towards me.

My back hit the ground. I bit back a scream as the impact jarred through my bones. Someone shouted my name. Kay. The world pieced itself back together in fragments—the blood-red sky, the misty cliffs behind the doorway, the magic-wielders heading that way, the kimaros now smaller and reduced to one shadowy body again, the bodies of the two summoners we'd killed lying near Mathran.

He wasn't unconscious. He clung onto the ground with both hands, grimly, and power surged from his skin and into the ground itself. The earth shook again, and the kimaros pushed back, even its insubstantial feet struggling to find balance. I pushed myself to my feet and nearly fell over again, the ground swaying and reforming in steep hills and plunging valleys.

Mathran must be using Aktha's power. He was helping us? Or maybe he'd realised if he didn't fight Veyak, we'd all die. Him included.

"Ada!" Kay ran towards me, aiming magic at the kimaros. His eyes flared black and a shadow fell over him. I choked on a warning, and the magic dissipated. He backed towards me, away from the beast.

"Veyak's making it impossible," he said, through clenched teeth. "All right. If I can't fight without provoking that deity, I'm going to have to go invisible and stop those crossing to the doorway."

"You can't," I said. "If run off without me, you won't be protected."

"Someone has to. The deity can't see me. When I turned invisible just a couple of minutes ago, it lost sight of me. I couldn't sense it anymore."

I stared. "You're kidding. The god couldn't *see* you..." My gaze drifted over the summoners. "Is it watching through *their* eyes?"

The deity had only attacked us when we'd been near the summoners. And when Kay had contacted it directly.

"Holy shit," I said. That explained why Veyak hadn't instantly struck us down as soon as we set foot on Vey-Xanetha. The deity was raging mad, but it could only sense us when we used magic to draw attention to ourselves, or when one of its puppets attacked us.

Did that mean—if we took out the summoners—we might have a chance of winning this?

I didn't dare consider the possibility that the fight could only end with the deaths of everyone on this world.

"Don't you dare get killed," I said to Kay.

"Wasn't planning to," he called, and only I caught the flash of fear in his expression before he turned his back. "Watch out for that deity." And he vanished, leaving a blurred impression on the magic in the air.

I turned back to Iriel and Raj to see them gaping wide-eyed at us.

"Tell me that wasn't the concussion," muttered Raj. "Did Kay just disappear?"

"It's a little complicated." I glanced up at the sky, which had returned to blood-red again. It really did seem like the god only appeared whenever one of us used magic. "And our friend is recovering."

The kimaros shook itself, trailing sparks. What Mathran did had affected it in some way. But it was part of Veyak, and I wasn't sure it *could* be killed. If Veyak was magic itself…

I reached for the magic, willing it to stay under control, and pushed at the kimaros. *Veyak, go away. I'm adamantine. You can't control me, and you have to stop!*

A shadow descended over my head and the lightning swallowed my scream.

20

KAY

I stared for a moment as Ada disappeared under a cloud of magic. That shadow again. I'd been dead right—Veyak and third level magic looked exactly the same.

The same shadow followed *me,* and the deity was closer to gaining power over me than the others.

But the other two gods were still alive. Mathran had channelled Aktha.

I couldn't worry about that now, not when the summoners were metres from the doorway, and on their feet again. Several seemed to have figured out what Mathran had done and were running towards him over the uneven ground.

Which meant the deity knew, too. And Ada and the others were over there.

But I had the element of surprise. I needed to stop the summoners and close the doorway, and right now, none of them had a clue I ran towards them, invisible—not daring to look back in case I lost it, ran to help Ada, and got myself killed.

A flash of lightning behind me told me another

summoner had died. There weren't many of them left. *Dammit, Veyak.* Sure, they'd walked into this, but the deity had manipulated them. Like it was trying to do to me.

If Ada wasn't here, it *would* have.

A glint caught my eyes from beneath the doorway. The three spheres had been placed at intervals

on the ground. They *were* holding the doorway open.

How to destroy pure magic sources without using magic? Ada could absorb magic to an extent, but this amount—it was like when the Campbells had used that bomb, surely too much for one person to contain, and Veyak was in the way. If I tried the same, I'd burn from the inside out.

The summoners turned around, as though sensing I was nearby. Shit. Maybe the deity could sense me after all, even though I was invisible. Or sense my magic. But I'd reached the first sphere. The heat pouring from it felt white-hot even from a distance. I crouched down, and immediately knew touching it would burn the skin off my hands.

Lightning flared above Ada again. *Hold off the damn magic force, Ada. If anyone can, it's you.*

A group approached the doorway, passing within a hair's breadth of me. I had seconds to make up my mind, and while I might not be able to use magic, I could stop them.

One blow brought down the first before the others realised something was wrong. I stabbed a second during the confusion, and though I missed the heart, the summoner fell immediately. They were effectively dead already, their lives burned out. *So why does Veyak want their sacrifice?*

Lightning flared up around the remaining two magic-wielders. The deity's presence pushed at me again, insistent and crushing. Being an amplifier probably aggravated it. *I don't need this.*

As magic flared, my hand appeared. Damn. The invisibility had worn off. The surviving summoners only needed to look up and they'd see me.

"Thanks a fucking lot," I snarled at the lightning flickering overhead, and prepared to face the two remaining opponents. But one had already slit the other's throat. I froze, eyes widening as he dragged his companion towards the chasm.

And a hand appeared from the fog behind the doorway, and dragged both men after it. A giant, stone-like hand.

I stared, the blood freezing to ice in my veins. What the hell was that thing?

What world was behind the door?

Veyak whispered in my ear, "I am as much a slave as you are, magic-wielder." No, the voice came from a summoner, the one I thought I'd killed. His head lifted slightly, but the gleam of red in his eyes was inhuman.

"You're not alive," I said, more to myself than anything, ignoring the voice of reason that posing existential questions to a mad deity wasn't going to end in my favour.

"You humans gave me life and consciousness. I feed on all, but I am the servant myself, magic-wielder." The summoner's head fell back, his eyes closing, as lightning flashed in the air above us again. I stepped back, and again, blinking rapidly, the deity's presence pushing against me like a pressure on my skull.

"No," I said. "I won't submit to you."

Something clamped around my legs. Swearing, I struggled forwards, but was snatched backwards again. My vision cleared, revealing a stonelike hand that held me, and it dragged me into darkness.

ADA

The lightning flared again, and this time, I pushed back. *Get away, Veyak.* I could feel the deity's rage, and Avar's words came back to me. Someone had shackled magic to a vessel. Not a human one. But I knew beyond all shadow of a doubt that though it might not be living in the usual sense, it was conscious. And angry.

A clap of thunder sounded behind and I whirled around to see smoke rising from somewhere in the distance, near the jungle.

"Stop that!" I shouted.

"It can't hear you, it's living magic!" Iriel barely kept her feet, and Raj all but clung to the ground, as though afraid it might throw him off.

Light flared across my vision again and despite myself, I found my eyes drawn to the doorway... which appeared bigger than before, filling the entire space between the canyon walls and blotting out the sky with white fog.

A gigantic, stone-like hand came from the mist beyond the door, pawing at the ground. Snatching at anyone who came near.

"Kay!" I shouted, running at the doorway, ignoring the others' shouts. Screaming his name, I ran full-pelt over the bumpy ground, paying no heed to the shadow rising behind me, and to the struggling, re-forming kimaros. A wall of energy knocked me off my feet in a flare of red lightning. I yelled, body convulsing.

Just as suddenly, it stopped. Gasping, I quickly checked for injuries. Nothing. I was pretty sure the third level shot would have killed anyone else.

The summoner who'd fired it marched towards me. I shakily stood up to face him. Undaunted by the shaking ground, the summoner watched me with those blanked-out, dark eyes. The mark of a powerful-magic-wielder.

Red smoke curled around him. *He's not really alive. Veyak's already killed him,* I told myself, ignoring my too-fast-beating heart, and calling magic of my own. Mine. Not Veyak's. I wouldn't let the god control me. Magic flowed through my fingers, building higher, and I let go as he fired a bolt of energy at me. I jumped out the way, the magic grazing my side in a shower of sparks and scorching another hole in the pitted ground. My own attack did likewise, missing the summoner as he dodged aside.

"Get out of my way," I said. *Kay.* He was on the other side of the doorway.

Smoke swirled around the summoner, enveloping the man in reddish-purple. He raised a hand and I dodged the attack, firing another of my own. I missed. *Damn.* Magic at a distance was too unwieldy, and too likely to hit the wrong target. I moved towards him, dropping into an attacking stance. If I could get him to keep still, maybe…

Not 'him'. He's not alive. Not alive.

I ran at him, firing magic at the ground in a diagonal pattern to drive him into my path. Tackling him, I took him by surprise and we both crashed to the ground, me pinning him in a perfect Alliance guard restraining position. His body shook all over, eyes gleaming red.

The kimaros charged at us. I pulled magic into my fingers, lightning flashed down from the sky, and I leaped back as it struck. His head hit the stone, unmoving. Dead.

And the kimaros charged at me, smoky feet blurring, pit-like eyes raging. Raj and Iriel attacked it from behind, but the bolts of magic they sent at it only seemed to fuel its rage. Raj moved slowly, injured, while Iriel's eyes flashed black and she cringed away, clearly aware the god was fighting for control.

It wanted us to be the next sacrifices.

Smoke struck me in a blast, sending me head over heels. My back hit the ground again, the world spinning. Dust filled my mouth and I coughed, turning onto my side. The momentum had carried me right next to the open door. *Kay.*

Another summoner approached. This one was armed with several of those arrow-like spears. I might not be able to die from magic, but I could be stabbed. Rolling to my feet, I took a step back, drawing my own weapon. But he was possessed by a deity, while I was only human, for all the magic I had. The whisper pressed against me again, insistent, angry.

A figure launched themselves at the summoner from behind, knocking him down. The two grappled on the ground, magic sparking.

Mathran?

Second level magic sent the old man flying back, but he hurled a spiked weapon at the summoner and brought him down. The possessed summoner stood, betraying no hint of pain or injury.

I couldn't breathe. I moved to enter the fight but the two had already clashed—the glint of a blade—and Mathran fell back on the ground, blood pooling from a wound in his chest.

The summoner was on the ground, too, crawling away, towards the door. "Die, magic-wielder," he hissed.

And the ground trembled. My last sight of Vey-Xanetha was of Iriel and Raj facing down the re-formed kimaros. A shot of guilt hit my heart, but it was too late to stop myself tumbling into another world.

21

KAY

Mist surrounded me on all sides. The hand held me loose enough to push myself upright, but I didn't dare jump until I saw what I'd be landing on.

Very good job, too. The mist cleared, revealing the ground... a fifty-foot-drop away. Marshy ground dotted with boulders.

Except the boulders weren't boulders, and the rock-like figure holding me was a bigger version of one of them. I knew which world I was on. One I'd never been on, though I'd come close enough in the lower levels of the Passages.

Cethrax was the world behind the door. And one of their kings held me in its hand. A giant head the size of a small car glared at me with wheel-sized black eyes. It was literally a colossal boulder, or an oversized version of the much milder mannered vox-kind that roamed around the lower levels of the Passages through Cethrax's many doorways. Its craggy face was offset by two curved horns the length of its head, its tusks at least five feet long.

Mother-fucker.

As unappealing as it was to be fifty feet off the ground in the hand of a giant stone monster, struggling would bring me a quick death. Cursing, trying to remember anything I'd picked up about negotiating with the vox-kind, I fought the instinct to panic. For one thing, there was nowhere to run, for obvious reasons. And on the other side of the white fog above, Vey-Xanetha lay out of reach, rampaging gods and all.

The shifting sensation beneath me was a jarring reminder that a very different kind of giant might drop me at any moment. I had only one way to get back to the doorway: magic.

No time to question. I shifted in the giant's hand and aimed a second level shot at the ground, enough to propel me up and through the doorway.

The giant's other hand moved to block it. *Shit.* I'd forgotten higher vox-kind had naturally magic-proof armour. Not enough to block third level—but I couldn't access that here.

Here, I was prey.

"Do not try it, human," hissed the Vox... in English. I'd forgotten how fucking clever they were. Though as far as Voxes went, they didn't usually need a translator to interpret the screams of any unlucky humans they caught straying into their swampland.

But nobody ever said I was sensible. "Who opened that doorway?" I demanded, fairly certain I'd join those unfortunate humans in a second.

"Magic-wielder," said the giant. "You are not a native of the Veyak."

"No, I'm from Earth," I said. "And your world has a treaty with the Alliance." I pulled out my communicator as a last resort, flicking the touch screen to show the Alliance's logo. Though Cethrax might hate the Alliance, their world was far outnumbered and they knew how swiftly the Alliance could retaliate if they provoked an attack by killing an Ambassador. Not that I really wanted to set an example.

The Vox hissed, but said nothing. Its hand shifted beneath me and for a heart-stopping moment, I thought that was it for me.

"Did you open the doorway?" I asked, putting my communicator away before I dropped it. My hands shook from the adrenaline. *Fuck me. I'm actually going to die on Cethrax.*

It gave a rumbling laugh. I hung onto the side of one of its gigantic fingers, swearing in seven languages. Including Cethraxian. The only words I knew in that crude language were curses, of which there was an abundance.

"I am the guard of the doorway, magic-wielder."

I stared. I hadn't expected an answer. I should be dead already, crushed in its hand or a snack for its servants fifty feet below. It hadn't killed me. And... the Vox wasn't just sitting here. Heavy metal chains covered its tree-trunk-sized legs, weighing it down, and it sat in a permanent crouch. *How* in the hell had that happened? Had something even more powerful chained it down?

"I am the guard, magic-wielder, and the commander of Veyak."

"On whose orders? Who opened the doorway?"

"My master."

That's helpful. Employing sarcasm against a fifty-foot giant wasn't the best plan, but urgency and fear for the others in Vey-Xanetha made it difficult to think clearly. It hadn't killed me already... and it was a prisoner itself. Which meant —no. Had the Vey-Xanethan people migrated from *Cethrax?* There *had* been people living there, a long time ago—that was why the Cethraxians retained a few characteristics which seemed oddly human compared to their otherwise brutish way of life, and they had technology they themselves didn't know what to do with. Nobody ever wanted to get close to the swamp and find out, for obvious reasons.

The humans were slaves and playthings of monsters. It actually made sense. The magic-wielders had combined their power together to open the doorway, the chasm. And the Cethraxian shadow-monsters were *remarkably* similar to the kimaros. I couldn't believe I'd never thought of it before.

"If you're not going to kill me, let me go back." I pointed to the doorway.

"You have trespassed here, magic-wielder."

Damn. I'd forgotten, of course, given the number of thick-headed foot-soldiers and idiot pain-tripping chalder voxes I'd fought, that Cethrax's leaders were far more intelligent. It had actually proven an evolutionary advantage, even if they only used their brains to decide how best to kill trespassers.

"Fine. What does your master want with Vey-Xanetha?"

"Sources," hissed the Vox. "I do not pretend to understand the whims of magic-wielders, but he was very insistent. The force known as Veyak can transfer power through the doorway."

Its master is a magic-wielder?

"So this master of yours is here?" Or *a source?* The god's power must be going somewhere.

"If he were, you would be dead, magic-wielder. He has already killed three of my brothers. I am the single remaining Vox in the Janx territory, by the undergods of—" The name came out as unpronounceable gibberish.

"Great," I said, caution fading. "So there's a mysterious magic-wielder who's using *you* to enslave Veyak, a living deity?"

Another rumbling laugh shook the world and I came close to dropping my communicator.

"Veyak is no deity, magic-wielder," said the Vox. "Veyak is power given life, power chained to a living creature from the rage of ancient magic-wielders. But Veyak will die along with the rest of its world, as will the other magic-creatures formed from its strength."

If Veyak was a source, it couldn't be draining the other deities at all. Which meant they were losing power because of the doorway, because that power was being drawn here, along with all other magic on Vey-Xanetha.

"Power chained to a living creature," I said slowly. "*Which* creature?" Stupid question. But that seemed to contradict everything I knew about magic.

"That is not for me to say, human." The Vox bared its teeth in a grin.

"Why *this* world? Why risk destroying yourselves?" I was sure the destruction would continue through the doorway if it carried on, especially with Cethrax's magic levels being amplified by Veyak.

"This one is the only high source we could reach. It is true there are many worlds with worthy sources, but most have burned out or are closed off even to us. Enzar. Thairon."

Those two words hit me like a double punch. The first, Enzar, I knew to be closed-off aside from the refugee tunnels... while Thairon was temporarily locked off from the Alliance, and had been so for five years. Since my father had left to negotiate with their council following a series of wars and attacks on the Alliance. And the deaths of several Ambassadors, including my mother.

I hadn't known there was a source on that world. I couldn't have, of course. But the idea of Cethrax taking an interest in that place... *and* Enzar?

"Why did they need you to guard the door?" I asked, keeping my expression as blank as I could under the circumstances. "Why Cethrax?" It had no sources, which was why those dreyverns had stolen bloodrock. They'd worked for the Campbells, then the Conners...

A chill went down my spine. Was someone else involved? This *master?*

"I am their shield," said the monster.

I swore under my breath. The Vox's skin was resilient to magic, which meant if Vey-Xanetha did destroy itself, the giant was chained in the way of the open door so the residual magic would hit the Vox. Even if Cethrax's king was destroyed in the process, Cethrax itself would be spared.

"The master promised to leave your world alone," I said. "Right?"

The giant bowed its massive head, and my heart sank. So it was true. Something could bend the will of the kings of one of the most dangerous worlds in the Multiverse.

How long had this been going on for? Far longer than Mathran had said, surely. But if the Alliance hadn't known, how had something like this stayed hidden?

"Let me go back," I said. "I can stop Veyak." I was less sure by the second, but the giant didn't need to know. Besides, if Veyak really was a living source, perhaps Ada and I could stop it. Perhaps...

The doorway above lit up with white light, and a body fell through, tumbling head over heels. A redheaded woman—in guard uniform.

"Ada!" I shouted, and ignoring all caution, pulled on magic, willing it to slow her down. But the Vox's hand had already moved to catch her, sending her tumbling into me.

"Kay," she gasped, then saw the drop and screamed. "Holy *shit!*"

"Hang on, Ada," I said.

"Did you think I'd let go?" She grabbed my arm with one hand, her nails digging in. "Oh... my... god. Tell me this isn't what I think it is."

"Apparently, Cethrax is in control of this doorway. But they're acting on other orders."

"God." Ada stared at the giant's face as it examined her. Terrified gasping noises escaped, but I was kind of impressed she didn't flip out and scream again.

"It's all right," I said. "I'll get us out of here."

"Seriously?" Her voice rose in pitch. "You'd better have something good to say, Kay Walker. I'm gonna scream in five seconds."

"Look," I said, pointing down at the chains. "It's trapped, same as us. Its master has it here as a shield to absorb the backlash once Veyak destroys Vey-Xanetha, but there's some kind of source they're charging..." I trailed off, while Ada breathed quickly, her eyes wide.

How to get out of this one? Whoever the Vox's master was, they were powerful. But as long as that doorway remained open, the Balance was at risk. Back in Vey-Xanetha, Veyak still rampaged, and the power flowed into Cethrax—no wonder the magic level was higher than it should be.

"It's talking to you," said Ada, half-hysterically. "Tell me I'm not going crazy here."

"We'll set you free if you let us go back through the door," I said to the Vox. Negotiating with one of Cethrax's leaders? Definitely not a job for newer Ambassadors. Or anyone with a lick of sense. Even the council didn't set foot in the place without signing a half-dozen agreements that nobody would murder one another in negotiations. It didn't always end well.

"You cannot break the chains," said the Vox.

"What are they?" I asked. "Adamantine? I think we can." I turned to Ada, who gaped at me in shock. "Sorry about this," I said. "We'll get out. Can you break the chains?"

"If I could I'd have easily escaped the cuffs when you arrested me." She gripped my arm convulsively. "Oh... my... gods."

"Tell me about it." I didn't dare use the world-key, and that wouldn't solve this. The Vox's imprisonment should have provoked a war across this district of Cethrax, which made me all the more certain this was a seriously powerful magic-wielder at work. But the problem at hand lay overhead. Veyak.

"All right," said Ada. Her hand locked onto mine. "If you can amplify anything…" She stopped, trembling, her gaze darting to the giant's stone face.

"I can," I said, "and you can do this."

"Nobody can break the chains," the Vox said.

"Veyak can," I said, and squeezed Ada's hand. Magic exploded in the air, glancing off the Vox's skin. I grabbed hold of the magic and pushed the level higher. The Vox shook its head, but I ignored it. *Veyak.* The energy came through the doorway, from Vey-Xanetha.

I could amplify that, too.

I reached with my other hand, to the doorway I couldn't quite reach, and pulled.

White lightning sparked and Veyak's voice echoed in my ears, enraged—but it couldn't stop me here. Not on this side of the doorway. The world turned white, Ada's hand gripping mine the only solid thing in existence. The white blaze obscured my vision.

Crack.

"Holy hell," Ada whispered in my ear.

My sight cleared. The stone giant stared at me, its pit-like eyes even wider. I moved to peer over the edge of its hand.

"Did we—?"

"Yeah," she said.

The Vox shifted again, kicking aside the remains of the chains. We'd actually broken whatever its master had used to chain it. Metal pieces scattered on the swampland below, amongst the boulder-like forms of the smaller vox-kind.

There'll be hell to pay for this.

"I told you," I said to the Vox. "Let us go back. We'll close the doorway. You won't have to stay here anymore."

"It is too late for that, magic-wielder," said the Vox.

For a moment, I thought it'd go back on its word and swallow us whole. But the giant stood, causing a small quake under our feet, and lifted us up. Ada clung to my side as the Vox placed us through the doorway to Vey-Xanetha.

Mist swirled around us, revealing a sea of dead bodies. The summoners lay scattered on the ground. None of them moved.

We *had* to close that doorway. Now.

The deity's presence pushed against me, the whispers coming back

"Go to hell," I said.

22

ADA

I staggered on the ground, hanging onto Kay as the giant's hand put both of us down. My head spun, my entire body trembling with the adrenaline and the rush of magic in the atmosphere. If not for Kay's presence at my side, I'd have dismissed the whole thing as a whacked-out hallucination. From the deity, maybe. But the doorway remained, shimmering behind us. And around us... blood stained the cracked earth.

"Hell." I stared around at the carnage. Most of the summoners were dead. Which meant Veyak was even stronger. Just ahead, Raj and Iriel fought against the kimaros with magic. *It's still alive?* But then, it was part of Veyak. Maybe it couldn't be killed. And it had driven the other Ambassadors right up close to the doorway.

No way. I ran towards them, firing a bolt of magic at the kimaros's back. I was certain it was the main manifestation of Veyak. If I could take it down—

The white lightning broke apart before it could hit. Crap. Looked like the creature was too strong for normal magic to affect it. Living backlash kept growing, kept gathering power. Power I felt in my own blood, under my skin. Those whispers. The beast's anger had grown as we'd defied it, and now it was furious enough to topple worlds.

I looked back at Kay, and my blood turned to ice. He stood vacantly staring into space. Smoke curled around him, red and sparking. Like the summoners.

The god had possessed him.

"No!" I shouted, torn in two. The kimaros renewed its attack on the others, and Raj collapsed in a heap on the ground. Iriel staggered to the side, barely able to stay on her feet. Magic sparked around her hand, but disappeared almost instantly.

"Veyak!" I shouted. "Stop! We're not your enemies."

The kimaros sent a shower of sparks into the air and spun to face me in a haze of swirling smoke.

"Let him go," I said. "You don't have to do this…"

The beast leaped at me, purple-red magic flaring around it.

I struck back with magic of my own, the hairs lifting on my arms, but again—my attack dissipated, absorbed into the beast. *How* could I possibly win?

Kay. I ran to him, grabbed his hand. "Please snap out of it."

I reached for the magic below the surface, the rage of Veyak. The charge built higher, making my teeth rattle in my head. Kay shifted forwards, and the gleam went out of his eyes. He shook his head. "Ada…"

"I'm not gonna let go of you until that deity's gone," I said, fiercely.

A bolt of lightning descended, and the world exploded in white.

Kay called my name again. I shook my head, my ears ringing. Somehow, my hand was still clenched around his.

The kimaros appeared again in a cloud of smoke, swirling

around our interlinked hands. I gasped and let go, and Kay swore, striking the beast with magic. The lightning rebounded, multiplying in two, three. I reached to the sky and the bolts sparked from my hands.

Holding onto the strands of lightning like ropes, I faced down the malevolent, snarling cloud. Veyak. It was like a king-sized kimaros, more force than monster, with the wicked hand of magic as the deadliest weapon. We had seconds before it obliterated one of us. It had hit us with third level magic once already, and if we hadn't been touching...

No. I felt Kay's amplifier supporting me, driving the monster back. But still not enough.

The sources were right there, the three spheres lying unprotected by the bodies of the fallen summoners. When the Vox had put us back down, it had knocked them out from under the doorway. If only there was a way to touch them without causing more damage.

Lightning burst overhead, and this time, there was no avoiding it. The ground shook, and I yelled, knocked off my feet again. Kay stood still, a shadow behind him. Veyak was back. I swore and jumped to my feet, bracing myself as the ground buckled again. Not an earthquake, not natural. Nor the deity.

Not *that* deity.

A hand grabbed my ankle. Mathran. I recoiled away from his grasping fingers—I'd thought he was dead.

"I am sorry," he whispered. "I have done such wrong—please, take what I have left. You... can absorb magic, can you not?"

I nodded. The amount of blood pouring from the wound in his chest told me he'd be dead in a minute. Magic took over, surging through my body, and to the earth. Aktha's power. I could absorb it directly from Mathran, because he was a source himself.

I sent another wave of magic downwards, at the red-scorched ground. I dug my heels in, but couldn't keep from staggering sideways. The earth trembled again and a crack appeared on the surface, a few metres away. I moved my hand and the crack spread, deepening, cutting into the dry soil. A wild force rose inside me and I trembled along with the world under my feet. I had to get control over this—had to aim the magic where it counted.

I splayed my hand and sent a bolt of energy at the ground, right beside the spheres. They trembled on the edge of the new crater I'd created, then toppled over, one at a time. I let the power surge widen and the chasm deepened, pulling the spheres along with it.

I let go. The two sides of the earth slammed into one another, and the spheres were swallowed up entirely.

And the fog-shrouded doorway winked out of existence, the kimaros dissipating, leaving the bare red ground of the canyon, and the clearing sky.

23

KAY

The calm hit harder than the rage, making me stumble over the already-unsteady ground. The light cleared from my vision and I could see the canyon again. There was no doorway, but barren, burnt-red ground, stretching towards the horizon. No voice whispered in my ear. Nothing but silence, and the light dimmed enough for me to see Ada. Relief knocked the rest of the deity's influence away from me.

She was alive.

And she'd closed the doorway. No one else could have done it. A crack spread across the middle of the ground but was already closing, two sides slamming together with a reverberation that shook the earth. I braced myself for a hit that never came, because the quaking ground calmed, and Ada bent over the body at her feet and spoke to—Mathran.

Raj and Iriel lay unharmed, though dazed-looking. The bodies of the fallen summoners surrounded the area where the doorway had been open. But I could no more turn away from Ada than I could make my own heart stop beating. *She's alive. She's alive.*

"Kay!" She stood, unsteadily, as I reached her, and threw her arms around me. "You're alive. Thank god."

"Not that god."

She laughed shakily. For a moment, I held onto her, feeling her own racing heartbeat alongside my own.

"We're still here," Raj shouted. "And I'm pretty sure I have a concussion."

"I think he's exaggerating," said Iriel, though she winced as she stood up. "Ow. Please tell me it's gone for good."

"Yeah." Ada pulled back from me and nodded to the space where the doorway had been open. "The spheres are gone, and they were fuelling the doorway. Now it's closed…"

"I can't feel Veyak." I scanned the area. Dead summoners, and scorched ground. Nothing more remained. The spheres had been swallowed by the earth.

"Damn," said Raj. "Is someone going to explain what happened?"

"I can try," I said, with a glance at Ada. "But to be honest, I'm not completely sure on some of it."

"Not here," said Iriel. "You have the world-key?"

"Yeah." We'd have to explain this one to the council ourselves, and who would believe it? Only Ada and I had been to Cethrax, and seen the monster enslaved. This was magic beyond any I'd heard of.

Later, I thought, taking hold of the world-key. I was far too tired to check the magic level was normal, or if it ever would be. That doorway might have drained half the magic from this world. There needed to be an inquiry, maybe even from the council… my head spun with it. *Later,* I told myself, again, using the world-key to open a doorway to the Passages.

∾

ADA

First, we needed proof the deity's rampage had stopped else-where in the world. Kay quickly opened a doorway to below the tree-city, which looked no different to the last time we'd been here, except nobody climbed amongst the trees. But when we moved directly below the tower, the sight of people moving inside it made relief flood me. They were alive. We owed them an explanation, but first, we had to check the base.

"We can't leave evidence here," said Kay, when we stood before the rubble, all that remained of the bronze stone building. "We'll need the fake spheres as proof for the coun-cil." The real ones, of course, had gone.

"This feels wrong," said Iriel, shaking her head at the ruins. "But these materials belong to the Alliance. They'll want to strip down the place anyway—look for any evidence. We're deep in the shit when we get back."

"Tell me about it," Raj murmured, rubbing his head. "Are our bags and stuff in there, too? The tech we were using?"

"Yeah," said Iriel. "Anything unbreakable survived."

Unbreakable. I bit my lip at the word. For someone who was supposed to be unbreakable, I'd come awfully close to dying out there. We all had.

I half-heartedly climbed over the ruins to search out anything I might have dropped. I still wore the earpiece, though I'd forgotten I did. Kay and I tried to explain it all to the others, as best we could. Raj and Iriel could accept the two of us weren't normal magic-wielders—like they hadn't figured it out already. Cethrax was the part which made them exchange raised eyebrows. Anything might have been on the other side of the chasm, but an imprisoned giant was way down the list of likely things. Cethrax didn't make deals with other worlds. And I'd thought the Vox was nigh on invincible.

Everyone else had thought that, too. Something—or someone—had wanted to use Vey-Xanetha's magic source. Wanted it badly enough to risk Cethrax's wrath.

"The council knows who the Alliance's enemies are." Kay closed the doorway on Vey-Xanetha for the last time. "They should have some clue. Unless it's... no. I'll think on it." He checked his communicator. "It's six. Ms Weston will still be around at Central."

Raj groaned. "I'm concussed. And tired. And starving. I can't handle an interrogation."

"You're not concussed," said Iriel. "But you have a point. We aren't *technically* supposed to go and report until tomorrow."

"I'm pretty sure they think we're dead," said Kay. "Come on. Let's check on the evening guard, at least."

We walked through the Passages in silence. I half expected hordes of Cethrax's monsters to be waiting, and kept glancing over my shoulder as we passed the stairs to the lower levels, but even the noise from the main Passage seemed to have died down. Hopefully that would be the end of the magic-related chaos on Earth. That'd be a relief to the Complaints Division. Maybe Nell would get some peace from the people asking her for help, too. I checked my communicator, but it was stuck on "no signal." The thing was pretty resilient considering I'd had it in my pocket the whole time we'd been on Vey-Xanetha.

Carl waited around the corner. "You're alive," he said. "Weston's been trying to contact you for hours." He looked tired, but the magic burn mark on his face appeared to have faded slightly.

"Told you so." Kay rolled his eyes. "Yeah. It's a long story. Is Ms Weston around?"

Carl's eyes narrowed. "I hope it's a good story, because Central detected some erratic use of a world-key. Wouldn't have anything to do with you, Kay, would it?"

"Not all of it," said Kay. "In fact, keep an eye out in here. Has Cethrax made any more trouble?"

"Cethrax?" Carl blinked. "Not that I know of. Been pretty quiet..."

"That's not right," Kay muttered, echoing my thoughts. Maybe not, but I was too tired to think about Cethrax now.

"What's that?" said Raj. "Come on. You're the one who wants to drag us back to Central. We nearly died," he added to Carl.

"He got hit on the head," said Iriel, in explanation.

We really did nearly die.

I couldn't take my eyes off Kay, but held back, aware of the others. We had some serious explaining to do to Ms Weston.

Late evening found us at the Blind Wyvern, of all places. I'd tried to call Jeth but my communicator's signal was scrambled from Vey-Xanetha. I'd left a message instead, and another for Nell. She was over at the Knights' place again, along with Alber, dealing with the latest in the chaos the rising magic level had caused. I'd dashed home to quickly shower and change out of my dust-stained, battered uniform, impulsively packing an overnight bag. I wanted my family, of course, but I didn't want to leave Kay yet.

If Iriel and Raj noticed we were sitting close together at the pub, they didn't comment. After another interrogation from the dragon, all we wanted was a decent meal and sleep. Though I didn't particularly look forward to more nightmares. The good news, though, was that Vey-Xanetha's magic levels were reported as back to normal. Ms Weston had finally contacted Kevar at the research base. And Earth was back to the way it should be—magic-free.

"Okay, I'm done," said Raj, standing up.

"Me too," said Iriel, wearily. "Are you two staying?"

Kay shook his head. "Ada, you should go home."

"Don't start lecturing me," I muttered, stifling a yawn. "In fact—that reminds me. I owe *you* a lecture."

"Huh? Now?"

I pretended to debate as Raj and Iriel left, though my heart beat fast. This was it. Our brush with death had swept away all doubt. "At your apartment."

His eyebrows shot up.

"It's not far from here, is it?"

He shook his head. "Your call."

I couldn't read his expression. And he didn't say anything as we walked through London. The cold night air, the gleaming lights of buildings and cars—it was all so surreal. My pulse raced. I didn't want to lose this. Not ever.

I didn't want to lose *him*.

Four flights of stairs were murder after the day I'd had, but I followed Kay into his room with no hesitation. He threw his jacket over a chair and set his communicator down on the desk. Unlike last time I'd been here, there weren't any boxes stacked in the corners and the punch bag was properly set up, though the room was still ridiculously neat. I hardly noticed, though, because my heart drummed with nerves and my pulse raced. *Get it together, Ada. You want this*. And I did. I shut the door behind me with a snap, making him turn around, startled.

"I'm not having you disappear on me again, whichever

universe might need saving. And that means *literally* disappearing, too."

"All right." He rolled his eyes. "Hit me."

"For one thing," I said. "What were you thinking when you ran after Veyak? You didn't even tell me you were going."

"I was going to be quick. I didn't mean to scare you like that."

"That's not the point," I said. "You keep rushing into danger without considering what it does to other people. What would you do if *I* ran up against a mad god without thinking?"

Kay shook his head. "Ada, that's not—"

"Not the same?" I crossed my arms. "Why shouldn't it be? Either you have a death wish, or you think your life isn't worth anything. You think no one would care, is that it? Well, I care, Kay. I care." I ducked my head, feeling myself blush bright red. "For what it's worth."

For the first time, I'd shocked him into total, slack-jawed silence. I thought he wasn't going to respond at all, and I backed towards the door. That's what I got for speaking my damn mind.

"Everything." One word, so quiet I barely heard it.

I stopped, inches from the door. "Huh?"

"You said, for what it's worth." He looked me in the eyes. "Everything."

I swore my heart stopped beating.

He just said that.

No way.

And now I was the one staring in disbelief. "You… really…" *Remember how to speak English, Ada.* "You could have fooled me. I thought you were a goner back then."

"Guess we got lucky. Reckon I've used up my good luck quota by now."

"Hmm." I moved several paces towards him. "I beg to differ."

His mouth curled up on one side. "Seriously?"

"Seriously." I moved forward until we were barely a metre apart, my heart fluttering in my fingertips. "Do I have to spell it out to you? I want you, and I won't stay away from you."

"What a pity," he said, giving me a slow, crooked grin. "And there I was, thinking I was shot of you."

"Tough," I said. "And by the way, I'll have you know I'm aware of several ways to kill a man with my bare hands."

And I placed said hands on his forearms, wrapping him into an embrace.

His lips brushed my ear. "Then it's a good thing I have a death wish."

He kissed me. Heat rushed through my body, and I let my jacket fall to the floor—though I had an inkling I'd need to retrieve something from the pocket very soon. I pressed myself against him until he broke the kiss with a groan —"*God,* Ada"—and my fingers found the hem of his shirt and tugged. He pulled it over his head in one swift motion, and I did the same, whipping my top off so fast my hair tangled in it. Both of us were breathing heavily. His eyes roamed over me, head to toe, and his hand left goosebumps where he brushed my cheek, my neck.

Then we were mouth on mouth, skin on skin, shedding the rest of our clothes as he steered me back onto the bed. We explored one another, slowly at first, the intensity building as his hands wandered south until I gasped his name. We came together in a rush of heat and need, like a flame kindled to life.

24

KAY

I lay still, not wanting to wake Ada. Almost afraid she'd disappear if I looked the other way.

Almost afraid I'd imagined the past few hours. Though imagination was no substitute for reality. Not with Ada. I listened to her steady breathing, breathed in the sweet-scented shampoo on her hair. I reached out, ran my fingers through it. Ada shifted, turning her head to blink at me. "You're still here?"

"Why wouldn't I be?"

She smiled, moving closer into my arms. "I thought I might be dreaming. It'd be a lot nicer than my usual dreams."

"Hmm." I closed my eyes for a brief moment. I'd lucked out and snatched a handful of hours' sleep before my subconscious had decided to replay the moment when lightning had pierced the sky and I'd almost lost her. A dozen bruises from the fight reminded me of their presence, but it could have been much worse. We'd been lucky. Really lucky.

And yet, I swore I'd overlooked something crucial. I checked the time on my communicator. Six a.m. We didn't have to be in work for a couple of hours, but I grabbed my clothes.

"What are you thinking?" asked Ada, as I started to pace the room. "You're trying to figure out who had control over that doorway, aren't you?"

"How'd you guess?"

"Because you can't stand not being able to solve a problem."

I had to smile. "I suppose. Come on, though. I can't believe the dragon just let that one slide."

"We did drop a bombshell on her," said Ada. "Hope the council listens. This is… big."

Yeah. Obviously, there was a force bigger even than Veyak and Cethrax at play—but *what*, I had no idea. I just couldn't conceive of anything powerful enough to subdue one of Cethrax's leaders.

"Damn right." I shrugged my jacket on. "To open a doorway, you need a world-key, whatever that's made of. So they must have had a magic source on the other side. I suppose it might have been those chains, but if they'd been adamantine, you wouldn't have been able to break them."

"*We*," she corrected. "I couldn't have done it without an amplifier."

"Hey, I have to be useful in some way." But the situation bugged me. Cethrax hadn't been making trouble. They'd been… what? Had they opened the doors, or someone else? More to the point, to move between worlds, there was usually only one place to go. The Passages. And the Alliance watched every inch of the place, even with the chaos happening now. They'd have noticed high-magic creatures travelling through, like these 'masters' supposedly were.

"This doesn't add up," I muttered. "Doorways. They'd *need* Passage access for their plan to work."

"Huh?"

"To get to Cethrax," I said. "The Passages *are* the only legal way. The Alliance might not understand everything about magic, but that's not just a truth, it's a goddamned principle. And they watch every single inch of the place…"

"God," she breathed. "I'm such an idiot. I didn't realise—I should have known. I think I know how they did it."

Wait. "You don't think—"

"The hidden Passage," she whispered. "New doorways to Cethrax open in there all the time."

"Shit," I said. "You're right." Why had it slipped my mind? "You didn't see anything…?"

"Apart from the monsters?" She gave a shaky laugh. "No. But I can't think of anything else. And they said magic was leaking out onto Earth from somewhere. We left the door near my old house open, didn't we? When we used it to find Alber."

I shook my head. "No, I closed it."

"But it isn't under extra security like the others," she said, hitting herself in the forehead with her palm. "Dammit. Why didn't I think of that before? The hidden Passage is right near Cethrax. *And* one of the hidden staircases is near the door to Vey-Xanetha."

Hell. Could she be right?

"I suppose we can check," I said.

"It'd be the obvious place to hide," she said. "Even we didn't know all the paths. I never checked… Kay, I totally forgot—some of the pathways are invisible to non-magic-wielders. Like the shielding they put on the stairs to the upper level, but stronger."

I stared. "What? Are you sure?" Stupid question. But I'd never even considered it. The hidden Passage had been taken out of my hands once I'd made my report following Ada's escape from custody, and aside from when we'd used it in an emergency, it honestly hadn't crossed my mind since.

"Yeah." She shifted from one foot to the other. "I didn't think. I mean, no one asked me about it when I joined the Alliance, and I forgot how few magic-wielders there were at Central—on Earth."

Which meant there was a high chance no magic-wielders had even been near the area. Carl would have mentioned it if he had, and none of the other magic-wielders had been guards, unless you counted Aric…

"If it's true, it'll have to be closed." Something didn't quite add up, but I couldn't put my finger on it. "All right. I'll check it later."

"*We'll* check it," she said, sternly, and then grinned. It was almost enough to make me give up on the whole idea and stay with her all day instead. I could get on board with that plan. Unfortunately, we had to be at work, to file written reports on the Vey-Xanethan fiasco. I wouldn't mind a quick detour into the Passages.

The shortcut was easy to find, and no one saw us—we were invisible, just in case, but we'd picked a time during guard changeover so there was nobody inside Central's Passage entrance. We climbed down the hidden staircase. *Just a look.*

I stopped. *No way.* Facing the stairs was a door, one which hadn't been there before. Magic buzzed in the air, almost tangibly. No way it came from Cethrax. I switched off the invisibility.

"Cethrax played us for fools," I said, unable to take my eyes off the door. "They must have known London's Alliance would cover up a hidden Passage and keep it a secret from the other Alliance members. It makes them look bad for not knowing it existed."

"The bloody idiots," said Ada, staring, too. "How do we close this one?"

"I'll call someone," I said. "Get hold of a world-key or whatever they use to close doors in here. You run and fetch the nearest guards, I'll make sure the door stays shut."

Ada hesitated, biting her lip. "All right."

Crash.

The door cracked apart before our eyes like something heavy had struck it down the middle. Another crack appeared, widening by the second—and a group of figures pushed their way through the remains of the door. Human-like figures. I took in the details while my brain struggled to catch up—their greyish skin had an odd, marbled cast under the cotton-like garments they wore, and all were bald, though half the group were female. Six in total, and more waiting behind the door, blocking whichever world lay on the other side.

"That was more dramatic than I expected," one of them said. In English.

I backed up, pulling out my dagger. *Who are these people? They're not from Cethrax!* Nor did they belong to any other world I'd recognise.

"You are not the one we want," said the first man who'd spoken. "We have come for the girl. The girl they say is unbreakable." He looked at Ada with flat black eyes gleaming. "This is she?"

"Who in the Multiverse are you?" I demanded. *Don't you look at her.*

"Yes," said one of the females. "This is Adamantine."

"You're not taking me anywhere." Ada crossed her arms in a familiar gesture, ready to draw her weapon at a second's notice. "Who even are you?"

"We are Stoneskin," said the leader, baring his teeth in a wide smile. "And it was you who set our prisoner free."

These were the ones who'd imprisoned the Vox? *Impossible.*

"You enslaved Veyak?" Ada's hand rested on her dagger in its sheath.

"Veyak was bound to the same chains we used on the Vox. You'll have plenty of time to question our master, Adamantine."

"What part of *I'm not coming with you* do you not get?" said Ada. "You almost destroyed the Multiverse." But her voice shook. How did it know her real name? *I'd thought only her family knew. This is wrong.*

"You will help us, Adamantine. We are unbreakable, like you."

"Like hell." Screw caution. I let magic flow into my palm, striking him with a second level shot. The magic dissipated as it touched his skin, and I followed it up with a punch that he blocked. Pain jarred my wrist, throbbing like I'd hit a wall, not a person. Ada was already using her communicator, calling for backup.

"Don't try it," said another, moving towards Ada. I blocked the way and agony exploded across my vision as my head connected with something as hard as concrete. My eyes widened, reactions slowing down—until I saw three of them held Ada between them. She struggled and kicked and screamed as the side of her hand struck one of their heads.

I raised my arm to block the strike of another attacker. Something cracked in my wrist and I clenched my teeth against the pain. They weren't human...

Stoneskin. They're made of adamantine.

But they were taking Ada. Disconnected thoughts jarred against one another in my head, but that one notion obliterated all others, and I ran through the doorway.

Jungle surrounded us in an instant. Vey-Xanetha? They

were using Vey-Xanetha as a doorway? I shook off the dizziness and ran after them.

A Stoneskin challenged me, stony teeth bared in a grin. I went for my dagger, ignoring the pain, and brought it in a stroke across its neck. The enemy didn't even try to block— but the blade shattered in my hands like cheap glass.

A roaring rose in my ears, insistent, powerful. *Ada.* The three dragged her between them, and two more barred my path. I had no weapon. Only magic. And another doorway lay open a few feet away. I couldn't see the world on the other side—

Pain exploded all over my body as a dozen steel punches hit, all at once. My head snapped back, vision blurring even as I knew magic wouldn't help. *They're not human.* The thought drifted through my mind, the world breaking into fragments. Somehow I was on the ground. A foot stamped on my hand and I felt the bones shatter.

Ada.

No.

The edges of the world fell away into blackness like an opening chasm, and the last thing I saw was the sliver of the door closing.

The doorway had closed. And she was gone.

ABOUT THE AUTHOR

Emma is the New York Times and USA Today Bestselling author of the Changeling Chronicles urban fantasy series.

Emma spent her childhood creating imaginary worlds to compensate for a disappointingly average reality, so it was probably inevitable that she ended up writing fantasy novels. When she's not immersed in her own fictional universes, Emma can be found with her head in a book or wandering around the world in search of adventure.

Find out more about Emma's books at
www.emmaladams.com.